Infinite Courage

Clay Warrior Stories
Book #8

J. Clifton Slater

Infinite Courage is a work of fiction. Any resemblance to persons living or dead is purely coincidental. I am not a historian, although I do extensive research. For those who have studied the classical era and those with exceptional knowledge of the times, I apologize in advance.

The large events in this tale are from history, while the dialogue and action sequences are my inventions. Some of the elements in the command and control of the Legions are from reverse engineering. The requirements necessary to carry a command from the General to a Legionary on the end of an assault line, who was fighting for his life, took imagination. Hopefully, you'll see the logic to my methods.

I need to thank Hollis Jones who kept the story on track and grammatically correct with her red pen. Without her, the project would have wandered far from my plan. And my writer friends and support group who keeps me sane. You are much appreciated.

J. Clifton Slater
Website: www.JCliftonSlater.com
Email: GalacticCouncilRealm@gmail.com

Infinite Courage

Act 1

Consul Valerius Mesalla and Consul Otacilius Crassus formed Legions and marched on Sicily. While they didn't participate in pitched battles with the Carthage Empire, their Legions fought many small battles. Each unique and all against some sixty odd cities and towns on the eastern half of the island. Welcome to 263 B.C.

Chapter 1 – Licosa

The sandals of thirteen handlers and hoofs of thirteen mules, loaded with fourteen tents, and fourteen sets of camp equipment, crunched on the stony beach. One of the pack animals and its handler marched with a Legionary at the front of the slow-moving caravan.

"Why does Centurion Megellus want us to set up at Licosa?" Alerio Sisera pondered.

"How would I know, Corporal?" the mule handler replied.

"It's a rhetorical question," Alerio told the man. "It's only twelve miles to Velia where Crassus Legions are training."

"Should we push on and join them?"

"No, Grilli. We follow orders," Alerio explained. The Legionary pulled out a goatskin map, identified a landmark, and called back to the lines of men. "Our campsite will be around the bend, on the other side of the villa, and just off the beach."

"Whose villa is that?" Grilli inquired.

The house and compound had come into view far down the beach. As they approached, details became noticeable. A balcony on the second story overlooked the sea and the Villa's compound was surrounded by a small unkept wall. Fallen stones from the wall and overgrown bushes and weeds showed the neglect of an absent owner.

"I don't know, and it's not marked on the map," Alerio informed him. "It looks like a vacation estate. Somewhere for a nobleman to get away from a city or a landowner from his farm in the heat of summer. A place where he can enjoy the sea breezes."

"I'd like to have a summer villa," announced Grilli. "Or a fishing boat. Or a farm."

"You have a job," Alerio pointed out. "As do I. Let's get to the site and set up the camp."

"This would be more fun if we were at Velia," Grilli suggested. "There are more games and entertainment where the Legions are training."

"Grilli, this is the Legion," Alerio corrected pointing back at the pack animals. "It's not supposed to be fun."

"No offense Corporal but, the Legions are twelve miles further south," the mule handler commented. "What you have here are tents and cooking utensils for a new, untested Century."

***

Alerio eyed the broad strip of flat land between the ocean and the toe of high hills to the east.

"Grilli. Have the handlers drop the Centurion's tent to the north and the squad tents in two rows," Alerio instructed. He stood in an area close to the foothills using his hands to indicate the placement. "The NCOs' tent goes on the south end."

2

"And the corral?" the mule handler inquired.

"Put the mules south of the handler's tents," Alerio told him. "I don't think the Optio would enjoy the aroma of mule. I know I wouldn't."

"Speaking of aroma, where do you want the latrines?"

"Beyond the corral," Alerio advised. "I'll have the Century build the practice field on the other side of the merda facilities."

Grilli dropped the reins for his mule and began directing the other handlers. Soon there were two rows of five tents between the large, folded Centurion tent and the NCO tent. Four handlers began leveling the ground, spreading sand, and setting up the officer's tent.

From the mule with the Optio and Tesserarius' equipment, Alerio extracted a coil of string on a stick, a hammer, and a stack of short stakes. After measuring out a length, he called Grilli over to take one end of the string.

"We'll align the camp off the Centurion's tent," he instructed the mule handler. "Pull it tight from the tent pole."

Alerio stretched the string, so the 1st Squad's tent rested far outside the centerline, spaced about two tent lengths away from the Centurion's tent. This gave privacy to the infantry officer and allowed him to talk without being overheard. Alerio pounded in a stake then moved to the other side of the camp and positioned 2nd Squad's tent.

They stretched the string, measured distances, rotated between sides of the camp, and lined up eight more tents. At each tent's location, Alerio tapped in a marker stake. On the south end, he pounded in a final stake for the NCOs' tent.

"This side is straight," Alerio asserted as he wrapped the string around the stick. After strolling across the width of the camp, he peered at the line of five markers on the other side and announced. "We have an ordered Century area."

"I'll have the handlers begin setting up the squad tents," offered Grilli. Pointing at the ten bundles of tents laid in the center of the camp, he added. "After we level the ground."

"Clear the brush, level the earth, and get buckets of sand for the tent base," Alerio directed. "Leave the tents where they are. I want each squad to erect their own tent."

"Part of the training, Corporal?" inquired the mule handler.

"More evaluation of how the men work together," Alerio corrected. "They should know how to set up a squad tent. Senator Maximus told me he was hiring experienced Legionaries when I was given this assignment."

***

Long after sunrise the next morning, a staggered line of thirty-two men appeared on the beach. They came from the north, sauntered into the center of the camp, and dropped their travel bags. After looking from the erected Centurion tent to the NCO tent at the far end and the rows of folded squad tents, their eyes locked on the mule handlers.

"Why aren't our tents set up?" one yelled down the length of the Century area. Beyond the NCO tent, a few mule handlers turned their heads to look at the newly

4

arrived Legionaries. The rest remained sitting at their campfires. "Get over here and do your job. Or do you need a good beating to teach you your place?"

From beside one of the fires, Grilli dipped his head in respect and lifted an arm to point eastward. Several Legionaries followed the direction of the arm. At the top of the high hill, they noted a man dressed in a loincloth with a gladius on his hip, wearing hobnailed boots.

"Who in Hades is that cūlus?" a Legionary questioned.

"No clue," another responded.

They watched as the man jumped from the crest, landed a body's length downhill, and began tracking back and forth. As he descended, they could see he glistened with sweat obviously from earlier exercises. Muscles straining from the run, the half-dressed man arrived at the foot of the hill. There he transitioned to a march while crossing a square of level sand the mule handlers had prepared for a squad tent.

"Good morning, Legionaries," Alerio greeted the group. He snatched a woolen shirt from the top of a folded tent, wiped off the sweat, and slid on the garment. Before it fell over his head, the Legionaries noticed his battle scars. "We're going with a contubernium, eight men to a squad."

"I've brought my own ten-man squad," the Legionary who threatened the mule handlers stated. "Who are you?"

"Corporal Sisera. Eight heavy infantrymen to a squad. Now, I'd suggest you set up your tents."

"I was supposed to be the Tesserarius," the Legionary challenged. "Optio Gustavi said it when I signed up with the Century."

Alerio looked over his shoulder at the NCO tent, then faced front and peered around the gathered Legionaries in the direction of the Centurion's tent.

"Nope. No Sergeant or officer to adjudicate your claim," Alerio commented. "How about you show some leadership and get your squad's tent set up? Eight men per, as this is a marching camp and, not garrison duty."

The Legionaries broke off and began erecting the first two tents on either side. Alerio watched from the center of the camp without saying a word. When they were finished, he wandered between tents checking the tautness of the guylines. At the complaining Legionary's tent, Alerio pulled on the lines, walked to the other side, and tested those.

Then the Corporal stood at one corner and looked down the front of the tent trying to see the next tent and the markers for the rest of the row.

"You seem to have an issue," Alerio mentioned while lifting an arm and holding it against the front flap. "Your tent is off the line."

"Who cares, this is a training camp. We're not even with the Legions," the Legionary offered. "Besides, there wasn't a marker."

"That does present a problem," Alerio responded.

Drawing his gladius, Alerio vanished around the side of the tent. When he reappeared, the tent was collapsing. The reason soon became apparent. With his blade, the Corporal also sliced the guylines on the other side and the entire structure fell. With his foot, Alerio kicked back a section of the goatskin material. Under the fold, he discovered a marker stake laying on its side and half buried in the sandy base.

"There's the issue. Someone stepped on 1st Squad's marker," the Corporal announced. He pulled out a piece of parchment and a nub of charcoal. While making a notation, he informed the Legionary. "I'll get your squad new ropes. But let's be sure the tent is on the line."

"What are you writing down?"

"The cost of new ropes," Alerio informed the squad leader. "Your squad will be charged for the resupply."

"It was you who cut the lines," the Legionary bellowed while stepping forward and placing a hand on the hilt of his knife. "If anyone should pay, it's you."

In two steps, Alerio stood nose to nose with the infantryman. When the Legionary attempted to pull his knife, the Corporal slapped his hand on the man's knuckles, preventing him from drawing the blade.

"What's your name?" Alerio questioned.

"Horatius Ostrei."

"We are going to have weapons training Decanus Horatius Ostrei. A lot of weapons training," Alerio promised with a wicked smile. "And I can assure you Lance Corporal Ostrei, you'll have plenty of opportunities to show me your skills. For now, I suggest you get your tent set up."

Horatius hesitated then glanced around. All thirty-one Legionaries and the mule handlers stood waiting to see the outcome of the confrontation.

"Fine," Horatius growled while attempting to step away.

7

But the Corporal's palm shifted from the back of Ostrei's hand and gripped the Legionary's wrist.

"Try that again," Alerio ordered.

Horatius Ostrei's body shook with rage, and he started to verbally challenge the Tesserarius. Just before he exploded, he caught the smile on the NCOs' face and noticed the joy in the man's eyes at the expectation of an outburst of violence. Ostrei had served five years in the Northern Legion, and he recognized the signs. He was being goaded into a fight. An engagement where he could be embarrassed in front of the other Legionaries.

"If you're finished, Corporal Sisera?" Horatius uttered. "I'll help the squad set up the tent."

"On the line, Lance Corporal Ostrei," Alerio reminded him while releasing the wrist. Then in the direction of the mule handlers, he shouted. "Grilli. I need new guylines."

Grilli already held the ropes in his hand. Everyone in the camp had watched the exchange with interest and different emotions. Some were amused at the audacity of the Corporal cutting the lines then charging the squad for the loss. Others were angry for the same reason. While suppressing a smile, the mule handler jogged to Tesserarius Sisera and delivered the new ropes.

***

Early in the afternoon, thirty-two more Legionaries made it to the camp. They were a little taller and fairer of skin and hair than the first group. Alerio recognized them but a Legionary in 3rd Squad vocalized it.

"Samnites," he exclaimed. "I didn't know they let tribesmen in the heavy infantry."

"The southern tribes are citizens. Don't be fatuus," a squad mate chastised him.

"I'm not simple. I'm just surprised," he responded.

Alerio met the new Legionaries. After a short greeting, he stood and watched them set up the next four tents. All went up correctly giving the Corporal no cause for worry about their skills. What did worry him, the squads who arrived earlier ignored and, some turned their backs on the Samnites.

After witnessing the tension between Latians and the mountain Samnites, Alerio made a note to not have the two groups skirmish. At least not until he knew the men better.

The shadows were long, and the orange ball of the sun floated a finger's width from the horizon when the last sixteen Legionaries appeared on the beach. They were Latian but their clothing and slumped postures displayed a downtrodden lifestyle. Several of them lugged heavy leather bags displaying bulges where flat and rounded objects inside pressed against the material.

He greeted the late arriving Legionaries, as he did the other groups, and set them to erecting their quarters. While they were setting up the final two tents, Alerio had to step in and issue corrections and instructions. Every Century had its weaker squads and the Corporal had just met his.

The sun sank into the ocean and night fell on the Century. Corporal Sisera looked over his campfire at the flames burning in the camps of the ten squads. Beyond the squads, the dark and empty Centurion's tent vanished in the fading light.

With no officer or Sergeant, Alerio had a decision to make. Set his own training schedule and get started on bringing the Century to fighting form or allow the Legionaries to lounge around until the Century's Optio and Centurion arrived.

Chapter 2 – Resistance in the Ranks

A pink haze brightened the eastern sky announcing the coming sunrise. In the dark, Alerio tossed back the flap, stepped from the NCO tent, and shouted.

"Maximus Century! Get up, get out, and get on the parade ground," the Corporal called. He repeated the order while strolling down the center of the area. At the end, near the Centurion's tent, he turned about and added. "You will get your swinging mentulas out of those tents, or I will burn them down."

The first squads to emerge from their tents were the Samnites. After them, a few more Legionaries came out and stood in front of their tents.

"Lance Corporal Ostrei. Is 1st Squad too busy having an amor fest?" Alerio demanded. "I suggest ending the warm embraces. Get your people on the parade ground."

Laughter came from the 2nd and 3rd Squads as they surged from their tents. Most of the Legionaries were in front of their tents when Ostrei and 1st Squad came slowly from theirs. It was obvious by the swagger that the delay was intentional.

"Columns of twos, on me," Alerio instructed. Once two lines of forty Legionaries formed and faced the Corporal. "Turnabout. Decanus Ostrei. 1st Squad has the rear. Century, standby."

Forty feet stomped, but the halting reply of, "standing by Corporal" was weak.

"Let's try this again," Alerio shouted while walking beside the formation. "For every sad response, I'm adding another hill to the run. Century, stand by."

"Standing by, Corporal," came the response with more enthusiasm.

Alerio began jogging to the front but stopped beside a Samnite. In the weak light, he noted the Legionary had reached out and shoved four men back into ranks.

"Name?" he demanded.

"Telesia Caudini," the tall Samnite replied. "I guess with 5th Squad, based on the tent's location."

"Lance Corporal Caudini," Alerio said acknowledging Caudini as the tent commander and Decanus for 5th Squad. "Pull your contubernium out and take the lead."

"Yes, Tesserarius."

When the eight Legionaries were positioned at the head of the columns, Alerio stopped by the 9th and 10th Squads.

"If at the end of this run, you are anywhere except right behind those eight, I'll make the next week the worst seven days of your life."

"Yes, Corporal," the men in the two contuberniums replied.

"Century, forward march," Alerio called. "Decanus Caudini, follow the beach."

The Century filed between the NCO's and the 10th Squad's tent. Soon, eighty hobnailed boots crunched gravel and sand as the Legionaries marched along the shoreline. Alerio trotted to the front and explained the route to Telesia Caudini.

***

Based on Alerio's pacing the day before, they had covered about seven miles. When Telesia Caudini and 5th Squad started down a steep flume, Alerio ran ahead, climbed the embankment, and dropped into the neighboring gorge. In front of him, Horatius Ostrei and 1st Squad pushed lagging Legionaries up the incline.

"Lance Corporal Ostrei. Isn't this great," Alerio said from directly behind the squad leader. "I could do the grind all day."

Horatius' head snapped around. From being one of the last Legionaries in the columns, sweat coated his face and dirt caked everywhere except his mouth, nostrils, and eyes where he blinked them clear.

"This is cruel," Horatius spit out the words along with a wet wad of dirt. "You don't know the conditioning of these men."

"You're right, Decanus Ostrei," Alerio admitted. "I don't know the conditioning of these men. But I know what's expected of a Legionary. The tail is lagging behind. Try to keep up."

Alerio put on a burst of speed and climbed to a break in the line where infantrymen were struggling. After scrambling out of the ravine, he dropped into the adjacent one and joined the men running downhill. The Corporal shouted encouragement while passing those on the downward slope.

***

Telesia Caudini and 5th Squad, although breathing hard, held themselves erect as they walked by Corporal

Sisera. Behind them, the Legionaries came into camp in stages of exhaustion. Further back, pain showed on their faces and near the end of the columns, a few were limping. Horatius Ostrei and 1st Squad braced up at the sight of the Century's Tesserarius.

Alerio sat at a camp desk beside the path. With a quill in one hand and a mug of water in the other, the Corporal seemed relaxed as if he had spent the day napping under a tree. Unknown to the Legionaries, he had raced ahead and ducked his head in a bucket of water to cool down. Then he peeled off the sweat-soaked tunic and replaced it with a matching one.

"Fall out," he called to each Legionary as they passed. "The run was a nice warm-up for the day."

When out of earshot, or so the squads thought, they marveled at the dry and relaxed Corporal. One overriding question, whether rhetorical or based on actual curiosity, was 'who is this guy?'

They didn't realize Alerio's stomach was in knots from the run and all he wanted to do was lay down and take a nap. He didn't. Instead, he smiled and welcomed the rest of the Century back to camp.

***

The Century spent the afternoon pulling weeds and digging brush to clear the practice field. Mounds were formed for archery and javelin practice. Even though they didn't have bows, arrows, or javelins to use on the targets, they did have muscles. A few engaged in wrestling in the fighting pit. Other's raced in sprints on the short, measured track. Once the gladius drill posts were set, Corporal Sisera ended the work details and gave the

Legionaries the afternoon off. He had no choice; they didn't have gladii or shields either.

As the sun moved lower in the sky, Alerio walked the camp talking with the men and getting to know them. Most of the Legionaries greeted him respectfully. Some were standoffish which was understandable, he was a new authority figure. What surprised the Corporal, the men in the 1st and 2nd Squads were openly hostile.

***

"Maximus Century! Get up, get out, and get on the parade ground."

Shadows moved from the entrances of five tents. Two more contuberniums joined them but the Legionaries from 1st, 2nd, and 3rd Squads, once again, hesitated to respond.

"Fall in on me, columns of twos," Alerio ordered.

The seven squads formed up facing their Tesserarius. Standing silently in the early morning light, they waited to see how the NCO would handle the disrespectful squads.

"I wonder if the missing squads realize that I control the pay records, the supply inventory, and the funeral funds?" Alerio called out. "Century, stand by."

Fifty-six Legionaries responded, "Standing by, Corporal."

"Turnabout, march," Alerio directed. He jogged to the head of the column and fell in beside the 10th Squad. "Who is your Decanus?"

A thick brute of a man replied, "I am Palinurus, and I command the tent."

"Decanus Palinurus, guide the Century to the beach."

"What about the missing squads?"

"What missing squads?" Alerio questioned.

"Corporal, the ones still in their tents?"

14

"I have no idea what you're talking about."

"But?"

"March to the beach and listen for my command," Alerio advised. Then the NCO shouted. "Left, stomp, left stomp."

At first, a ripple rolled through the columns. After a few more cadence calls, the Legionaries caught the rhythm and the hobnailed boots on the gravelly beach crunched down as one. The Corporal jogged to the front, passed Palinurus and 10th Squad, and stopped.

"Column left, march," Alerio ordered when the front of the column reached him.

Decanus Palinurus missed his mark and the man to his left slammed him with his shoulder when he turned left. The big Legionary shoved the man and was pushed back in return. Behind the scuffling pair, the infantrymen bunched up and the columns stopped.

"Palinurus. Raise your right hand," Alerio requested.

The Legionary lifted his left. Looking around for approval and seeing none, he raised his right arm.

"Column left, march," Corporal Sisera ordered while pointing up the bank in the direction of the practice field.

Coming off the hard surface of the beach, the Century's steps were ragged in the loose dirt. Once on the flat of the practice field, the NCO called the Century to a halt.

"Breakdown by squads," Alerio directed. "We're going to run contubernium shield drills."

"But we don't have shields, Corporal," Palinurus reminded him.

Lifting and bending his left arm as if holding a shield, Alerio called out, "Get them up. Draw."

He mimicked pulling and holding a gladius down by his right side.

A Legionary laughed and put his hands on his hips.

"This is ridiculous," the man proclaimed.

Alerio marched over to him and inquired, "Your name?"

"Lance Corporal Acharis Enitui of 4th Squad. And this is foolish and useless without shields and gladii."

With his left arm bent and held up, and the right down by his side, Alerio's arms appeared to hold a shield and blade.

"That is an interesting observation, Decanus Enitui," the NCO offered. "Let's test the opinion. Advance!"

The motion as proscribed by the Legion involved a smash with the shield, and once it was withdrawn, a thrust with the blade. Although Alerio had neither, Enitui caught a forearm in the chin before the Corporal hammered a fist into the Legionary's chest.

"That wasn't fair, I wasn't ready," Acharis Enitui complained. The strikes had driven him back into the arms of 4th Squad.

"Do they not teach the advance command in the Northern Legion?" inquired Alerio. "I assumed it was a standard tactic."

"Of course, they do. But we use real weapons," Enitui replied. He shook off the arms of his squad mates and leaned forward putting his face close to Corporal Sisera's. "We don't play at war."

"I'm going to give the advance command again. But I want to be sure you're ready," Alerio cautioned. "Here we go, advance."

Acharis threw up both hands in a wrestling guard and spread his legs. Because he was leaning forward, the Corporal's forearm drove the arms up and out of position. On the way down, the forearm smashed Enitui's nose. Then the forearm withdrew, and the NCO's right fist came up and buried itself in the Decanus' solar plexus. The squad leader for 4th Squad doubled over in pain, bleeding from his nose, gagging and gasping for air.

Alerio leaned down and put his mouth by the distressed Legionary's ear.

"I don't play at war, either," he whispered. Then to all the squads. "We are the Legion's heavy infantry, craftsmen of war, and because we are journeymen warriors, we fight with whatever is available. Lance Corporal Enitui forgot that every advance is a killing move. With or without weapons. Now, pick up your shields and your gladii. If you can't find them, I'll come over and instruct you."

Looking around, Alerio noted the fifty-five Legionaries on the practice field holding out their bent left arms and pressing invisible gladii against their right hips. Slowly, Acharis Enitui straightened, wiped the blood from his nose, and lifted his arms as if holding a weapon and a shield.

***

"Flank march, advance, step back," Alerio shouted. "Right pivot."

On the practice field, the seven squads moved at an angle, shoved their pretend shields forward, withdrew them, and struck out with their fists. After taking a step to the rear, they swung their line to the right. All of them

17

maintained the shoulder-to-shoulder formation, except for 10th Squad.

"Decanus Palinurus, do you like being a squad leader?" Alerio asked as he marched up to the eight, out of line, Legionaries. "Because I look at you and see an unmovable stone pillar. If I was building a solid shield wall, I would want someone of your stature as an anchor."

"I can fight," Palinurus informed the Corporal. "It's just repeating your commands and remembering to follow is hard."

One of his squad mates raised a hand and patted the big Legionary on the arm. The calming gesture of reassurance came from the smallest man in the contubernium.

"Palinurus. I think this squad requires protection on their right side. A powerful, unmoving shield. You will be 10th Squad's right pivot," Alerio announced. Then he examined the small Legionary. "Your name?"

"Lucius Tescum, Corporal."

"Palinurus, I'm making a change in 10th Squad. As the right pivot, I need to know if you'll protect Lucius Tescum. Can he depend on your fist, gladius, and shield to defend your new squad leader from harm?"

A smile crossed the big man's face as if a weight had been lifted.

"10th Squad's right side will never falter and will never be breached," Palinurus swore. "Decanus Tescum has my gladius to command."

"Then straighten your line," Corporal Sisera instructed. To the Century, he ordered. "Turnabout, left pivot, advance, advance, advance."

Seven squad leaders repeated the commands while performing them. In the chaos of combat, their voices would be recognizable to their squad members allowing a contubernium of eight heavy infantrymen to fight as a unit.

***

Before mid-morning, three squads marched from the beach. Lance Corporal Horatius Ostrei strutted at the side of the formation calling cadence. They topped the rise from the beach and came to a staggered stop.

1st, 2nd, and 3rd Squads gawked at the shouting and repeating of orders as the bulk of the Century moved, attacked, and pivoted. A few chuckled at the unarmed men acting as if they had weapons. The more experienced Legionaries took in the maneuvering and nodded their approval.

"What's the plan now, Ostrei?" one asked.

Another added, "I don't think the Century missed your leadership."

Before Decanus Horatius could think of an answer, Corporal Sisera called the Century together. Once formed, the seven squads marched off the practice field and passed the three disobedient squads. No one said a word or acknowledged Horatius Ostrei's revolt or resistance.

Chapter 3 – Wet Threat

Alerio hung back to allow the seven squads to go ahead. It was tempting to confront Horatius Ostrei about the missed training and disrespect. But he was only a Tesserarius, and heavy punishment required a Sergeant or an officer. Besides, his throat was sore from yelling

19

commands and hunger pains gnawed at his midsection. Looking around the camp, he noted the Centurion's tent remained empty and there was no sign of the Century's Optio. Resigned to shouldering the divided Century by himself, he climbed from the beach. Suddenly, his senses were assaulted by the smell of hot camp stew.

'One of the squads has a cook,' the Corporal thought before turning the corner of the NCOs' tent.

Grilli squatted at a fire in front of the tent, stirring the aromatic substance in an iron pot.

"Is that for me?" Alerio questioned. "If it's not, I'm willing to wrestle you for a bowl."

"The mule handlers took advantage of the leisure you've provided and baked bread this morning," Grilli said while spooning meat and vegetables into a bowl. He handed it to Alerio then unwrapped a loaf of bread. "You haven't assigned any of us to squads. We're curious if it's an oversight or part of your strategy."

"Having a servant is important for freeing up infantrymen so they can fight," Alerio replied between mouthfuls of stew and bread. "While training, mundane tasks fill the days. And help strengthen the bonds between members of a contubernium."

"No offense Corporal Sisera, but you seem to have military wisdom beyond your years," Grilli commented.

"For years while I was growing up, an experienced Centurion and Optio came to my father's farm for the harvest," Alerio explained. "They were both unmarried and childless. I think they pounded lessons into me as if I was their son. From weapons training to tactics, to the best practices of the Legion, I was drilled, punished, and tested. All of the training gives me an edge. However, it doesn't give me all of the answers."

"You're referring to Lance Corporal Ostrei's actions," Grilli pondered. "If I might, I have a suggestion."

"Please tell me. An experienced Legion animal wrangler's idea can't be any worse than a new Tesserarius'," Alerio said while dipping a piece of bread into the bottom of the bowl.

"Solve the issue with Horatius Ostrei before Optio Gustavi arrives," Grilli offered. "Make him respect you. If that's not possible, make him fear you. Become his worst nightmare."

"It might be easier to just slice him into pieces in a duel," Alerio pondered.

"There is always that approach," Grilli confirmed. "More stew?"

***

When he was finished eating, Alerio began walking the camp. And doing something unexpected.

"9th Squad, are you the Decanus?"

"Quiris Stulte, Corporal Sisera," a man acknowledged. He had no fat under his flesh to cover his muscles. As he stood, the rope-like cords under his skin flexed with the slightest movement. "Is there a problem?"

"Get your squad out here and let me see their feet."

"Feet, Tesserarius?" Stulte inquired with a raised eyebrow. Even that small movement sent ripples through his facial muscles. "You want to look at men's feet?"

"Toes actually. Specifically, between the toes," Alerio corrected.

"9th Squad. Gather around, the Corporal wants to see your toes," Quiris Stulte informed his contubernium.

21

"But I haven't painted mine today," one Legionary exclaimed in a high-pitched voice.

"I pity you. My feet are so pretty, they need no embellishment."

"I've seen your feet. They are as ugly as an old knotty oak."

"That's your opinion. Let's see whose feet the Corporal proclaims are the cutest."

The comments brought chuckles from the rest of the squad and Alerio ignored the taunting. He wanted to laugh but thought it would undermine his authority. Instead, he stood stern-faced with his arms folded across his chest. When all eight Legionaries had their boots off, he bent and inspected their feet.

"I was recently on a Greek boat," Alerio began when a Legionary interrupted.

"Oh, that explains it."

More laughter accompanied the comment.

"As I was saying, I was on a Greek transport. The sailors weren't big on bathing," Alerio informed them which brought about sounds of yuks and disgust. "But none had any skin problems with their feet."

"Because they're not stomping through mud during rainstorms," Quiris Stulte remarked.

"True, and because they hung their feet off the side of the boat," Alerio offered. "The salt water kept their feet free of sores."

"You want us to soak our feet in the sea?"

"Just two of you. Those are some of the most disgusting feet, I've ever seen."

"Seen a lot of feet, have you?"

Alerio looked away and scanned the camp.

"Unfortunately, not yet," he said as he moved to another squad's area.

***

"Maximus Century. Get your boots off, strip down, and join me on the beach," Alerio announced.

With the memory of the Corporal studying everyone's feet fresh in their minds, the Legionaries began accusing each other of having ugly feet. While they undressed and continued the teasing, Alerio marched to the NCOs' tent. He unstrapped his boots and pulled the tunic over his head.

"Are you injured?" Grilli inquired.

He indicated the silk wrapped around the Corporal's waist.

"No. I have a dagger hidden in there."

"Very wise, Corporal Sisera. You never know when you'll run into a sea monster."

"Or two-legged fish with iron teeth."

Alerio picked his way across the gravel area with only a few dealings with pointed rocks. On the sandy section, he stood letting the waves roll over his feet. The Century filed onto the beach and to Alerio's surprise, Horatius Ostrei and his rebellious men stood among the other squads.

"Every Legionary can swim," Alerio called out as he backed into deeper water. "Some enjoy the exercise. Others swim only when necessary. And a few, wouldn't take time to wash their feet."

A round of accusations bounced through the Century and Alerio let the good-natured ribbing go unchecked. When it died down, he raised his arms.

"Who is a fast swimmer?"

23

Pentri Umbria, Decanus for 6th Squad, stepped forward.

"Lance Corporal Umbria, you are first in. I'll signal with a wave," Alerio ordered. "When you get back to the beach, there shouldn't be anyone to meet you."

Pentri nodded his understanding.

"I'm going to swim out. You will come out, swim around me, and head for shore," Alerio continued. "Questions?"

"I have a question," Horatius Ostrei remarked while pushing through the crowd of Legionaries. "If you drown, who is in command?"

"If I drown, then you, Lance Corporal Ostrei would be the new Tesserarius."

"Thank you," Horatius acknowledged before turning and walking back to his squad.

***

Gentle waves rolled by lifting Alerio and for a moment he could see the shoreline. Then it moved on and, from the trough between waves, his vision was restricted to the high ground above the beach. On the crest of the next wave, he lifted an arm and signaled for the swim to begin.

Pentri Umbria raced into the water followed by four others. The aggressive swimmers splashed into the sea then Alerio lost sight of them as he floated between waves. On the next lift, he noted the beach was mostly empty. Only a few hesitant Legionaries remained but they were walking into the shallows.

He was far enough out to make the swim challenging without being an endurance course. Once the Optio arrived, they would organize a swim to test the Century's skills.

A single swimmer came out of the swells and Alerio assumed it was the Decanus from 6th Squad. Behind the lead, four more stroked and kicked the surface trying to catch Pentri. But they didn't seem to be gaining on the swift Legionary. The five rounded their Corporal and headed for the beach. Treading water, Alerio rotated to watch the race for second place. Then the splashing of arms and hammering of feet by a multitude reached him and, at the top of a wave, he saw the bulk of the Century approach. Resembling a school of fish breaking the surface or an isolated storm creating white caps, they churned the water and kicked sprays high into the air. If there was a sea monster in the area, the chaos of the Century swimming around Alerio was sure to drive it away.

The stronger swimmers positioned themselves on the outside of the pack. They swung wide to avoid the mass of lifting arms and thrashing legs. Closer to the turning point, some attempted to cut the distance by crowding to the inside. To prevent from being overrun, Alerio shoved a few back, making them swim around him. It worked and swimmers following those in front flowed by at a distance.

The first segment of the Century had completed the U-turn and was heading for the shore. Behind them, the bulk of men had just reached Alerio's position and begun to circle. Further back, the slowest segment had yet to reach the turning point.

On a wave, Alerio looked for the beach. It was empty. Just before the wave passed, he noted a single figure nearing the shoreline. Lance Corporal Umbria was indeed as swift as he claimed.

A swimmer nudged his right shoulder. Believing the line of returning and circling swimmers was about to swim over him, Alerio fluttered his legs and swung his arms to turn and fend off the mob.

Then webbing flew over his head, sunlight filtered momentarily through a checkerboard pattern, before a fishing net descended over his head and shoulders. Three pairs of arms slammed into him and shoved Alerio under the water.

The natural tendency when something falls over your head was to lift your arms and attempt to dislodge the object. Alerio began to reach for the fishing net. But the hands pressing down on his shoulders helped the weapons instructor focus. Instead of trying to fight the hands and the net, he dug under the silk bandage around his waist.

Between the small lead weights distributed around the edges of the net and the pressure of the hands, Alerio sank. His lungs cried out for air, and he wanted to battle his way back to the surface. Shoving aside the urge to take in a breath, Alerio concentrated on locating his assailants.

The thought of turning the water red with their blood and leaving their traitorous bodies for the fish ran through Alerio's mind. Resisting the temptation, the Corporal jabbed out with the Ally of the Golden Valley dagger. The long double-edged blade pushed through the netting and sank into flesh. Before the wounded man could backstroke away, the dagger retreated, swung to Alerio's front, and again breached the rope. After deeply puncturing another man's flesh, the blade withdrew.

Far under the surface and free from the grips of two men, Alerio could have cut the net and escaped. But then the third assassin would swim away unmarked. Scissoring his legs, Alerio fought the weight of the net, moved upward, and shoved the blade at the last assailant. He was rewarded with the satisfying feel of a blade entering skin and slicing flesh. The Legionary assassin must have twisted away from the sharp edge, causing the blade to slice sideways.

There was a cloud of blood in the water when Alerio retracted the dagger and guided it up along the profile of his face. When the blade reached the fibers on his head, Alerio cut the net and allowed it to settle on his shoulders. He wanted the net, he wanted the men who attacked him, and he wanted the man who planned the mission. But mostly, Corporal Sisera wanted a breath of air. With powerful thrusts, he kicked for the surface.

***

The thrashing of the weaker swimmers hid the attack. None noticed and that was fine with Alerio. He wanted revenge not their help. But a Tesserarius lacked the authority to order a hearing or a session on the punishment post. What he controlled were pay and supplies. While those tasks wouldn't satisfy his immediate need for retaliation, one of his jobs did. Dragging the fishing net, the Corporal swam behind the last Legionary in the Century and thought of the best Legion practice for doing his duty and punishing the offenders.

At the beach, Alerio dunked his head and slipped the fishing net from around his neck. He left it underwater and strolled onto the beach directly to the section with rocks and gravel. As if following a ritual, he selected and stacked larger stones.

"What are those for, Corporal Sisera?" a Legionary inquired.

"An altar to my personal Goddess," Alerio replied while arranging the rocks into separate columns.

"Who is she?"

The Legionary didn't get an answer. His Tesserarius was already moving away from the little shrine and marching in the direction of the NCOs' tent.

***

"Grilli. I need two favors."

"Whatever you need, Corporal Sisera."

"I want a limb about the length of my arm and as thick as my wrist," Alerio replied. "And I need the mule handlers to go on a hunt."

"A few handlers spotted boar tracks in the hills," Grilli reported. "It shouldn't take much to gather a hunting party. And finding the stick isn't a problem. Can I inquire why you need it?"

"In your own words, I'm about to become someone's worst nightmare," Alerio said as he ducked into the tent. Moments later, he emerged wearing a tunic, his hobnailed boots, and a dual gladius rig strapped on his back. "Just leave the stick by the tent. I'll collect it later."

Decanus Tescum watched as the Corporal crossed from the NCOs' tent to 10th Squad's area.

"That is an interesting harness, Tesserarius," observed Lucius.

"It comes in handy at times, Lance Corporal Tescum," Alerio offered. "Go to the beach and call in the Century. Once everyone is gone, have Palinurus locate a little temple I built. Straight down from it, he'll find a fishing net in the water."

"We'll retrieve the net for you," Tescum promised.

"Keep it hidden until I call for it."

The short squad leader started for the beach and Alerio wondered why he didn't order the squad to follow him.

"Lucius is moving," right pivot Palinurus announced. "10th Squad, get up, and get moving."

The big man lumbered after his Decanus followed by the other six men of the contubernium. Alerio started to ask about the unusual command structure when Lucius turned his head, winked, and faced back towards the beach. As long as the squad performed, Alerio would let them work things out their own way.

Corporal Sisera marched to the Centurion's tent, turned about, and marched back down the length of the camp. During his patrol, the Legionaries who lingered on the beach returned. When 10th Squad appeared, he noticed Palinurus had a large bulge under his tunic.

"Maximus Century. We have a grave issue," Alerio announced while turning to check each squad. Then he paused and eyed one in particular. "We have infantrymen missing. 1st Squad, you are short three men."

"Three of my contubernium have fallen ill," Horatius Ostrei answered. "If we had servants, it wouldn't have happened."

The statement surprised Alerio. Was that Ostrei's problem with him? No, the Lance Corporal expected to be the Tesserarius. The lack of servants was probably just one issue Horatius used to gather sympathy for his claim.

29

"If they are too ill to appear, we'll send them to the Legion for treatment," offered Alerio. "4th Squad, send a runner to the mule handlers. Have them prepare litters. The rest of you help Decanus Ostrei bring his men out of the tent."

Lance Corporal Acharis Enitui turned to one of his 4th Squad Legionaries and started to issue the order. Ostrei spoke up and halted the process.

"That won't be necessary," Horatius stated. "They just need a little rest and they'll be fine."

"My information is for every heavy infantryman in the Century," Alerio advised. "They don't have to stand to listen. Call them out."

Horatius crossed his arms, elevated his chin, and stood in the defiant pose daring the Corporal to challenge him.

"Century. On your feet," Alerio ordered. Of the Legionaries in the other nine squads, about half were sitting. They stood and the NCO called out. "Stand By."

"Standing by, Corporal," Seventy-two men replied while stomping their right feet.

Dissention in the ranks wasn't unheard of in the Legion. Aggressive Legionaries clashed over everything from personalities to rations. The disputes were handled in one of two ways. A fight under an Optio's supervision or a ruling by an infantry officer. Alerio had neither handy, so he used the one tool at his command. Despite what any of the Legionaries felt about Corporal Sisera, discipline and pride wouldn't let them sit down, fix dinner, or even move without his release.

An ominous calm fell over the camp as the squads waited. Some Legionaries shuffled their feet but were quickly silenced by their squad leaders. They realized the conflict between Sisera and Ostrei needed to be resolved for the good of the Century.

Birds chirped as they flew overhead and the sounds of waves crashing on the beach carried to the Legionaries. The stillness stretched out until Ostrei broke.

"Help them," he ordered the other members of 1st Squad.

The four healthy ones ducked into the tent. Moments later, they reappeared supporting wounded men.

One had a bloody wrap on his thigh, another held a red-soaked compress to his side, and the third clutched a piece of blood-stained cloth to his left shoulder.

"What's this?" Alerio shouted. "These men have been attacked."

Ostrei's mouth fell open at the surprise in the Tesserarius' voice. Grumbling came from the rest of the Century as they saw the bloody injuries.

"This cannot stand," Alerio announced. "There may be retribution. Who knows if the assailants will come for 1st Squad in the dead of the night?"

Horatius Ostrei flinched at the wording. None of the other squad leaders picked up on the threat.

"Orders, Corporal?" asked Telesia Caudini from 5th Squad.

"We will protect 1st Squad," Alerio replied. "Every tent will have a Legionary on watch throughout the night. No harm will come to our 1st Squad. Century, stand down."

Ostrei and the 1st Squad relaxed. Corporal Sisera hadn't accused them of attempted murder. And having to post a watch, wasn't really a punishment.

Alerio strolled to 10th Squad, took something from Palinurus, and carried it back to the Centurion's tent. Reaching up, he hung the fishing net on the front tent pole. As he walked away, Alerio looked into Ostrei's eyes and smiled a toothy, silly grin.

It was going to be a long night for 1st Squad. They didn't know it yet, because Corporal Sisera made an announcement giving them another worry.

"Tomorrow, we're holding a hill climbing competition. Squad against squad elimination rounds. Get lots of rest tonight, you'll need every man in your contubernium at his best."

A Century's Tesserarius could short pay a Legionary, sink a promotion, or withhold supplies. In this case, Alerio used his position as the training NCO to schedule a brutal form of conditioning. Unfortunately for Lance Corporal Ostrei, the 1st Squad wasn't at their best.

Chapter 4 – Victoria Hill

"In the name of the Goddess Victoria, we dedicate this competition," Alerio announced.

The Century stood in ranks facing their Corporal and behind him the nine-hundred-foot hill. They nodded reflexively at his words, but the heavy infantrymen were distracted. Drifting on the early morning air, the aroma of roasting swine made their stomachs rumble and their mouths water.

At the end of the practice field, two large boars crackled on spits. Mule handlers rotated them over fires and, based on the smell, had been since last night. In addition to the meat, wineskins and loaves of bread were lined up and waiting for the winning squads.

However, before the Legionaries feasted, they had to claim victory over the hill by beating other squads to the top. The promise of food almost overcame the apprehension of the steep climb.

"Lance Corporals, on me," Alerio directed. The ten squad leaders marched from the ranks and formed a semicircle around the Tesserarius. "The rules are simple. Win two heats and your contubernium eats. Lose, and your squad keeps climbing."

"I object to the competition," Horatius Ostrei complained. He pointed at the murderous incline and added. "1st Squad has injuries."

"If all the squads can't participate, we'll cancel the climb," Alerio announced.

A smile came over Ostrei's face then it fled from his features.

"Grilli. Take the pigs and the bread and throw them in the ocean," the Corporal ordered while he walked away. "We'll not have games today or a feast. 1st Squad has issued a protest."

Sixty-three voices roared their disapproval and turned angry faces towards the seven Privates of Ostrei's contubernium standing in ranks. Several heavy infantrymen up the stakes by pointing at 1st Squad and mouthing threats. The danger to the contubernium didn't go unnoticed by the squad leaders.

"Corporal Sisera, hold that order," Trax Dircium, the Decanus of 2nd Squad, requested. "We'd like to discuss a resolution."

"There's only one acceptable solution," Alerio remarked as he continued to walk away. "Grilli. How tender is that boar?"

The mule handler drew a knife and sliced off a piece. With it between his fingers, Grilli held it aloft and allowed the juice to drip from the fresh pig. Then he put his face under the meat, caught some drippings in his mouth, and took a bite.

"Corporal Sisera. It must be the salt grass they feed on," Grilli reported. "This boar is some of the tastiest pig I've ever had. It will be a sin to waste it."

Groans came from the ranks as the Legionaries smacked their lips in anticipation of having a taste for themselves.

"Ostrei. What happened to your men?" Lucius Tescum demanded.

"Watch your tone with me, little man," Ostrei warned.

"He asked a valid question," Telesia Caudini observed. "And if you want to threaten someone, try me."

"Bickering isn't getting us anywhere," Acharis Enitui, Decanus of 4th Squad, pointed out. "How did your men become injured?"

"We'd all like an answer to that question," added Quiris Stulte from 9th Squad. "No one saw them attacked by another contubernium."

"It's complicated," Ostrei offered.

"A simple answer is not complicated," Hallus Italus from 3rd Squad stated. "Dealing with angry Legionaries in my tent is. Your men have knife wounds, not stomach ailments or fevers. How did they get them?"

"I don't know," stammered Ostrei.

"You strut around telling everyone you should be the Tesserarius," responded Pentri Umbria. "Yet you don't know when your own contubernium takes knives to each other. And now you want the entire Century to suffer from your neglect?"

"There is one possibility," Trax Dircium suggested. "Unconscious men can't run. I volunteer the 2nd Squad to beat them. At least I'll get some pig and not have to listen to my contubernium complain for a week."

"9th Squad will join in the punishment," added Quiris Stulte.

"You would beat me and my squad over a little pig?" Ostrei asked in horror.

"Hades man, heavy infantrymen would certainly beat you over roasted swine," Caricini Aternus from 7th Squad assured him. "Up north during one campaign, I watched two men die while fighting over a rotting elk corpse. And even after cooking, you could smell the death."

"From the elk or from the Legionaries?" Trax inquired.

"From all three," Caricini replied. "We still ate the meat before burying the men."

Horatius Ostrei peered into the stern faces of the other squad leaders. His dream of being the Century's Tesserarius, as did his defiance, died at that moment. Even if selected by the Optio or Centurion, these men would never accept his authority.

"1st Squad will climb," he declared.

"Corporal Sisera. In the name of the Goddess Victoria, let the games begin," announced Acharis Enitui. "1st squad will climb."

35

Cheers from the ranks drowned out Corporal Sisera's words but the arm gesture to Grilli was unmistakable. The feast would not be discarded. As the yelling faded, Alerio strolled back to the squad leaders.

"Two wins and you feast," he repeated then added. "We'll use a reverse line up. The first match is 1st Squad against 10th Squad. Then 2nd against the 9th."

As the squad leaders went to their contuberniums to explain the rotation, Lucius Tescum moved alongside Ostrei.

"Let's see if you can keep up with this little man, cūlus," Lucius whispered. "And later, maybe you and I should have a discussion about respect."

***

Corporal Sisera picked up a large stick from the ground and stood at the base of the hill.

"Two wins and you feast," he said while tapping one end of the branch into the palm of his hand. The motion resembled a man threatening to attack someone with a club. "Squads, stand by."

"Standing by, Corporal," the sixteen racers responded.

"Go!"

10th Squad managed to run up the face before the steep incline forced them to lean forward and use their hands. While Tescum's contubernium moved steadily up the hill, Ostrei's struggled. The leg wound caused immediate issues and required two men supporting the injured man. They fell behind. Then the Tesserarius dashed up beside them. As he climbed, he offered encouragement.

"1st Squad, you are falling behind. At this pace, you'll be on the hill all morning," Alerio informed them. "When I was at Volsinii, I watched heavy infantrymen die on slopes not much steeper than this. You won't die today. But you'll feel like it."

Corporal Sisera moved on and reached the top just behind the 10th Squad.

On the practice field, the waiting Squads appreciated the Corporal taking time to motivate the distressed Legionaries.

"Come on 1st Squad, put your hearts into it," Alerio called down while tapping the stick into his palm. They reached the top and fell on the crest. Alerio lifted the stick, waved it, and shouted down to the practice field. "2nd Squad and 9th, on the line. Go."

While the next two contuberniums raced up the grade, the first two squads picked their way down to the base of the hill. One needed to race and win one more heat before they were done. 10th Squad had a chance. The 1st Squad didn't. The man with the wound at his waist was already bleeding through his bandage and bending over favoring his side.

It went unnoticed that Corpora Sisera didn't tap the club into his palms once Ostrei's unit left the course. He held the stick along his leg or waved it overhead to signal more starts. But the next time 1st Squad came to the line; the branch dropped and began tapping Alerio's palm.

**

For the fourth time, 1st Squad staggered to the base of the hill. With them were the Legionaries of 8th Squad. All sixteen were covered in dirt, sweat, and blood. Most from cuts on their hands and skinned knees. But the bandages on Ostrei's men were saturated and the wounded Legionaries had their eyes compressed against the pain. Seeing the struggling unit, the caring Corporal Sisera scrambled down to the starting line.

"I feel terrible about the suffering of this contubernium," the Tesserarius proclaimed while tapping the club into his palm. "Maybe we should call off the rest of the games. I fear the squad can't continue. The six remaining squads will return to the Century area and forgo the feast."

"Hades Tesserarius, I can't help it if 1st Squad is dēfutūta," a Legionary announced. "I've been up this hill and I've earned my share."

"But if 1st Squad doesn't make it to the top," Alerio mentioned as the stick continued to tap his hand. "Then your victory won't count."

"They will make it up the hill," promised the Legionary. "Even if I have to kick their cūlī almost to the top."

"If that's what it takes to keep the competition going. Stand by. Go!"

The five healthy but exhausted members of 1st Squad attempted to help the three injured men. When they faltered, Apulia Frentani's 8th Squad stepped up behind them and shoved, kicked, and even picked up two and tossed them up the hill. As ugly and brutal as the climb was, Corporal Sisera watched impassively while tapping his palm with the club.

By the sixth round, Horatius Ostrei and 1st Squad were on their knees at the starting line. Only one other squad stood with them. The remainder of the Century lounged around eating slices of boar and bread. Between streams of vino, they called out insults at the final two squads.

"Lance Corporal Enitui. Take 4th Squad to the top then join me at the feast," Alerio directed.

"What about the 1st Squad?"

"Once your contubernium has been served, they are welcome to crawl over like snakes and join real men at the feast."

While the eight men swarmed up the slope, Corporal Sisera marched to Horatius Ostrei. The Lance Corporal knelt in the dirt with his forehead resting on the ground. Alerio squatted beside him and leaned close to the Decanus' ear.

"The next time you want someone dead, be sure the job is done right," Alerio whispered. "And maybe come for me yourself. It'll save me the trouble of cutting your throat in the night."

The stick hit the ground and bounced. Then another item clicked as it landed by the club. Horatius raised his head and gawked at his own coin purse.

"And fix the slit in the back of your tent," Alerio ordered as he stood and peered up at the eight men almost at the top of Victoria hill. "Dig deep 4th Squad, you're almost there."

Act 2

Chapter 5 – Usurped, mangled?

Three days later, while the Century ran unarmored shield drills, five wagons appeared on the beach. Rolling from the south and with an Optio on the lead wagon, suggested the caravan was coming from the Legion camps at Velia.

"Corporal Sisera. Looks like we'll soon be doing this with real shields," Trax Dircium said while pointing to the supply caravan.

"And none too soon," Alerio replied. "I'm sick of watching you show off those titan-like arms."

"They do make the other lads jealous."

"Lance Corporals. Work with your contuberniums," Alerio shouted. "I'm going to greet our visitor."

Alerio dropped down the embankment from the practice field and marched partway across the gravel zone. While he waited for the slow-moving wagons to reach him, the Corporal took the measure of the Sergeant sitting on the first wagon.

He was a middle-aged man with a shot of white in the short hair at his temples and wore a frown on his lean face. The Optio didn't look in Alerio's direction. Rather the Sergeant sat stiffly on the seat board, stretching his long neck to observe the Century's empty-handed drills.

"Optio Gustavi?" Alerio inquired

The wagon driver reined in the horses and the first rolled to a stop.

"I'm Ibis Gustavi. Who are you?"

"Corporal Alerio Sisera, Tesserarius of Maximus Century," Alerio reported. "We're glad…"

The Sergeant cut him off with a sharp jerk of his arm.

"First off, it is Megellus Century," Ibis stated before swinging down from the wagon seat. Once on the ground, he spun and looked down his nose at Alerio. "And I haven't appointed my Tesserarius, yet."

"Yes, Optio," Alerio replied then attempted to explain. "It's just that Senator Spurius Maximus ordered me here as your second in command NCO."

"Senator Maximus is in the Capital and not in Licosa," Gustavi advised. "Whereas Centurion Fenoris Megellus is here and in command."

"The Centurion is here?" Alerio asked.

"In the villa up the beach and has been for two days," the Sergeant informed Alerio. "The slow dances the squads are doing on the practice field, is that your work?"

"Yes Sergeant. We didn't have equipment so I thought the drilling would help with unit cohesion," Alerio reported.

"They look silly, and the drills are unnecessary," Gustavi commented. "It's not why the Century was formed."

"It's not?"

The Sergeant didn't respond to the question. He turned and spoke to the wagon driver.

"Drop my gear at the NCOs' tent and take the wagon to the villa," Gustavi ordered. He lifted an arm and indicated for the remaining wagons to head for the camp. Only when the horses were in motion did the Optio address Alerio.

"Corporal Sisera. Seeing as you've usurped command, order Megellus Century to the camp," Gustavi instructed. He emphasized the new name of the unit. "Let's see how badly you've mangled the squad assignments."

Usurped, mangled? Alerio's head buzzed with the words as he marched off the beach. When he met with Spurius Maximus, the Senator had been clear in his goals for funding the Century.

***

A few weeks ago, Alerio stood in front of Maximus' desk as the Senator finished reading a missive. Laying down the parchment, he looked up and smiled.

"Stand easy Corporal Sisera. For the Legionaries in a shield wall their motivation is to live and remain uninjured," the former General stated. "Killing the enemy assures the first two. Walking away from a battle healthy, as well as, receiving steady pay and full rations is their reward."

"It is that sir," Alerio agreed.

"Step back one layer from the battle line and the Corporal's goal is to assure his squads take ground and perform as a unit. His pay is higher, rations more substantial, and he may receive a little extra if they win the fight with a heroic deed or two," Maximus stated. "Step back, metaphorically, and the Optio has responsibility for the discipline of his Century. Pay, yes, and rations absolutely but, his drive goes beyond the immediate fight. If successful in routing the foe, a Sergeant may receive a bonus from the capture of soldiers and enemy weapons."

"It's a rather simplified way to look at the duties of a Century's NCOs, sir," remarked Alerio.

42

"I have a point to make and while your observation is correct, you'll miss it if you focus on the mundane," the Senator cautioned. After his protégé dipped his head in acknowledgment, Senator Maximus continued. "An infantry officer has additional motivation beyond pay, food, and bonuses. Showing his courage to his Century and the senior officers may get a Centurion a small piece of the slaves, weapon sales, and confiscated goods. And if he and his Century show extreme bravery, they are used in strategic areas with more chances to collect honors and accolades."

"You make the Legion sound like craftsmen in a marketplace," Alerio observed.

"Now you're beginning to understand this lecture," the Senator commented. "The Senior Centurion and Senior Tribune are beyond caring about their pay schedule or worry about their next meal. They have more on the line, so to speak, with concerns about keeping their positions. Success brings them shares of spoils and rewards from the battle commander and the General. Plus, the senior staff may collect accolades from the Senate with the promise of bags of gold. I'll not talk about the Coronels. They are professional military with designs on a Senatorial position or being selected by the next General as a battle commander. But what about the Consul/General? A parade through the city with throngs singing his praises or orders from the Senate isn't why he risks life and reputation to march a Legion off to war."

Alerio shifted his feet, feeling uncomfortable at someone discussing a Consul in mercenary terms. But Spurius Maximus was a prior Consul, a General, a hero of the Republic for his campaigns against the Samnites, and a powerful Senator. While a farm lad wouldn't, a politically astute man of Maximus' status could describe motives in any manner he saw fit.

"A winning Consul when he returns to the Senate owns far more than when he marched out. What comes back to the Capital as a victorious General are acres of land, sacks of gold, and personal trade agreements with important people in subjugated cities," the Senator explained. "But there are hidden men behind it all. Men who loan money to the Republic to fund the Legion. Armor, weapons, rations, pay, and the means to transport the Legion to battle are expensive. To gather the amount necessary, the Republic reaches out to these wealthy men."

"Men like you, sir," Alerio suggested.

"Yes. And I expect victory and a return on my investment. But there is another side to this. My desire to protect the Republic. Between the barbarians to our north and the encroachment by the Qart Hadasht Empire to our south, we must defend the Republic," Maximus professed. "In the end Corporal Sisera, war is about profit and protecting our wealth."

"Sir, I appreciate you educating me, but as a simple infantryman, I have no investment funds. And unfortunately, no head for business or politics," Alerio exclaimed. "There has to be another reason you ordered me here."

"You are about to be put in a position to start reaping some of the benefits of war. As the Corporal of a combat Century, your assets will increase. Earn glory and victory and you'll soon be an Optio. As your patron, I can promise you the promotions won't stop with the Sergeant's rank," the Senator assured Alerio. "I wanted you to understand the monetary side because I'm funding a Century and you're going to be the Tesserarius."

"I'm honored, sir. But the Corporal is chosen by the Century's Optio and Centurion," Alerio reminded him. Then he thought for a moment and questioned. "You've just explained the monetary advantages of war by a Legion. What is the upside of funding a Century?"

"Almost none, unless the Century does something extraordinary," Maximus admitted. "I have a friend who lost most of his merchant fleet over the last year. He had purchased a Tribune position for his son. Unfortunately, Fenoris Megellus got stationed with the Northern Legion in a support command. For three years, the young noblemen supervised the building of bridges, roads, and Legion posts. In the end, he earned no glory or bonuses. Now my friend's son is without means. As a favor, I'm funding a Century for Fenoris."

"Wouldn't it be cheaper to buy him a Tribune position on a General's staff?"

"Sisera, you may not have a head for business or politics, but you do form interesting questions," teased the Senator. "While helping a friend, I also aim to help his son. Being an infantry officer will mature him and place him under strict Senior Centurions."

"Or get him killed, Senator," Alerio suggested.

"That's why I want you there to train the Century," Maximus remarked. "Centurion Megellus and his Optio, a man named Ibis Gustavi, are recruiting infantrymen and buying armor and weapons. Belen will give you coins to purchase tents and camp supplies."

"Thank you for the opportunity, General."

45

"Don't thank me yet, Corporal Sisera," Maximus warned. "You'll be an outsider forced on the Century. I have no concerns about you gaining the respect of the Legionaries. I fear your bigger challenge will be winning over the Centurion and the Optio."

The Senator's words faded and Optio Gustavi's words returned, "Seeing as you've usurped command, order Megellus Century to the camp. Let's see how badly you've mangled the squad assignments."

Chapter 6 – Ill-equipped for War

As the Legionaries marched in, Ibis Gustavi came out of the NCOs' tent. He strolled the length of the camp as each contubernium fell out of formation and positioned themselves at their tents. Alerio followed the Sergeant to the infantry officer's tent.

"Horatius. What is that fishing net doing on the Centurion's quarters?" the Optio demanded of the Decanus from 1st Squad.

Horatius Ostrei shifted his eyes from the sliced net to Gustavi, to Sisera, and back to the Sergeant.

"It was found, and nobody claimed it," Ostrei replied.

"Well, it doesn't belong on Centurion Megellus' tent," Gustavi declared. He took the net down and tossed it towards the center of the camp. Then, the Sergeant scanned the squads. "Not how I would have placed them, but it's acceptable. Good job, Horatius."

"Optio, I didn't place the squads, Corporal Sisera did," Horatius corrected the Sergeant.

"You were signed on as the Tesserarius. Why haven't you taken charge?"

Alerio stared at Lance Corporal Ostrei and allowed a tight smile to crease his lips. Horatius paused before answering.

"Corporal Sisera and I discussed the position and we decided he should be the Century's Tesserarius."

"Since when do junior NCOs make command decisions? This is not a democracy," bellowed Gustavi. A moment later, he calmed down and instructed. "Horatius. Move your gear to the NCOs' tent. Sisera, you will take over 1st Squad."

Ostrei's squad shifted nervously. The prospect of living in close quarters with a man who might hold a vendetta against them sent chills up four of their spines. The other three reached for their wounds and cupped their bandages.

"It's your Century, Optio Gustavi," Alerio remarked.

"Yes, it is. Now move your gear, Lance Corporal Sisera," Gustavi ordered. His choice of words implying a reduction in rank for Alerio.

"I wish you luck with it," Alerio added. "I'll be moving to the Legions at Velia."

1st Squad relaxed at avoiding the new squad leader.

"You'll do nothing of the kind. I gave you an order," Gustavi informed him. "Maybe a session on the punishment post will teach you to respect an order from your Optio."

"Sergeant Gustavi. I suspect you had every man here sign an enlistment form and gave them an advance in pay."

"Of course, that's the usual procedure," the Optio responded.

"I never signed my name or accepted pay," Alerio informed the Sergeant. "Thus, you are not my Optio, I am not part of this Century, and I am not going on the punishment post."

"Then pack your things and go," ordered Gustavi. "Corporal Ostrei. 1st through 4th Squads equipment is in the front wagon. The rest of the gear is in the other wagons with supplies. Instruct the men to unload them."

Alerio was halfway to the NCOs' tent when Horatius cleared his throat.

"Century, stand by," the newly promoted Corporal Ostrei shouted.

No stomp or vocal reaction came from the squads. Silence fell over the camp. The only sound was the crunch of Alerio's hobnailed boots on the sand.

"Your Tesserarius has called for your attention," Gustavi growled. "I expect results. Corporal Ostrei, again."

"Century, stand by!"

All ten squads including 1st turned and faced their tents. Respect for their NCOs was the thread that held a Century together. Heavy infantrymen were expected to hold a shield wall and maneuver while engaged with an enemy. They could only do that if the men giving orders were revered. Punishment for a few rule breakers was expected and necessary for discipline. But an entire Century voting with their backs spoke to their lack of esteem for Horatius Ostrei.

"Century, stand by," Sergeant Gustavi ordered.

For a moment, he feared a total mutiny. Then, the squads turned about and replied, "Standing by, Optio."

"Fall out and empty the wagons."

***

Alerio took time bundling his gear and strapping his armor, helmet, and shield together. After shouldering the awkward load, he pushed through the tent flap and was greeted by cursing and grumblings of discontent.

Immediately, he spotted the source. At the area of the first four squads, new shields were stacked, and the Legionaries fitted on pristine chest armor, skirts, and helmets. Starting at the 5th Squad, the gear was scarred and bent with cracked and dry rotted leather straps. At first glance, the equipment appeared to be badly used. He looked closely at 9th and 10th Squads and saw that most of the gear was unserviceable.

Ibis Gustavi scurried down the length of the camp with his eyes locked straight ahead. He ignored the calls for an explanation and complaints from the Legionaries. Almost as if he harbored guilt for the ruined equipment, the Optio fled towards the NCOs' tent.

"Sergeant Gustavi. Is that the best you could buy with Senator Maximus's coins?" Alerio inquired.

"There were other expenses," Gustavi mumbled while brushing Alerio aside before disappearing through the tent's opening.

Alerio wanted to walk away. His impression of the Optio and the absence of the Centurion already gave him a feeling of mistrust. And now, most of the heavy infantrymen didn't have the equipment they needed to face an enemy.

5th Squad attempted to stack their shields, but the iron bands were bent and the shields so warped, the stack fell over. One of the Legionaries kicked the pile, easily flipping two of the heavy infantry shields into the air.

'The wood is rotted,' he thought before dropping his gear and spinning around.

He paused, questioning his actions for a heartbeat, before marching into the NCOs' tent to confront the Sergeant.

***

The Optio sat on a camp stool with his head resting in his hands. Glancing up with a worried expression on his face, he seemed surprised at seeing Alerio, yet relieved. Probably because it wasn't one of his squad leaders demanding an explanation.

"What are you doing here?" Gustavi inquired.

"I could ask you the same thing, Sergeant."

"Clarify that comment, Corporal."

"That equipment tells me two things," Alerio replied. "You siphoned off funds for yourself."

"What's the other thing you think you know?"

"You are not an experienced infantry Optio."

"What makes you say that?"

"Because if you had ever stood behind a shield wall, you'd want the best equipment and best-trained men between you and the enemy's spears."

"You're right. My experience is with building for the Legions," Gustavi informed Alerio. "But I didn't take the Century's funds for myself. The coins were necessary for the villa where Centurion Megellus is staying."

"Instead of shields and armor, you diverted the funds to fixing up a summer villa?" questioned Alerio. "How is

50

a heavy infantry Century supposed to defend themselves with inferior equipment?"

"That's where you're wrong," Gustavi informed the Corporal. "This isn't an infantry unit."

"You try convincing a battle commander of that when he puts you in a maniple."

"Centurion Megellus is working the political angle," Gustavi reported. "and I've staffed the Century with Legionaries who are craftsmen. The 9th and 10th Squads specifically."

"What about the others?"

"The Samnites are here because Consul/General Otacilius Crassus is of Samnite origin. And we want to be attached to his Legions," Gustavi confessed. "General Valerius Mesalla will be marching on Syracuse. While he is laying siege to miles of defensive walls, General Crassus will be dealing with smaller cities. He'll require infrastructure and that's where Megellus Century will be needed."

"Senator Maximus expects this Century to be a line outfit and part of a battle maniple formation," Alerio remarked. "He has most likely sent word to the Legion's command staff informing them of the fact."

"Centurion Megellus is working his contacts to assure the proper outcome," Gustavi declared.

"I hope your plan works. Because I've faced Qart Hadasht mercenaries. At the present state of your squads, the soldiers will kick their way through those rotten shields and butcher you and the entire Century," Alerio warned. Then, he added while ducking through the exit. "You can expect a communiqué from the Senator after he receives my report."

"Corporal Sisera. I might have been too hasty in judging your qualifications," Sergeant Gustavi called from inside. "Come back and let's talk about the Tesserarius position."

Alerio's stomach soured but Senator Maximus ordered him here and depended on him to build this Century. Despite his sense of pride and self-preservation, Corporal Sisera turned and walked back into the NCOs' tent.

***

"How bad are they?" Alerio asked as he squatted by Pentri Umbria from 6th Squad.

The Decanus spun the shield on a corner then punched it with his fist. Rather than the sound of flesh and bone on hardwood, it resembled a hand slap against a wet surface.

"I've peeled off the covers from four," Pentri replied while cutting the dried leather facing. "We may be able to rebuild one by scavenging from two others."

"At the best, we can rebuild sixteen out of forty-eight," Alerio counted. "That leaves us short thirty-two shields. How about the armor?"

Pentri kicked a helmet to the Tesserarius, and the headgear wobbled to Alerio's feet. The motion of the shell unimpeded by cheek guards, they were missing, and the wobble due to the misshapen helmet.

"Did they give us parts or extra leather bindings?"

"It seems the distressed sale this junk came from didn't include repair items," Lance Corporal Umbria spit out. "Do you want to see the armored skirts?"

"Strip what you can and start rebuilding the shields," Alerio instructed while ignoring Pentri's last comment. "I'm going to see if any squads have it better."

As the Corporal crossed to the 7th, Optio Gustavi emerged from the NCOs' tent and marched to the 9th and then the 10th. Moments later, both squads followed him with their leather bags of tools. He also collected the first four squads and marched the six contuberniums out of camp, down to the beach, and northward in the direction of the villa.

"You and the Optio don't like each other, do you?" inquired Caricini Aternus.

"I don't know him well enough to dislike him," Alerio replied to the Decanus of 7th Squad. "Let's just say I'm disappointed in Sergeant Gustavi."

The Lance Corporal held up a section of twisted breastplate and added, "You are not alone Tesserarius."

Chapter 7 – Craftsmen Legionaries

While the Squads attempted to salvage gear by combining the best parts, Alerio went to the NCOs' tent. Inside, he placed the Century's fund box on the camp desk, sat on the stool, and removed the straps from around the box.

Alerio pulled out a bottle of ink and a quill. Then he picked up the Century's roster and unrolled it. Horatius Ostrei was changed from Tesserarius to Lance Corporal, Lucius Tescum's promotion to Lance Corporal was noted, as well as Palinurus' demotion back to Private. Then Alerio hesitated. The final change to the Legion payment document had to be made but, it carried consequences.

Once Alerio Sisera wrote his name on the roster, he'd fall under Ibis Gustavi's command. The Sergeant's next order, be it good or bad, required obedience. Alerio thought for a moment before adding his name to the list of personnel. Then he rolled it, placed the roster in the box, and extracted the accounting document.

"Let's see how badly you've hurt the Century's funds, Centurion Fenoris Megellus," Corporal Sisera whispered as he unrolled the parchment.

Anger flashed through Alerio as he ran his eyes over the listed items. The cruelest accounting trick wasn't the expenses for a wagon full of building supplies for the villa. They weren't listed. Instead, the document showed every Legionary had been issued new equipment. When the Century reported to the Legion, the quartermaster would issue new helmets, shields, armored skirts, chest guards, and gladii to replace the broken, worn out, and bent. And the individual Legionary would have the expense of replacing his gear deducted from his pay. As a result, forty-eight of the eighty infantrymen in the Century would shoulder the bill for repairs to a summer villa.

Alerio rolled the accounting document and placed it in the box. With shaking hands, he opened the coin pouch and began counting. A quick estimate showed the Century had enough for another pay cycle. Only enough. Then the Century would have to report to the Legion and begin drawing pay from the General's fund. A sad thought crossed his mind as he tied the pouch and closed the lid.

There were no additional coins for a funeral. If a Legionary died and the proper procedures for a funeral weren't observed, his soul might wander for one hundred years before being allowed to cross the river Styx and enter the Elysian Fields. A priest, sacrificial animals, and a burial required currency. Thanks to the Centurion and Optio, the Century had none to spare.

***

Alerio left the tent and marched to the rear of the NCOs' quarters. Moving towards the wagons with the Century's javelins and food supplies, he called to the mule handlers as he passed through their camp.

"Grilli. Tell your handlers their recreation period had drawn to a close," he informed the head mule handler. "Assign a servant to each squad. Make sure your most talented are with the ones mending gear."

"Tesserarius Sisera, you seem troubled," Grilli observed.

"Me?" challenged Alerio. "I've savored victory and tasted defeat. The sour bile on my tongue is neither."

"If not victory or defeat, what are you tasting?"

"Vexation," Alerio declared as he climbed onto the first wagon to check the supplies.

***

Once back in the squad area, Alerio looked around as the Legionaries hammered and twisted metal trying to get the armor and helmets back into the proper shape.

"Lance Corporal Aternus, 7th Squad has first watch on the NCOs' tent," Alerio instructed. "Get with Frentani and rotate the guard with 8th Squad."

"And where will you be Corporal Sisera?" Caricini inquired as he attempted to tap an old band around a newly constructed shield. At two deep impact dents, the iron stretched and snapped. Decanus Aternus threw the pieces to the ground and spit after them.

55

"To see the Optio and Centurion about that," Alerio replied while raising an arm to point at the broken strips of iron.

Caricini looked up with a scowl on his face and assured Alerio, "Corporal Sisera, we have the NCOs' tent secured."

Of all the property in all the tents, including the Centurions, the Century's funds were the most valuable. When the Optio and the Tesserarius left the area, a Legionary stood guard to protect the unit's wealth. Even if the funds were depleted.

With the thought of the coins and gear in mind, Alerio marched up the camp, moved between the officer's tent and 1st Squad's, and stopped. Down on the beach, a Centurion trotted from the North. He rode past the Legion camp without a sideways glance. Although not sure, Alerio guessed the rider was Centurion Fenoris Megellus. Deciding he could at least have a conversation with the Sergeant, Alerio marched down to the beach and headed towards the villa.

***

Private Palinurus stood on a line of scattered stones. A few days before, they had been a wall of the compound with only a few lose and fallen rocks. Now one complete side of the barrier had been dismantled.

"Building a road?" Alerio inquired as he walked up from the beach.

"Shoddy workmanship, Tesserarius," the big Legionary replied. "They used mortar to hide their lack of knowledge. Stone has character. You cannot place angry on top of angry."

"Angry?"

56

"Let me show you," suggested Palinurus. He selected two rocks and stacked one on top of the other in the palm of his hand. Then he vibrated them by shaking his hand from side to side.

"They appear stable," offered Alerio.

"Watch," instructed Palinurus. His hand dipped slightly to the side for less than a heartbeat then flattened. The top rock shifted, rotated, and then settled crosswise to the bottom stone. "Terminus, our God of boundary markers would be insulted if I forced these rocks together with mortar."

"I don't know about Terminus. But from your description, I imagine the rocks would be outraged if you bedded them together in the wall," Alerio guessed. He had no idea what the Legionary was talking about. "Where can I find Optio Gustavi and Centurion Megellus?"

"Centurion Megellus rode out right after he stormed from the villa asking what I was doing ripping down his cousin's wall," Palinurus replied. "I showed him the results of improper mixing rocks, but he tossed up his arms and went to find the Sergeant. A little while later, the Centurion was on his horse heading south along the beach."

"Is it going to take long to rebuild the wall?"

"I have them sorted by temperament," Palinurus assured him. "They'll practically set themselves."

Alerio nodded his head at the Legionary stonemason and picked his way over the stones. While growing up on his father's farm, Alerio had participated in building miles of stone walls. Never once did they consider angry stones. But every spring, some of the walls, no matter how carefully constructed, had fallen, and needed to be rebuilt. Maybe his father should have considered the temperament of the rocks.

***

As he walked the lawn beside the villa, Alerio heard the crackling of hot burning wood. Then the metallic smell of molten metal and charcoal assaulted his nostrils. He located the source of the sound and smells in an elevated rear courtyard.

Quiris Stulte from 9th Squad stood over a trench directing Legionaries who dug out shovels of sand. Behind him, a furnace made of stone blocks flashed flames with each pump of the bellows.

"What are you working on, Decanus Stulte?" Alerio inquired.

"Water flow, Corporal," Quiris responded. "The bath and fountain need new piping."

"I don't see a lot of clay around here. Are you getting it from up in the hills?"

"Not clay pipes, we're constructing lead pipes. Metal doesn't require the curing period of clay," the Lance Corporal informed him. "We're using that stone."

Alerio gazed at a long flat rock. Out of place resting on the patio bricks, the surface had dulled metallic residue around the edges.

"I thought you said you were making pipes not lead sheets."

Quiris moved to a position over the brick furnace, picked up a pair of tongs, and removed the top brick.

"Spoon," he ordered holding out a hand. A long-handled steel ladle was passed to the Lance Corporal. He reached into the furnace and dipped the spoon. "We've melted the lead and I'm going to skim off the dross."

From the furnace, he lifted out the spoon's head and poured hot liquid into a clay bowl. Then he pulled a thumb-sized lump of bee's wax from a pouch and dropped it to the furnace. Alerio moved closer to looked into the kiln. A container, filled with molten lead, rested in the flames.

"The wax works as flux and will cause the other impurities to clump together," Quiris explained as he dipped the spoon into the lead. After stirring, he lifted out a couple of small balls from the container and deposited them in the bowl. Handing off the spoon, he took the tongs and warned. "Hot metal."

Quiris lifted the container from the kiln, walked it to the flat stone, and began pouring lead. In a pattern resembling a cook making pancakes, he drizzled the lead onto the stone being careful not to splash any of the hot liquid. When there was an even layer coating the surface, he put the container back into the oven.

"A lead sheet," observed Alerio. "I don't see a pipe."

"Cool it," Quiris instructed.

Another Legionary tilted a bucket and water hissed and steamed when it hit the lead. By the bottom of the bucket, the water pooled on the sheet and bubbled a little. With a hatchet, a third Legionary trimmed the edges until the lead sheet was cut into a long rectangle. Then he worked the flat tool lengthwise down the surface of the lead until it was level.

"The thickness is good, and we have a smooth interior," Quiris proclaimed after squatting down to inspect the lead sheet. "Roll it."

Using the blade of the hatchet, the Legionary peeled the long edge of the sheet from the stone. When the edge resembled the crest of a wave, another man placed a pole against the curve and began beating along the edge with a wooden mallet. His hammering rolled the lead around the pole until a tube of metal formed.

"Good shape, cut it," Quiris ordered.

In response, the hatchet man sawed down the side of the tube separating it from the lead sheet. Once free, the mallet man hammered the seams together leaving a thin gap. Quiris took the ladle, dipped it into the hot lead, and poured the liquid into the seam. A few more taps to spread and flatted the hot lead closed and sealed the seam. Then the Legionary with the mallet pulled the pole from inside the form and held up a length of pipe.

"Quicker than clay and we can carry the water around bends," Quiris announced.

"Impressive," acknowledged Alerio. Not seeing any flowing water, he inquired. "Where does the water come from?"

"There's a spring on the other side of the hill. A small tunnel carries it to the castellum where it's collected," Quiris described while pointing at a round structure higher up on the hill. "I've got the rest of my squad pulling a shovel head attached to a rope through the tunnel cleaning out the gravel, dirt, and sand."

"And how do you get the water into the villa?"

"It'll flow from the castellum, fall into a pipe leading under the patio, and come out at a fountain," Quiris replied. "When we're done, this villa will have running water. As good a system as you'll find in any grand estate in the Capital."

"Why are skilled craftsmen, like your squad, in the infantry?" Alerio asked. "There has to be a demand for your services in every major city."

"Most of us are younger sons," Quiris informed Alerio. "We grew up learning our craft. But we'll always be under the thumb of our older brothers. At home, we'd be nothing more than servants. In the Legion, we get to travel and get paid for it."

"And maybe die on the tip of a spear," suggested Alerio.

"Not according to Optio Gustavi. We'll be building roads and Legion posts."

"Where is the Sergeant?"

"In the villa, Tesserarius," Quiris answered.

***

Alerio stomped across the patio with fury twisting his guts. Command staff's fantasy of being some kind of special unit had spread through the ranks. Instead of mentally and physically preparing to man a shield wall, the Century envisioned themselves far behind the line happily plying their trade.

He passed a dry fountain. In his haste, he barely paid attention to the statue of Faun with a hole in the half-man half-goat figure's mouth for the water pipe. Deeper in the great room, his eyes scanned the buffed floor tiles and the newly painted walls. Down a short hallway, he located the Sergeant and the Lance Corporals from 1st, 2nd, 3rd, and 4th Squads. They sat around a table, talking and sipping mugs of vino.

"Corporal Sisera, grab a drink and join us," Horatius Ostrei invited.

61

"I need to have words with the Sergeant," insisted Alerio.

"This is an NCO meeting, Tesserarius," Gustavi stated. "Whatever you have to say, can be said in front of our squad leaders."

"If that was the case, you're missing six squad leaders," Alerio pointed out.

"Do you always have to play the hard-nosed veteran?" Hallus Italus questioned. "It gets old fast."

Alerio started to explode on the gathering but caught himself. Two deep breaths later, he nodded and replied.

"Have any of you been to Sicilia?" he inquired.

"We've been stationed north and to the east," Acharis Enitui ventured. "Mostly it was boring and difficult building situations. So, an island to the south can't be much different."

"More heavy infantrymen marching around banging shields and beating themselves with gladii while we did the difficult work," Hallus Italus added.

Alerio clenched his fists and fought the urge to shout.

"I was in Messina when the Legions crossed over and faced impossible odds," Alerio lectured. "And I marched down the coast to face city militias. We retreated leaving half our Legionaries dead on the road. Sicilia is a battleground with walled cities and armies of Qart Hadasht mercenaries. There are no building projects to create infrastructure or units needed to build things. Only Legions on war footing every day, week in, and week out."

"We all know your opinion," Gustavi responded dismissing the warning. "Centurion Megellus is more than capable of handling the politics of placement."

Alerio's mouth fell open at the gullible attitude.

"Optio Gustavi. I'm going to train this Century in an attempt to save lives," he spoke in an even tone.

"Fine, Corporal Sisera. We're almost done with the villa," Gustavi responded with a dismissive wave of his hand. "Do what you must to satisfy your view of the world."

Alerio didn't bother to request permission to leave. He just spun on his heels and left the villa. On the beach, he ran southward hoping the physical effort would burn off his rage.

Chapter 8 – The Day After Tomorrow

The craftsmen and work detail squads returned from the villa the next afternoon to find the other squads out on the practice field. Javelins flew and the rattle of wooden gladii on practice posts carried to them.

"Looks like Sisera is playing with his Samnites," Hallus from 3rd Squad sneered.

"Better them than us," Horatius remarked as the squads moved to their areas.

To their delight, a servant waited at each tent. 9th and 10th Squads filtered through and continued to their areas.

"Our Tesserarius finally gave us some help around camp," Trax commented. "I wonder what changed?"

"Because you were supposed to be training before," Alerio said as he stepped from between tents.

"We still are, aren't we?" questioned Acharis.

"No. Now it's time to become a fighting unit," Alerio informed the squads. "Strap on your gear, grab your shields, and meet me on the practice field."

"It's been a long day, Corporal," Trax suggested as he flexed his arms. "Maybe tomorrow, after I get a good night's sleep."

Laughter escaped the lips of several Legionaries.

"Gee, why didn't you tell me you were dēfutūta?" Alerio asked. "If I had known, I wouldn't have set up this demonstration."

"What demonstration?"

"Grilli, if you please," Alerio called over his shoulder.

From the other side of the camp, the mule handler strolled into view carrying an infantry shield. He crossed to the 2nd Squad's area, handed Alerio the shield, and quickly went back the way he came.

"Shield against shield? Or do you want to go for the gold, and we'll include gladii?" Alerio inquired.

"Look Tesserarius, you seem like a decent enough NCO," Trax offered. "Save yourself some pain and leave me alone."

Behind their Decanus, 2nd Squad nodded in agreement. Their squad leader had shown them his temper more than once.

Alerio's infantry shield never rose, dipped down, or wavered to the side. But when he took a giant step, the heavy shield shot forward and smashed Trax in the face. The force of the blow drove the squad leader back and off his feet.

"I asked you a question," Alerio reminded the Lance Corporal.

Trax Dircium came off the ground and bull rushed the shield. Everyone expected Corporal Sisera to be knocked onto his back. But the moment Trax got a grip on the shield, Alerio bent his knees, powered forward, and used his body to lift his left arm.

Lance Corporal Dircium found himself tossed into the air, clinging to the face of the shield. Then Corporal Sisera spun, jumped up and, putting the full weight of his body behind the shield, drove it and the squad leader into the ground. Trax, caught between the heavy shield and the soil, grunted as the air was forced from his lungs.

Alerio stood up, stepped back, and looked over the top of the shield.

"I asked you a question."

Blood dripped from Trax Dircium's nose and a cut on his forehead. Gasping for breath, he looked up at the Corporal.

"I wasn't ready," he complained between breaths.

"Get your shield," Alerio instructed. "and get ready."

Trax rolled away from Alerio almost as if fearing the shield would come at him again. While the Lance Corporal went to get his shield, Alerio talked to the astonished squads.

"In the street fighting to take Messina, if you were fourth in the ranks, you had to learn to unload your shield. There were just too many Qart Hadasht mercenaries coming at us, and we couldn't afford to get weighed down," he explained. "Granted, the twist and pound at the end is my invention."

Dircium returned with his shield and a grim expression on his face.

"What, no gladius?" Alerio questioned. "I was hoping you had bigger cōleī."

"What did you say to me?"

Alerio's left arm rotated upward putting his shield parallel with the ground. Using the flat edge, he shoved it at Trax's face while circling the Legionary. The Lance Corporal flinched and Alerio moved swiftly behind the man's guard. There the Corporal slammed his right hand into the end of the shield. The solid hardwood snapped forward and smacked Trax in the back of his head.

The Lance Corporal stumbled forward barely keeping his footing. Alerio helped by lifting his foot and kicking him in the back. Trax flew half a body's length before crashing to the ground. As Dircium rolled over, preparing to stand, he stopped. The iron band of Corporal Sisera's shield rested on his throat.

"When given a choice always choose a weapon," Alerio instructed. Then he pressed down and both of Trax's hands rose to hold the shield off his windpipe. "Although it's been argued a shield is a weapon. But think, if my right hand was occupied with a gladius, you wouldn't have a headache."

"What headache?"

Alerio removed the shield, pivoted on one foot, and kicked Trax in the head. Lance Corporal Dircium's hands went from protecting his throat to cupping his aching skull.

"Get on your gear, take your shields, and meet me on the practice field," Alerio ordered the squads. Then he looked down and added. "Don't forget that disrespectful piece of merda and his equipment."

"But Trax is injured," Horatius Ostrei protested.

Alerio was partially turned. He stopped and slowly looked over his shoulder at the Lance Corporal for 1st Squad.

"Shield against shield? Or would you like to include gladii?"

***

For three days, Alerio drilled the Century. When not having Squads smashing into each other, he had them on the gladius post practicing their skills. Javelins flew, contuberniums sprinted, wrestled, and the entire Century ran through basic maneuvers.

With sore muscles and fatigue from continuous movement, the squad leaders complained but not within earshot of the Corporal. One did and after the demonstration, the Lance Corporal required help to get back to the squad area at the end of the day.

On day four, the squads rested on the practice field at midday with uneasy minds. Victoria Hill loomed as did the dreaded squad races. There was no feast waiting for the winners. Just the over-enthusiastic Corporal Sisera lurking on the slope for the losers. Before the call came to get on their feet, Sergeant Gustavi marched from the camp.

"Ostrei, Dircium, Italus, and Enitui, collect your squads and report to me at the villa," the Optio ordered.

With the first four contuberniums out of the races, Alerio changed the afternoon's training.

"Go swim," he instructed.

While the remaining squads joked and relaxed on the way to drop their gear, Alerio stripped down and went to the supply wagon. After selecting two of the heavy practice gladii, he carried them to the training posts.

***

Unseen by Corporal Sisera, a group of riders came up from the south. Fifteen in all, they joked and rode easy. Then one noticed the Legionary across the practice field. With two wooden gladii, the man wailed on the posts. Without missing a strike, he shifted between practice posts in an amazing display of swordsmanship. The rider broke from the group, nudged his mount up the embankment, and crossed to the Legionary.

"You there," he called down from the horse.

Alerio stepped back and swung a couple of side strikes to slow down his arms. When the momentum dissipated, he rested the gladii on his shoulders and turned to face the rider.

"Tribune. Good afternoon. What can I do for you, sir?" Alerio greeted the staff officer.

"I know you are way out here with Centurion Megellus' Century," the staff officer acknowledged. "but there is a sword competition the day after tomorrow. From your gladius work, I would think you could pick up a few coins before being eliminated."

"Thank you for the information, Tribune," Alerio replied. "But as you said, we are way out here."

"Just thought a talent like yours shouldn't go to waste. Carry on."

The Tribune reined his horse around and encouraged the mount with pressure from his heels. As the officer rode to catch up with the group of riders, obviously heading for the villa, Alerio strolled to the supply wagon.

He found Grilli sitting on the tailgate.

"What did the Tribune want?" the mule handler inquired.

68

"There's a sword competition in the Legion camp," Alerio replied while sliding the practice gladii under the goatskin cover.

"That sounds like an opportunity. Are you going?"

"I'm the only one here who believes this Century is going into combat," Alerio explained. "And the only one who cares to teach these Legionaries how to survive."

"Go for a swim. I'll get your supper and a wineskin ready," Grilli suggested. "The rest of the Century's command staff is celebrating tonight, why shouldn't you?"

***

Qart Hadasht mercenaries kicked through the Century's rotted shields and soldiers poured through the breaches. Soldiers and Legionaries fought but the flow of Empire forces soon overwhelmed the Legionaries. Shouts for Corporal Sisera to help echoed in his ears. But his gladius and shield were too heavy to lift, and he stood helpless watching his men die.

Noises outside Alerio's tent pulled him from the nightmare. Throwing off the blanket, he staggered to the tent flap, tossed it aside, and walked out to find four Lance Corporals sitting in front of the NCOs' tent.

"Good morning," he greeted his Samnite squad leaders. The sky showed pink, but the camp lay in darkness. In the campfire light, he made out four serious faces. "Lance Corporals Caudini, Umbria, Aternus, and Frentani, do we have a problem?"

"We do, Tesserarius," Telesia Caudini from 5th Squad replied. "We'll be moving to the Legion camp soon. When we get there, they'll issue us new equipment. The

God Sterculius knows we need to exchange the merda for better gear."

"No argument there," Alerio acknowledged.

"And we'll be charged for it," Telesia continued. "Our pay will be docked. In short, we'll be paying for the remodeling of a villa. It's not fair."

"What does 9th and 10th Squads say about this?" questioned Alerio mentioning the two missing Lance Corporals. "They have the same shoddy equipment."

"I talked with Stulte and Tescum. Those men are so accustomed to being used as craftsmen, they haven't pride enough to complain."

"There is nothing I can do," admitted Alerio after a moment of thinking. "Optio Gustavi purchased the equipment without consulting me."

He didn't mention that the accounting form showed the entire Century had been issued new gear. Although he told the truth, it would be disrespectful for a Corporal to openly criticize a superior or go into details.

"We didn't think you could fix the problem, but we needed to voice our concerns."

"Your issues have been noted."

The four squad leaders stood and silently went back to their areas. Alerio's gut tightened, and he swore that somehow or someway in the future, he would make it up to the squads for the swindle. Looking at the sky, he realized there was time to eat before starting the day's training.

***

He was down to the last bites of bread and cheese when a shape came from out of the dark.

"Corporal Sisera. What happens the day after tomorrow?" Grilli inquired.

"And good morning to you," Alerio replied. He took a swallow of water to wash down his breakfast and asked. "Is that a riddle?"

"I have five handlers at the villa looking after the Tribunes horses," Grilli said. "It's funny how the nobles and Legionaries ignore animal wranglers and talk freely in our presence."

"Am I to guess at the conversations? Or is there a reason you feel the need to report gossip?"

"If you don't want to hear, Tesserarius, then I'll keep my own counsel," offered the mule handler.

"Excuse my poor attitude. I've just had a troubling meeting," Alerio explained. "Despite my curt replies, I am curious."

"Last night, Centurion Megellus paraded the Tribunes around the villa. He pointed out the quality of work done by the Century on the repairs and the new water system. All the while, he assured them, his Legionaries were available to do the same for the Legion," Grilli described. "The staff officers were full of the Centurion's food and vino, so they agreed with him."

"Was a Senior Tribune or a Senior Centurion at the party?"

"No, Corporal Sisera, they were not."

"Then our officer was pleading his case to be a construction Century to a bunch of junior Tribunes," Alerio commented. "I don't understand his reasoning."

"His experience is with the permanent Northern Legion," suggested Grilli. "Tribunes in garrisons have a lot of power in assigning details. Can I assume by your

71

response, things work differently in a Consul's marching Legion?"

"Any construction required to advance on the enemy is handled by engineers and whatever Centuries are close by," Alerio stated. "In a fighting Legion, a heavy infantry Century has one primary use. It's why I'm pushing the Legionaries so hard."

"Let me restate my original question. What happens the day after tomorrow?"

"Tomorrow is the Legion games at Velia," Alerio answered. "The day after is payday for the Century. Why do you ask?"

"The other thing reported to me was a conversation between Optio Gustavi and a squad leader," Grilli related. "The Decanus complained about your harsh treatment of the Lance Corporals and your impossible standards."

"If they think my training is hard, wait until they encounter the Legion's weapons instructor or the Senior Centurion," Alerio laughed. "Then they'll be delighted with my gentle mannerisms."

"But that's just it, Tesserarius," Grilli advised. "According to the Sergeant, you'll be gone the day after tomorrow."

Alerio closed his eyes. How could Sergeant Gustavi get rid of him and avoid bringing Senator Maximus' wrath down on the Optio and Centurion? Then a thought formed and Alerio tried to push it out of his mind.

A disgraced Corporal's word wouldn't carry much weight. And the most devastating accusation against a Tesserarius was the theft of Century funds. Considering the skimpy bank in the coin pouch, it wouldn't take much to fall short while paying the Legionaries and mule handlers. Angry squads and the charge of larceny would follow.

"A summary crucifixion," Alerio mumbled.

"Excuse me, Corporal Sisera. I didn't catch that?"

"Grilli. Thank you for the warning. I need to do some accounting before we start the morning," Alerio stated as he stood. "Would you mind getting the Samnite squad leaders for me?"

Corporal Sisera didn't wait for a reply. He ducked into the tent and went to the Century's fund box.

Act 3

Chapter 9 – Larceny and a Goddess

Late in the morning, the six contuberniums were in a two wide, three deep formation. Their used and trashy armor and shields left in camp the Legionaries practiced the craft of war dressed in their tunics.

"Assault," ordered the Corporal.

Lunging and lifting their empty left arms, they mimicked a surge, then withdrew the left and followed up with gladii thrusts. Alerio walked between the ranks adjusting stances, hand positions, and the angles of the gladii.

"Advance," he ordered again.

On the beach, horses appeared from the north. The Tribunes, many still drunk from the night before, didn't ride as sharply as when they headed for the villa. Mounted in the center of the group was a Centurion talking and gesturing towards the practice field. None of the Tribunes paid him any attention. But several noted the lack of armor, shields, and helmets on the Legionaries doing unit drills.

Once the riders vanished around a bend in the shoreline, Alerio called for a rest period and walked to the mule handlers' camp.

"Grilli. Are you sure you and your men want to be involved in this?" he asked.

"Old mule handlers tell stories about what happens when Legions break," Grilli replied. "The stories aren't pretty. If this is what you need to keep us safe, then we're willing to help."

"Bags of onions, beets, radishes, and turnips, and three chickens," Alerio directed while handing Grilli a pouch of coins. "And be sure your wagons are in place tomorrow."

"We'll be there," the handler assured him as he snapped the reins on a team of horses.

His wagon rolled out followed by another wagon pulled by a team of prancing horses. Finally, the driver on the third wagon urged his four mules forward with a snap of the lines. Slower, and with some argument from the animals, the third wagon moved out of the mule handlers' camp.

Alerio watched the wagons until they were on the beach heading southward. Then, he marched back to the Legionaries, "Flank march. Turnabout, brace. Testudo."

***

Before daylight, Corporal Sisera walked to the 5th Squad's tent and ordered the sentry to wake the squad. He moved to 6th, 7th, and 8th and alerted those watchers. Then, he strolled to the beach.

"It's twelve miles to Velia," Alerio stated softly when the squads assembled. "We don't have space in the schedule for injuries. Move quickly but, be careful. Lance Corporals, move them out."

Soon the four squad leaders had the twenty-eight Legionaries stepping off and heading south. Alerio relaxed his shoulders, swung his arms, and matched their stride.

The timing was important. They wanted to reach the gates of the Legion camps fresh and not spent from a run. Yet, arrive during the heaviest flow of morning wagons through the gates when the sentries were the busiest.

At the six-mile mark, the squads approached a dry stream bed that angled up and off the beach. It rose gently into the hills to a flat grassy field.

"Lance Corporal Frentani, give me two men," Alerio called to the squad leader from the 8th.

The Corporal pointed up the stream to where four mules, a wagon, and a driver were camped. After a signal from Decanus Frentani, two Legionaries fell out of the march. As they strolled along the banks of the creek to the camp, the remaining members of their squad continued marching southward with the group.

Velia appeared off the beach and the squads left the shoreline heading towards the metropolis. By mid-morning, the city was closer and Alerio spotted the Century's wagons. Grilli had them parked in the shade of the city's defensive wall.

"Lance Corporal Aternus, give me two men who like to chat on each wagon," Alerio ordered the squad leader from the 7th.

"Shouldn't we be using stealth?" question the Decanus.

"Not at all. I want our people bragging about the luxuries at our camp," Alerio explained. "Stress how they can't wait to get back with the vegetables. Make it memorable for the sentries."

When they reached the wagons, Aternus gave instructions to four of his Legionaries before sending them to the transports. Alerio went directly to the lead wagon and greeted the driver.

"Grilli. Good morning. How went the purchases?"

"We have bags of vegetables, and I included several bags of apples," the mule handler informed him. Then he lifted a goatskin cover to expose a crate. "and three sacred chickens."

"Were they raised by priests?" asked Alerio, knowing chickens' bred and blessed by priests in the Capital were expensive.

"No. But these chickens don't have enough meat on their bones to feed a squad," Grilli ventured. "I assume they're for a sacrifice. Although, the scrawny fowls won't provide the best of gestures to the Gods."

"They'll do as a substitute for the grandest of sacrifices," Alerio stated before ordering. "Follow us through the Legion gates."

"Wait. What do you mean?" stammered Grilli. "The grandest of sacrifice is…"

He didn't finish the sentence because it was an uncomfortable subject. The greatest of animals that could be offered to the Gods was a human sacrifice.

Alerio ignored the question and the reference. He marched to the front of the formation.

"Squads, stand by," the Corporal shouted.

"Standing by, Tesserarius," came the response with a stomp of hobnailed boots on the road.

"Forward march. Left, stomp."

***

The sentries at the gates watched as twenty-six infantrymen, a Corporal, and two wagons with drivers and another four Legionaries approached the gate.

"Good morning," Alerio greeted the guards. "I'm Tesserarius Sisera and I am in command of four squads

77

from Megellus Century. I'm delivering a report to Crassus Legion North. And maybe doing some other business."

"Found an excuse to come for the games, Corporal?" one guard inquired.

"Like my first Optio used to say, never pass up a good fight," Alerio replied.

"Let me get a head count and the correct spelling of your name."

After logging in the size of the unit, the NCO in charge, and inspecting the content of the wagon beds, the sentries waved them through. They weren't impressed by the number of sacks in each wagon.

"I am not enthralled with the Legion camp," one of Aternus' men commented from the lead wagon.

He reached back, grabbed a bunch of radishes, and tossed them to one of the sentries.

"We have all the best any Legionary could want," the sentry protested as he caught the vegetables.

"Our camp is so close to the sea we swim every morning," offered a man from the second wagon. "After we finish eating stew with boar and vegetables so thick, we have to cut it with a knife."

The other man from the 7th Squad lifted the cover to display the wagon load of vegetables. He snatched up a pair of onions and threw them to the other sentry.

"It's almost embarrassing how delicious our rations are," he bragged. "How is the chow in the Legion camp?"

"Move along," the other sentry ordered, not bothering to answer. "Keep it moving."

The sentries sneered as the wagons passed. Their squad rations were a handful of grain, a little salty meat, and a few wilted vegetables. Once the Legions reached

Sicilia, they would receive normal rations. In the meanwhile, the description of the food enjoyed by Megellus Century, and the wagons piled high with sacks of vegetables made their mouth's water.

***

A block from the gate, Aternus leaned out from the ranks.

"I think the gate guards will remember we're hauling wagons full of vegetables."

"And piles of vegetables are what they'll expect to find when you leave," Alerio replied to Aternus. Then he shifted to the 5th Squad. "Lance Corporal Caudini, when we get to our campsite, I'll need four men."

"And where will that be, Corporal?" the squad leader asked.

"Near the armory for Consul Valerius Mesalla's Legions," Alerio replied. "We'll probably be assigned to one of the Crassus Legions. What we're about to do shouldn't be done to our own people."

"You mean what we're attempting to do," corrected the Decanus.

Regimented squares of tents and facilities for four Legions took up half the Velia valley floor. Sixteen thousand eight hundred heavy and light infantrymen, four hundred artillerymen assigned to the bolt throwers, twelve hundred cavalrymen, eight hundred people in direct support, and a few thousand more for indirect support. All the Legionaries lived in the precisely constructed Legion camps. The layout made it easy to locate the armory of Consul/General Valerius Mesalla's Legion.

"Park the wagons in the grassy area on the forge side," instructed Alerio. "Set up campfires and boil some vegetables. Give some away to any NCOs who pass by. Act as if we have a lot but don't give it all away."

***

A roofless brick structure anchored the armory complex. Large tents attached to one side created the armory's footprint and housed the armor, shields, and helmets. Right away it became clear why no organization or unit used the space next door to the brick structure. Sharp, loud hammering, yelling, and smoke from the metalworkers' forges filled the air.

"There must be fifty Legionaries in the armory," Pentri Umbria from 6th Squad guessed. "We can't get much done with them watching."

Alerio stretched and swung his arms to loosen up the muscles. Finally, he looked from the armory entrance to Lance Corporal Umbria.

"Just be ready when they clear out," the Corporal offered as he pulled his armor, helmet, and shield from under the bags of vegetables. "Grilli. When you're loaded, don't wait for me. Get the wagons out of the Legion camp and on the way to ours."

"I got you, Tesserarius," the mule handler assured him. "Where will you be?"

Alerio lifted an arm and pointed far up the valley. At the end of the Legion tents and before the foothills, a wooden forum had been constructed. High bleachers wrapped around a lower section that was out of sight below the tops of the Legion tents.

"Lance Corporal Caudini, pick three men who know how to gamble and another who is fast on his feet," Alerio

80

ordered. Then he spoke to the other squad leaders. "When Mesalla's Legionaries clear the armory, fill our shopping list, and roll out with the wagons."

"What makes you think the armorers will leave?" questioned Lance Corporal Aternus.

"They will leave, how could they not?" suggested the Corporal. Indicating the cage, he advised. "Lance Corporal Caudini, don't forget my chickens."

He distributed his war gear to the three gamblers and the runner. Then Alerio and his small detachment left the rest of the squads sitting around pots cooking vegetables.

***

Followed by the five Legionaries, Sisera marched through the Legion camp down a major road and finally reached the forum. It wasn't difficult locating the signup table for the gladius and shield competition.

"Optio. I assume this is the registration station," Alerio exclaimed while throwing out his arms as if he'd uncovered a secret.

The Sergeant glanced up from the stacks of parchment. Clearly written on the documents spread across the tabletop were the names of competitors. Large signs identifying the desk as the registration area rested on the corners of the table.

"Name and record?" the NCO inquired in a weary voice.

"That's just it, Sergeant, I have never lost a sword fight," Alerio bragged. "Do yourself a favor and keep your best fighters away from me until the later rounds."

"And why would I do that?"

"To save them the embarrassment of being eliminated early," explained Alerio. "Not to tell you how to run a competition, but if I was in charge, I'd want the best fighters in later matches. It'll please the crowd."

Experienced Optios loved to be told explicitly how to do their job. The Sergeant's jaw tightened, his eyes bulged from the pressure of a near exploding head, and he crushed the quill in his hand. While he searched through the correspondence box for another, the young Legionary stood across the table beaming with pride at helping the NCO.

"Name?" the Optio asked while grinding his teeth.

"Corporal A. Sisera," Alerio replied. "That's S. I. S. E...."

"I knew how to spell it," barked the Sergeant. "You're registered Sisera. Staging for Mesalla Legions are to the left and Crassus Legions to the right."

Alerio looked around the forum. Tunnels in the base allowed competitors to pass from the center area to the outside without having to walk around the structure.

"Excellent, Optio. You are very proficient at your job," Alerio complimented the NCO.

He marched off with an exaggerated swing of his arms and his chin lifted so high he appeared to be looking down his nose at everyone nearby.

The Sergeant picked up the sheet with the Corporal's name and placed it on the tabletop. Then, he searched through other piles until he located two notorious fighters known for brutalizing their opponents. He put the two experienced men into an early rotation in the competition. The crowd and gamblers would appreciate named fighters coming out early. And, the Optio would get the satisfaction of watching the first fighter beat some humility into young Corporal A. Sisera.

***

Alerio signaled for his Legionaries to follow him through the tunnel to the Crassus Legion side. A staging area for the fighters included individual zones divided off by bales of hay. Additionally, provided were three side curtains of tent material to give the competitors privacy. And in case a fight went bad, the areas were arranged around a central medical area for stitches and treatment.

Team Sisera placed the armor, shield, helmet, and the cage with the chickens on the hay bales.

"Corporal Sisera, I still don't know how you plan to draw the armorers and metalworkers away from the armory," Caudini questioned.

"Give the coins to our betters," Alerio responded as he dropped onto a bale. "The first two matches will be lopsided against me. Let's win and increase our Century's funds on those. After that, the odds will shift to being against my opponents. If during the afternoon, there is an opportunity, they can take advantage by making small bets."

"You seem very confident in all of this," Telesia Caudini suggested.

"I'm depending on something a friend told me," Alerio confessed. "Not much good being famous if people don't know who you are."

"Are you famous, Tesserarius?"

"We'll see after the first fight," Alerio promised as he began strapping on his armor. "Pull out a chicken and when I call for it, come quick."

"Why the rush to kill a chicken?" Caudini questioned.

"It's better than the alternative," Alerio suggested.

He slipped on his helmet and went to join the parade of fighters leaving behind a confused squad leader. Caudini stared at the cage with the three undersized chickens as if they could provide an answer.

Chapter 10 – A Rumor of Infamy

The Forty-five Legionaries signed up for the competition marched around the inside of the forum. Of the fighters, a few carried fearsome reputations, several were recognizable to a multitude of the Legions, but most were simply favorite fighters from their Centuries. As they circled, calls of support rained down from the tiers of seating as well as shouts of anger at the named fighters. Beating foes and causing men to incur gambling debts had that effect on people.

Alerio kept his helmet on and used the walkaround to observe his competition. If his jabs at the competency of the scheduling Optio worked, one or more of the more notorious fighters would be assigned to the first round. While punishing the brash Corporal A. Sisera was the aim of scheduling a top fighter early, it made Alerio the underdog and created an opportunity to build the Century's funds. Provided, he won the fight.

The line of fighters circled the forum before they tightened the formation around the arena part of the floor. Stopping, they each faced outboard and accepted more cheering from the audience.

"These are your fighters for the day's competition," a Sergeant announced from the center of the sandy combat area. "Some you know. Some you don't care to know. And some, by the end of the day, you will not be able to forget."

Cheers erupted at the promise of a day of shield and gladius combat. Every man in the stands depended on his weapons for survival. Today gave the infantrymen a chance to watch skilled people fight with the tools of war. Plus, the competition allowed the Legionaries to relax with a wineskin while placing a few bets. Games were motivation and entertainment for the Legionaries, as much as they were for finding the best fighter.

"The first match of the day," the Optio continued. "Pits Optio Recultus against a newcomer…"

Cheers and boos in equal measure rolled from the crowd at the mention of Recultus' name. Alerio looked around to see which newcomer would have the honor of opening the games by falling victim to the well-known fighte

"Corporal A. Sisera," the Sergeant said finishing the announcement. "Fighters, get your gear."

Alerio took the tunnel to where Lance Corporal Caudini and the runner waited.

"We got a named fighter," Alerio stated happily as he picked up his shield. "The odds will favor Recultus. We can capitalize on that."

"I asked around and Recultus is a brute," Caudini reported. "He never makes it to the finals, but he breaks a lot of Legionaries before he gets eliminated. I don't think I'd be as pleased if I was in your boots."

"But you're not me. Private, you have two jobs," Alerio informed the runner. "One is to filter through the crowd and repeat any bad rumor about me you hear. I want the word to spread quickly of how little chance I have against Recultus."

"What's the other thing, Tesserarius?"

"At the end of every fight, I like a snack," Alerio replied. "Apple cakes, meat on a stick, and, especially, those little meat pies. Make sure I have one when you report on how fast the tales are spreading."

"What tales, Corporal?" the Private inquired. "I haven't heard any yet."

"If there aren't any after the first part of the fight, my entire scheme goes up in flames," Alerio offered. "Let's hope there are rumors. The uglier the better."

Then Alerio whispered into Lance Corporal Caudini's ear before marching to the tunnel and the arena. He left the squad leader and the runner standing with puzzled expressions on their faces.

***

The Sergeant officiating the match held up his arms, turned his face to the stands as if looking at everyone in the forum, and shouted, "Fight!"

His arms dropped and the Optio ran for the edge of the sand.

Thinking he'd have a moment to set, Alerio inhaled and prepared to adjust his feet. Suddenly, he spun off to the side, almost losing his balance. Only experience and a rapid shuffling of his feet allowed Alerio to stay upright.

Recultus charged by him and began a tight turn for another attack. Howls of pleasure echoed around the forum. It seemed the quick assault was Recultus' signature move and expected by the official and the crowd.

86

'Like an angry bull,' Alerio thought as he waved his gladius to get the big Legionary's attention. It worked. Recultus dipped his left shoulder and blindly attacked.

Their shields collided and from the initial impact, Alerio gained an appreciation for Recultus' shield work. The NCO was one of the strongest men Alerio had ever faced.

Rolling his shield off to the side, Alerio used the last contact between the edges to go into a power rotation. Combining the push off from the shield and a kick out with his left leg, Alerio whipped around. Halfway through the rotation., he planted a foot and stopped.

Reaching out with his gladius, Alerio slammed the blade into the back of Recultus' helmet. Realizing his attack failed and his opponent had gotten behind him, Recultus moved off, came about kicking up sand as he dug in for another charge.

"Recultus. Pay attention for a heartbeat," suggested Alerio. "My name is Alerio Sisera."

"I never bother learning the names of first-round losers," he boasted. "I leave that for the medics."

"If you must, come on. But you should know, I'm going to hurt you," warned Alerio.

"That's where you're wrong," Recultus bragged. "I give the pain."

Solid legs, thick back, and heavy arms, there seemed no weakness in the powerful Legionary. Recultus shuffled forward, tracking Corporal Sisera with his shield, and preparing for a knockdown thrust.

Alerio's stood with his body rigid. Only his head moved. It dipped from side to side as if he was idly stretching his neck muscles instead of bracing for a

87

hammering. While not threatening, the neck motions gave his attacker pause.

In a gladius and shield fight, one clue for where your opponent planned to move was the angle of his head and direction indicated by his eyes. Alerio's rocking masked any forewarning of his planned defense or next move.

Recultus judged the distance and pulled back the shield as if winding up a ballista. Then, he stepped forward sharply and, using the momentum, drove the shield at his rival.

At the pullback, Alerio rested the bottom of his shield on the arch of his right foot and removed his hand from the cross grip. When Recultus thrust forward, Alerio kicked his shield into the air and dramatically leaned back. Catching it with both hands, he threw the shield, so the iron band slid over Recultus' shield and towards his face through the opening in the Legionary's helmet.

The iron band heading for his eyes caused Recultus to flinch back which halted his charge. His momentum stopped, Recultus raised his shield, ducked down, and stepped backward.

Something caught between his legs. His knees were forced into a painful twist and his legs, as if a master baker were making braided bread, spiraled, and tangled. The big fighter fell onto his left side.

After throwing the shield, Alerio dropped to his belly and crawled under Recultus' shield. He thrust his gladius between the big man's legs and torqued it hard to the left.

Steel beats muscles and bone. Recultus toppled over, falling onto his shield. Before he recovered, Alerio jerked the blade free, swung it up and over, and slammed the pommel into the man's helmet.

"Stay down," warned Alerio as he climbed onto the big man. While wrapping his arm protectively across Recultus' shoulders, he raised the gladius and hammered the helmet again. "The Goddess is near, and she is demanding a death. Stay down and pray she overlooks you."

Even in Recultus' dazed state, the mention of a Goddess seeking vengeance or punishment filtered into his brain and he remained on the ground.

***

The forum exploded in roars and boos when the crowd's favorite was upended. They expected Recultus to throw off his opponent and come up fighting. But the only figure to rise was A. Sisera. And his antics were confusing at first.

Ripping off his helmet, Sisera glanced up and over his right shoulder. Then his left hand gripped his gladius arm and he seemed to be fighting with himself. While he struggled to control the arm, he shouted over his shoulder as if arguing with someone or something floating above him.

During the struggle with himself, Alerio paused and waved briefly at the tunnel entrance. Then he went back to the gyrations and speaking to the empty air.

Far from the sand and watching with a group of NCO friends, the Optio referee was out of position. In the moments before the Sergeant realized the danger, Sisera circled the huddled Recultus. Clutching the gladius arm, A. Sisera seemed to be holding it back, preventing the blade from sticking the downed man. The official charged towards the arena hoping to prevent a death or serious injury.

As the Optio raced towards the combatants, a Lance Corporal sprinted from the tunnel. Clutched between the squad leader's outstretched arms was a scrawny chicken.

"Sisera, step back," the Sergeant bellowed over the distance. "Back away, now."

As if convulsing, Alerio's head jerked from facing over his shoulder to down at Recultus. Then it popped up and his wide opened eyes locked momentarily on the running official. Finally, his head snapped up and Alerio looked over his shoulder.

"Goddess Nenia. No one dies today," Sisera pleaded. "Nenia Dea, I beg of you."

Lance Corporal Caudini leaped Recultus' form, dropped to one knee, and held the chicken up as if presenting the bird to Alerio's back. Without looking, Corporal Sisera cycled his gladius down and under his shoulder. It swept by his thigh and rose, unguided, behind his back.

The blade ripped through the bird and Lance Corporal Caudini parted his arm. In each hand, he held half of the neatly cleaved chicken. Shocked by the swiftness of the blade as it passed between his hands, the squad leader spun on his knee, staggered to his feet, and ran stumbling for the tunnel.

Alerio fell to his knees with his arms outstretched to the sky and his head thrown back.

"Recultus. It's safe to move," he advised the big Legionary. "The Goddess is appeased."

***

On one knee, the fighter studied Alerio before asking, "Who are you?"

90

The Optio slid to a stop, glanced at the uninjured Recultus and Sisera in the submissive pose, and asked the same question, "Who are you?"

"My name is Alerio Sisera, and I am beloved of the Goddess Nenia," Alerio explained while still on his knees. "Last year in Messina, I had the honor of washing the dying and singing for the Goddess to free the Legionnaires from their ruined bodies."

"Death Caller," the Optio whispered.

"Not a name I embrace," Alerio informed the NCO.

"You're Death Caller?" babbled Recultus. "I did battle with Death Caller and survived?"

"Hold on Recultus," instructed the Sergeant. "This fight isn't over. You may continue."

"Optio. When I was on the ground, I could feel Sisera's hot breath on my cheek warning me to stay down," Recultus related. "But there was something else. A cold pouring over his shoulder as if the Goddess of Death was looking down at me. This fight is over, and I need to find a temple and make an offering to my household God for deliverance."

"In that case, stand Corporal Alerio Sisera," ordered the Optio. Alerio stood. The NCO waved his arms over his head to get the spectator's attention. Then he brought both arms down and pointed them at Alerio. "The winner of the first fight in the first round, Alerio Sisera, also known as Death Caller."

Pandemonium broke out at the ground level seating. Then as the Optio's words were passed up the stands, mayhem erupted on each tier as they heard the nickname. Many had no idea of the meaning. But the veterans from Messina soon told the story of a tough Legionary priest, his long hours of singing, and his gentle care of the fatally wounded.

Alerio bowed to the crowd and marched to the tunnel. He hoped the runner brought back gossip and one of those tasty meat pies. And that Caudini had an accounting report from the Legionaries placing the bets.

***

Lance Corporal Apulia Frentani squatted by the pot of boiling stew. One of the Legionaries from his 8th Squad had ventured away from the armory area and returned with slabs of salted pork. The aroma of boiling meat and vegetables carried across the temporary camp making the waiting squads hungry.

"So far, I don't see any sign of the armorers leaving, do you?" inquired Aternus from the 7th squad.

"Nope. I guess we'll have a good meal and head back," Frentani replied. He dipped a ladle into the pot, lifted out a chunk of pork, and inspected it. Before dropping it back into the stew, he added. "Almost done."

"What I don't understand is why Corporal Sisera thought they would desert the armory."

"Wishful thinking?"

"I'm hungry," Aternus announced. "I'm getting a bowl."

While the squad leader marched to one of the wagons, a runner pounded down the street. Without breaking stride, he ducked into the armory and vanished inside. Moments later, he appeared and sprinted down the street towards a group of supply tents.

Decanus Aternus had a bowl in hand and was about to return to one of the stew pots when armorers began rushing out of the armory. The ringing of hammers on

92

steel creased and the rhythmic breathing of the bellows stopped. Metalworkers, leatherworkers, and the men who beat armor into shape left the armory and headed for the forum. The last man out tied the door flaps together before jogging to catch up with his companions.

"What just happened?" asked Aternus while reaching for the ladle.

"We just received our signal," Lance Corporal Pentri Umbria advised. Then he kicked over the pot spilling delicious stew on the ground and shouted. "We have an opportunity, people. Let's not waste it."

Frentani ran to the entrance of the Armory and began untying the flaps. Staged behind him were most of the Legionaries from the squads. Those not in line were at the wagons unloading sacks of vegetables.

"I really wanted a taste of that stew," complained Aternus.

"Lance Corporal. We've got a shopping list to fill," a Legionary pointed out. "And our day at the market needs to end quickly and we need to be on the way back to the Century before the shopkeepers return."

Frentani shouted once the flaps were free, "Done. Go, go, go."

The squads leaped through the entrance and began gathering new gladii and armor pieces, and shields. Soon one wagon was filled and, as they raced back to the armory to get more, the men assigned to the wagons covered the stolen gear with sacks of vegetables.

***

"Lance Corporal Caudini, what news?" Alerio inquired as he approached his fighter's rest area.

Telesia Caudini sat on a straw bale with his head hanging between his knees.

"Caudini, talk to me," demanded Alerio when the Decanus from 5th squad didn't respond. "What is the count from the betting booths and the gossip?"

Telesia raised his head and Alerio could see his face was pale and his eyes were enlarged.

"You sliced that chicken from between my hands," Caudini gasped.

"It was a nice piece of blade work," Alerio offered. "I'd think you would appreciate the skill."

"That wasn't skill. You didn't even look where you swung," Caudini pointed out. "It was as if your blade was guided by another's hand, Death Caller."

"Don't you start. It's a nickname. A title forced on me that I hope to use to help the Century," Alerio explained.

The runner came from between other fighter's areas. Gripped in his hand was a large meat pie.

"Finally, something to celebrate," Alerio exclaimed as he focused on the food. "Give that to me and a report, Private."

"Death Caller," the Legionary announced while holding out the meat pie as if afraid to get too close to his Corporal. "Messengers left the stands to tell everyone in the four Legion camps that you have returned."

"Try calling me Tesserarius or Corporal Sisera," ordered Alerio. "What news traveled fast?"

"Between the Legionaries in the Central Legion who read about Death Caller and the veterans from Messina, everyone has been curious if you would show up for another campaign in Sicilia," the runner described. "At first, when you began struggling with the Goddess, we couldn't figure what you were doing. Then, when you sacrificed the chicken and dropped to your knees, we understood. You were begging Nenia for Recultus' life."

"A nice piece of theater, don't you think?" Alerio suggested between bites.

"No Corporal Sisera. In the dust, we saw a shape over your right shoulder," the Private exclaimed. "We all saw the Goddess."

"We fought on sand, there was no cloud of dust," Alerio corrected.

"Of course not, Corporal," the Private assured him as he edged away.

Before Alerio could question him more about the shadow over his shoulder, the three Privates charged with placing the bets strolled to the rest area.

"Hades, Corporal, no one placed any coins on you," one announced. "When Recultus walked off the sand, we collected twenty to one."

"The next fight won't pay nearly as well," another of the men charged with placing the bets declared. "But they put Hiematus in the first round. Probably to make an interesting fight for Recultus in the second round."

"But you'll be facing him," the third better informed Alerio. "Hiematus is a hammer. Weak on shield work because he depends on beating his opponents into the sand with his gladius. If you can beat him, we can make better coins on side bets than going through the gambling tents."

"We don't have time for you three to be chasing down winnings," Alerio warned. "Give the profits to Lance Corporal Caudini and go see about making us some more. And for your information, once I beat Hiematus, we need to leave, fast.

"We'll be ready," the first one assured him.

Caudini took the coins, placed them in a pouch, and walked to Alerio.

"I sent the runner to check on the armory," he said shaking off the shock from before. "Make the next one quick, Tesserarius. Because shortly, we'll have every staff officer in the Legions after us."

"Not after us, Lance Corporal," Alerio corrected as he took the last bite of meat pie. "They'll be searching for people with extra Legion gear."

"I wish I had your confidence," commented Caudini.

"It's not confidence Decanus," Alerio informed him.

From the arena inside the forum, a voice called out, "Second round. Sisera and Hiematus, report to the sand."

"It's fatalism," Aleris suggested while picking up his shield. As he walked to the tunnel, he added. "The result of doing nothing is worse than getting caught doing something wrong."

The Squad Leader was confused. Paying for new armor would hurt the Legionaries purse but, it was only money. He didn't realize his Tesserarius was facing a death sentence for theft from the Century's funds.

Chapter 11 – Fight and Flight

Hiematus lacked the stout build of Recultus. Instead of a thick waist and legs, the Legionary carried his muscles across wide shoulders.

"I saw the Goddess fiasco you pulled," he boasted while twirling his gladius. "That merda isn't going to work on me, Sisera. You'll be eating sand before your first prayer."

"I am so glad to hear that, Hiematus," Alerio assured him. The Corporal's gladius rested in its sheath, and he waved his empty right hand around as if this was a lighthearted conversation and not a prelude to a fight. "Because with skinny legs like yours, I was worried you might not make it across the arena."

Hiematus jumped from one side of the sand to the other while swinging his gladius overhead and bringing it down towards Alerio's head.

Sisera's shield shifted at the last instant, and he managed to stop the blade. Stepping back and to the side, Alerio peered around the band as if afraid to look.

"That's a powerful whack you have there," he observed while shaking his shield to loosen his left arm after the heavy blow. "You must get it from your mother."

"From my what?" demanded Hiematus.

"Your mother," repeated Alerio. "She must be great on wash day with a slapping motion like yours. Help her scrub clothing against rocks when you were growing up, did you?"

"Are you calling me a washerwoman?"

"Oh, oh, I see the confusion," Alerio explained. "I simply observed that you have a powerful slap for a washerwoman."

Hiematus leaped at his adversary and struck the shield six quick blows. Sisera staggered back under the assault. Stumbling to the side as if injured, he stopped and swayed on his feet.

"Yield now and spare yourself the agony," suggested Hiematus.

In the attacks so far, Hiematus hadn't used his shield or a proper stance. Normal tactics would be to use a shield to throw Alerio off balance or to position him for a blade attack. And the jumping put the Legionary's feet out of position. This told Alerio a lot about his foe.

People extremely talented in one area often neglect or ignore secondary weapons or methods of balancing an attack. In this case, it was obvious Hiematus' prowess with a blade allowed him to shun proper stances and the advantage of a shield.

"Hold for a heartbeat, so I can draw my blade," begged Alerio.

"Go ahead, it won't do you any good," Hiematus advised. "I'll just beat it and you into the sand."

"One question before we continue," Alerio inquired. "Is it your mother or your father you resemble?"

"Why do you ask?"

"Because you got the ugly one," Alerio stated. "Unless they are both…"

Hiematus reached out with his gladius in a snake quick strike and hopped forward. In a blur, his blade slashed at his adversary's neck.

Alerio didn't draw his gladius. Instead, he placed his right hand on his left giving him more control of his shield. When Hiematus moved, Alerio swung his shield to the left driving his foe's right arm outward. A hard tilt, a jerk back, and the iron band smacked the inside of Hiematus' elbow. The fighter barely hung on to his gladius as he lost the feeling in his fingers.

Then Alerio bashed his shield back to the right. Hiematus stumbled while attempting to lock in his stance and defend against the full body slaps by the shield. All the while, he flexed his fingers on the hilt hoping the numbness would fade. But the side-to-side smacks of the shield accompanied by its insistent crowding drove him back on his heels.

Hiematus attempted to reach over his rocking shield and stab downward. But Alerio's shield jutted upward throwing the arm and the loosely held gladius out of position. Suddenly, the forward pressure lifted for an instant. Hiematus shifted his feet trying to assume a proper stance. His feet were almost in line with his shoulders, his grip improved and, he thought, he might get control of this fight.

Alerio's leg shot out and kicked Hiematus right knee. The leg folded and the swordsman crumpled to the sand.

Expecting to defend against a gladius, Hiematus lashed out to fend off the blade. But it wasn't a gladius that smashed into his helmet.

The iron band on Alerio's shield struck a glancing blow to Hiematus' helmet. His head snapped to the side and before he could collect his thoughts, the band whipped back in the other direction. Back and forth the bottom of the shield smashed and the man's head rocked in rhythm with the slashing of the iron band.

It didn't stop until the official wrapped Alerio up in a bear hug and wrestled him away from Hiematus.

"Nenia," Alerio screamed as he shook off the Sergeant's arms and tossed his shield away. Then he drew his gladius, looked up, and spun in a circle seeking a target.

Lance Corporal Caudini sprinted from the tunnel with a chicken tucked under an arm. He crossed the sand, gripped the animal by its feet, and threw the bird into the air.

Alerio raced across the arena, used Hiematus' chest as a launch point, and jumped into the air. With his gladius raised, he cleaved the soaring chicken in two. The fowl's guts and blood followed him to the ground. Landing on both feet at first, Alerio dropped to his knees, thrust his arms into the air, and allowed his head to fall back.

"Goddess Nenia. I thank you for sparing Hiematus' life," he cried out.

***

Two additional Optios rushed onto the sand. After examining Hiematus to be sure he didn't have a broken neck, they converged on the referee. The three NCOs walked over and stood looking down on the Legionary covered in chicken gore.

"Death Caller, I'm going to declare you the winner of this fight," the referee informed Alerio. "However, we've decided it's too dangerous for you to continue in these games. Withdraw or I will eject you."

"Call a priest," Alerio suggested.

"You think a priest will plead your case?" one of the Sergeants questioned.

"No. A priest will prevent a riot if you toss me out or I quit," suggested Alerio.

A runner was dispatched to summons a high-ranking priest. While waiting, the Optios talked, Alerio remained on his knees in the pose, and the crowd consumed vino.

***

The spectators drank more, became bored, restless, and unruly. They settled a little when an old holy man limped into the forum. He crossed the dirt floor and stopped at the arena.

"Why was I called to the fighting sand?" the priest demanded.

"Death Caller wants words with you," the referee replied.

"I didn't choose the nickname, Priest," Alerio advised as he dropped the gladius and brought his hands down. Taking the Cleric's hands in his, he pressed a handful of coins into the priest's palms. "It would be best for all involved if you waved off the Sergeant and escorted me from the forum."

A quick glance at the handful of gold coins brought a smile to the holy man's face. It faded rapidly as the priest reached down and assisted Alerio to his feet.

"The winner of the first fight of the second round is Alerio Sisera," the Optio announced.

Then, the priest poked a finger in the Sergeants' face as if scolding the Optio. With an arm around Sisera's shoulders, he escorted Alerio to the tunnel.

"The Priest has declared that Death Caller is too close to the Goddess to continue," the Sergeant exclaimed. "For the safety of all involved, the Priest has forbidden Sisera to fight today."

The stands erupted in angry responses. But Legionaries stood in shield walls with death a hand's width away and none would argue with a priest's decision.

***

"Corporal Sisera, the wagons left before the last fight started," the runner informed him. Then he held out a strip of beef on a stick. "For you, Tesserarius."

101

"Where is Lance Corporal Caudini?" Alerio inquired as he took the stick and bit into the juicy meat.

"He went to find our betters," the Private replied. "I'm here to help you get out of the armor."

***

By the time Caudini and the three money men returned, Alerio's gear was resting on straw bales, and he was finishing up the meat. The squad leader directed the Privates, and each took a section of armor and the Corporal's helmet leaving Alerio with his gladius.

"We will stroll out of here not in a formation," Alerio instructed. "Don't rush but don't delay. Once outside the Legion gates, we'll jog and catch up with the wagons. Move out."

The six Legionaries took the trail from the forum, turned on the main road, and a quarter of a mile later, they passed through the gates.

"Detail, double time, march," Alerio ordered.

They hit the Legion pace and soon reached the walls of Velia. Beyond the walls, the road branched in several directions. The detail took the northern route, heading towards the beach. Once on the shoreline, Alerio spotted the wagon tracks in the sand and pebbles. An urge to rush touched every Legionary at the sight but they resisted sprinting. The Legion jog, they all learned in recruit training, was a proven tactic for delivering men to a battlefield with enough strength left to fight. They didn't expect a fight. But they had stolen a fortune in Legion gear and didn't know what to expect.

***

When the sun was low in the sky, the wagons came into view. They sat beside the beach road near a dry stream bed. Sprawled on the ground near cooking pots were with the squad members.

"Corporal Sisera. I trust you and your detachment are hungry," Grilli suggested.

"I believe we are, mule handler," Alerio replied.

Bowls were handed to the arriving Legionaries. They lined up at cookfires and heaping ladles of stew filled the dishes and chunks of bread were passed out.

"This has been a long day," commented Alerio.

"Corporal Sisera. You didn't tell us you were Death Caller," challenged Lance Corporal Aternus from 7th Squad.

"If I had mentioned that I had a moniker, would it have made any difference?" inquired Alerio. "As a matter of fact, would any of you have understood the reference?"

Faces twisted up in thought and after a while, Frentani from 8th spoke up, "No. But it would have been nice to know you were a celebrity."

"We walked in the Legion gate, no one cared about me," Alerio described. "We went to the forum, and nobody cared. It wasn't until I announced my nickname that people cared. My celebrity is about the same as Lance Corporal Umbria's fame."

"I'm not famous," Umbria pleaded.

"How many people would bet against you in a swim race?" Alerio asked.

"No one with any brains," 6th Squad's Decanus replied. "I see, you are famous for one thing. But carrying death around in a backpack is a pretty heavy load."

"That it is," Alerio agreed.

From the south, horses' hoofs pounded on the sand and gravel. Soon, a troop of cavalrymen and a Tribune rode up to the squads and the two wagons.

"Who's in command?" the staff officer demanded.

"Sir, Corporal Alerio Sisera. I'm in charge of the detail," Alerio reported with a salute.

"Get those covers off. We will search those wagons," ordered the Tribune while pointing at the cavalrymen.

Four dismounted, broke into pairs, and marched to the wagons.

"What's this about, Tribune?"

"Mesalla Legion's armory was robbed this afternoon," the staff officer replied. "Have any wagons passed your detachment?"

"No, sir. We've been alone the entire trip from Velia. Although we did see several wagons headings east," Alerio said. Then he shrugged and nodded his head as if figuring something out. "Did you say Mesalla's armory?"

"That's right," the Tribune answered. But he wasn't looking at the Corporal, his eyes were on the cavalrymen peeling back the covers from the wagons.

"There's an issue," Alerio advised. "We're attached to Crassus Legions. We wouldn't have any reason to be in Mesalla Legion's area."

The mounted Legionaries began shifting bags of vegetables and apples. From side to side and front to back, they exposed the floorboards then moved the sacks to lay bare another section.

"Nothing here except vegetables," a cavalry Optio reported.

"Mount up," the Tribune ordered. "We'll go back to Velia and search eastward."

"May the Goddess Fortūna guide you," Alerio called as the troop turned their horses and kicked their mounts into motion. Then he whispered. "And may she smile on us."

"Get up, pack it up, and get on the road people," Lance Corporal Caudini ordered. "We have six miles to the Century area, and I don't want to do it in the dark."

The wagons rolled out and the Legionaries fell in behind them. Far to the north, the tracks of a single, heavily loaded wagon pulled by four mules appeared in the sand.

"How far up did you have the men brush out the tracks?" Alerio asked Frentani.

"About a mile and a half," the Decanus of 8th Squad replied. "Any further than that and the cavalry would have spotted them anyway."

"I agree," Corporal Sisera said.

***

The sun hung low over the water when the Century's tents came into view.

"Lance Corporal Frentani. Did you fill out our shopping list completely?" Alerio questioned.

"To the exact piece of equipment," the Decanus assured him.

"Squad leaders on me," Alerio instructed. The four Lance Corporals walked over and strolled along with their Tesserarius. "Create a circuit. From the tents to the sea, to the wagon and back to the tents. I want every piece of old gear taken out to deep water and sunk. Then have the men come back to the wagon and collect the new issues."

"But Corporal, we can sell the old stuff," Pentri Umbria suggested.

"No. Every piece of used gear needs to disappear," instructed Alerio. "Double check your contuberniums. Everything goes, no argument or hoarding."

When the wagons left the beach and bounced up to the mule handler's area, the drivers pulled in next to the mule-drawn wagon. Further up the beach, the Legionaries left the shoreline and marched to their tents.

"Stulte. Tescum. On me," Alerio called to the squad leaders from 9th and 10th. "Follow the Samnites lead and dump your old gear."

"But we can sell it," Decanus Stulte protested.

"You could also get caught with extra gear and die on the wood," Alerio countered. "No exceptions. Stick with the plan."

As the squads went to their tents, selected their old equipment, and carried it to the beach, the first four squads came out and watched.

"What are you doing?" Ostrei asked.

"We're washing our armor, helmets, and shields," Caudini replied.

"At dusk?"

"Corporal Sisera's orders."

That brought a chuckle from the Decani of 1st, 2nd, 3rd, and 4th Squads. But the smiles transitioned to curiosity when the first set of Legionaries returned to the camp with new, shiny equipment.

Alerio watched the process until half the contuberniums had returned to their tents and stacked their new shields. Confident the squads were getting everything in order, he walked to the NCOs' tent and threw aside the flap.

Chapter 12 – Pay Call

By candlelight, Alerio took inventory of the Century's funds. As expected, the coins and the balance sheet didn't match. When he last checked, there was just enough to meet payroll. Now, there wasn't enough in the chest to pay all the Legionaries, mule handlers, the Optio, and the Centurion. It was a ham-handed conspiracy but effective enough to cast blame on the honesty of the Century's Tesserarius. His one question revolved around how Megellus and Gustavi planned to blame him for the theft.

He moved to his bedding and belongings and patted them down searching for lumps and hard bumps. When he couldn't find a stash of stolen coins, he relaxed. Maybe they simply wanted to get rid of him. Then he began to pick up his personal gear. Again, no extra weight in his pouches or spare clothing signaled the illicit placement of coins.

Alerio had pretty much exhausted all of the likely search areas. For comfort, he placed a hand on his dual gladius rig and idly turned one of the hilts. The steel blade scraped on metal. Testing the second gladius, he heard the same sound. After smoothing out a blanket, he upended the rig and pulled the blades. Gold coins came tumbling out of both sheaths.

Someone had painstakingly fed the stolen coins into the gaps between the blades and the sheaths. A quick count showed that not all the missing coins were accounted for, and the payroll funds were still short. Thankfully, he had the gambling winnings to add to the funds. But first, he needed to adjust the Century's accounting forms.

"Megellus Century. Get up and get out," Optio Gustavi announced as he walked between the tents. There was a lightness to his voice, and he seemed pleased with himself. "Get up and get out. It's payday."

His voice started at the Centurion's tent and climbed in intensity as he approached the NCOs' tent.

"Tesserarius Sisera. Get up, you are wasting daylight," Gustavi stated from outside the tent. "The Legionaries and handlers want to get their pay."

His almost manic style of speaking was obviously as false as his enthusiasm for getting the pay distributed. Alerio had no delusions about the real reason for the Sergeant's excitement. This could be the last day Corporal Sisera would be around to counter the Centurion's plans for the Century.

"Good morning, Optio Gustavi," Alerio greeted the NCO when he pushed through the tent flap. In his arms were the Century's fund chest, a quill and ink box, two camp stools, and a folding desk. "Are there any half pay punishments due?"

"No, Tesserarius Sisera. Everyone receives full pay," the Sergeant declared.

The two NCOs marched through the camp. Their passage was watched by the Legionaries and handlers standing in front of their tents. When the NCOs reached the Centurion's tent, Alerio put down his load and set up the table.

"Will Centurion Megellus be joining us?" Alerio inquired while placing the chest on the edge of the table.

"The Centurion will be along shortly," Gustavi answered. "We have his permission to begin without him."

"What order is your pleasure, Optio?" asked Alerio.

"Let's start with 10th Squad," declared Gustavi. "They have worked hard this pay period."

During their year of service in the Legion, Legionaries would receive four payments. This was the initial payment. The next two would be adjusted for food and the cost of replacement equipment. Any bounties or bonuses the Century earned would be included in the final payout.

"Decanus Tescum, present your contubernium," Alerio ordered. "You will sign as a witness that the Legionaries in your charge were paid."

The 10th Squad lined up. One by one, Alerio had them sign or make their mark by their name as he counted out a quarter of their base pay. Once the squad members had their coins, Lance Corporal Tescum signed and received his pay as a squad leader.

"Decanus Stulte, present your contubernium," instructed Alerio.

While the 9th accepted their pay, Optio Gustavi shifted uncomfortably. As if impatient for the process to be over, he attempted to look beyond the Tesserarius and get a glimpse into the fund's chest. But it rested on the far end of the table, and he couldn't judge the number of coins in the bottom.

"Decanus Frentani, present your contubernium."

***

The sun climbed into the sky as the squads lined up, accepted their pay, and moved away. They were down to the last four squads with the Optio, Centurion, and the mule handlers to follow.

"Decanus Enitui, present your contubernium," Alerio ordered. "You…"

"I know how this works," Enitui sneered. "4th Squad, line up."

Alerio laid down the quill and stared at the squad leader. Even when the eight Legionaries were lined up, he continued to glare at them.

"Is something wrong?" Gustavi questioned as if he hadn't heard the disrespectful interruption of the Tesserarius' instructions. "A problem with the funds, perhaps?"

"Enitui. You and I are going to have a conversation about etiquette later today," Alerio warned.

The Lance Corporal allowed a smile to cross his face before replying, "Sure whatever you say Sisera."

Alerio started to stand and correct Enitui's attitude. Then he remembered that he was in the middle of an ambush. When under attack, a Legionary was taught to follow his training and not allow emotions to take away his discipline.

"You will sign as a witness that the Legionaries in your charge were paid," Alerio informed the Decanus while picking up the quill and offering it to the first Legionary in the line. "Name?"

***

"Decanus Italus present your contubernium," Alerio said calling 3rd Squad to the table. "You will sign as a witness that the Legionaries in your charge were paid."

While Italus shoved his Legionaries into line, the sound of a horse coming from the north reached the

Corporal and Sergeant. They turned to see Centurion Fenoris Megellus ride up the embankment, cross the flat, and rein in his mount beside the Centurion's tent.

"What's this? The Century is short of funds?" shouted the infantry officer as he leaped from his horse. He seemed to be performing from a script but was far out of sync with the rest of the actors. "Who is to blame for the inability to pay the squads?"

Optio Gustavi's face flushed turning a deeper red and he waved a hand to get the officer's attention. But the lifting arm triggered a Legionary from 2nd Squad. He sprinted away in the direction of the NCOs' tent.

Centurion Megellus strutted into the crowd of waiting Legionaries. Turning to face the table and NCOs, he put his fists on his hips and announced, "My men work hard and deserve their pay."

"Isn't there enough coins to pay us?" blurted out Decanus Ostrei.

1st and 2nd Squads began to yell about not being paid and that someone should be held responsible. During the outburst, the missing Legionary came back from the NCOs' tent holding Alerio's dual gladius rig over his head.

"What do we have here?" demanded the Centurion as the Legionary held out the leather straps with the two sheaths and gladii. "Pull the hilts and let's see what's in there besides blades."

The Legionary pulled the first gladius and turned the sheath over as if to empty a pitcher. Nothing fell out. But he noticed a piece of parchment tied around the steel blade. Raising the blade to his eyes, the Legionary read the note.

"What does it say?" someone called to him.

He didn't answer. Instead, he pulled the second gladius and read the note attached to that blade. His face paled and he squinted as if in pain.

"What do the notes say?" demanded Trax Dircium, the Decanus from 2nd Squad. "Spit it out."

"They both say, you have violated my personal equipment," the Legionary reported. "Cut yourself now or I will cut you later. It's signed Death Caller."

"Who is Death Caller?" asked Centurion Megellus.

The squad members from the four Samnite squads and the 9th and 10th all pointed at Corporal Sisera. In response, the Tesserarius handed the quill to the next Legionary from 3rd Squad and smiled.

"Name?"

***

When 3rd was done, Alerio called for 2nd Squad to line up.

"Aren't we out of money?" someone asked.

"No. We have coins for everyone," Alerio assured him. Then, the Corporal raised his head and looked down the line of Legionaries to the one holding his rig. "I suggest you put my dual sheaths back in the NCOs' tent. And I better see blood on both blades."

While Alerio went about the business of paying the Legionaries, among the squads, the talk centered around the sword fights from the day before. Specifically, the legend of Death Caller and the respect and fear the name generated around the Legions. Lance Corporal Enitui began to sweat but not nearly as much as the Legionary holding the two-gladius rig.

1st Squad filed by and drifted away. Then Optio Gustavi and Centurion Megellus drew their pay.

"Master Grilli, present your handlers," Alerio called to the head of the animal wranglers. "You will sign as a witness that the men in your charge were paid."

"I can do that, Tesserarius," Grilli assured him.

Not until the last handler collected his due did Alerio pass the accounting sheet to Gustavi.

"Please witness my pay draw," Alerio requested. After counting out a stack of coins, he signed and handed the quill to the Optio. "Please witness my signature."

"I don't know how you did it, but you managed to get everyone paid," Gustavi offered as he signed his name beside Alerio's signature.

Before they could breakdown the table, a cavalry troop and two Centurions rode up from the beach.

"Centurion Megellus?" a Senior Centurion asked.

"I'm Fenoris Megellus."

"Good. Let's go into your tent while the cavalrymen search your camp."

"Searches for what, Senior Centurion?"

"Stolen armor, helmets, and gladii," the senior infantry officer replied as he slid off his mount. "Come with me, Centurion."

Megellus sheepishly followed the Senior Centurion to his tent. Once they vanished and the flaps closed, the second Centurion dismounted and marched to the NCOs.

"Payday?" he inquired.

"Yes, sir," Alerio answered.

"I'm the Tesserarius for Crassus Legion," the officer explained. "When you join, you'll be under me for pay and requisition. Show me your accounts."

Optio Gustavi stood and went to watch the cavalrymen as they entered and exited tents.

"New equipment?" the Legion Tesserarius commented while reading the ledgers. "And what's this about construction material for a villa?"

"Those supplies and the Legionaries' equipment were purchased before I reported to the Century," Alerio explained.

"It appears your Legionaries are ready to go to war."

"I need a few more months for that, sir," Alerio suggested.

"You've got a week," the Centurion informed him. "The Senior Centurion wants his Centuries drilling together. Describe your Century."

"Second maniple at best," Alerio reported. "Some experience but not enough to rate third maniple and more than enough to rank above first."

"You're a veteran and could claim a spot in the ranks of the third maniple," advised the Centurion. "Or even join the 1st Century."

"That's very kind of you, Centurion," acknowledged Alerio. "But my patron wants me here and here I'll stay."

The cavalry officer marched from the far end of the Century's area and stopped at the table. Optio Gustavi arrived a half step later.

"No extra gear," the mounted officer reported. "But most of what they have is new."

The Centurion held up the accounting form and eyed the lines.

"It's what the Legionaries were issued when they reported to the Century," the Legion Tesserarius explained. "And you found nothing extra. No spare shields, armor, or helmets?"

"Nothing. Just lots of new equipment."

"Senior Centurion Publius. We are done here," the Centurion called to the officer's tent.

Inside, Fenoris Megellus stood stiffly in the center of the empty tent. Publius prowled the interior but managed to have his lips a few fingers from Megellus' ear whenever he spoke.

"There is a reason Centurions drill and live with their men," Publius barked. "From the looks of these quarters, I'd say you not only didn't live with your Legionaries, but I would bet coins that you haven't drilled with them."

"Senior Centurion, I've been busy."

"Mister Megellus. I have thirty-six other infantry officers and every one of them drills with their Centuries," Publius advised. "Any one of them not proficient will be helped by some of my more experienced Centurions. But you have an advantage. Corporal Sisera is a veteran and a weapons instructor. Let him help you before I do. Understand?"

"Yes, Senior Centurion. We'll be ready in a month or so."

"No, Centurion Megellus. You'll pack up and join the Legion within the week," Publius ordered. "And when I signal an order, your Century better be the first to respond."

The Senior Centurion marched through the flaps leaving Fenoris Megellus shaking. Some of it was anger but mostly it was fear. He never wanted to be an infantry officer for the heavy infantry.

Act 4

Chapter 13 – Part of a War Machine

Two sheep peered over the crest of the hill then topped it and started down the far side. Behind the flock leaders, the rest of the sheep ambled to the top. At the rear of the flock and further down the reverse slope, the shepherd nudged the slower animals with a tap from his staff. Encouraged by sharp words and raps, the stragglers hurried up the slope. The shepherd wasn't concerned about predators but the thought of his sheep spreading out on the broad downhill slope was a concern. Once the slower ones began moving, he put on a burst of speed and hiked to the top of the hill. He needn't have worried. His sheep were clustered in a grassy area peacefully munching on the spring shoots. However, in the valley below him, the scene was anything but peaceful.

Four hundred and thirty-two heavy infantrymen grunted and pushed against an equal number of opposing shields. Directly behind each line, a second rank pushed the first rank while jabbing javelins over their heads. The two front lines shouted and yelled at each other over their shields.

Behind the javelin line and stationed at every twenty-fourth man in the shield wall, an Optio and a Tesserarius flanked a Centurion. Behind the Century's command staff another twenty-four Legionaries waited to be called up. Further to the rear of each Century stood four Legionaries on resupply duty and standing by to act as body bearers for any wounded. Behind them, two mule handlers waited with mules carrying water and vino, wheat cakes, cheese, and olives, plus additional javelins, and bandages.

No one was supposed to get injured during the mock battle. The exercise allowed the Legion's command staff to have a look at the individual Centuries. Static inspections and gladius drills could only tell Senior Centurion Publius, Senior Tribune Nictavi, and the battle commander, Colonel Bacaris, so much about the men's fighting ability. But pitting heavy infantrymen against each other would reveal weaknesses. With the information, the commanders could put their strongest Centuries where they would do the most good. And, adjust their weakest Centuries so they would do the least harm while getting annihilated. No one was supposed to get injured in training. That wasn't the case when the Legion went to war. Then a lot of men on both sides would be wounded or killed.

***

"Senior Centurion. Can you explain why that Century is a half a beat behind the rest?" challenged Colonel Bacaris.

Publius followed the battle commander's eyes. As he'd come to expect, Fenoris Megellus stood at the apex of the slow Century.

"Move them away from my center," Bacaris warned. "If I find them at a critical location in my battle line, I'll have the 1st Century remove them."

"I understand, sir," Publius replied as he kneed his mount. A short gallop later, he reined in behind Megellus. Waving across the shield wall to the other Century, the Senior Centurion chopped his right hand into his left. Then slashed the knife edge of his palm across his throat.

117

The Centurion on the other side of the grunting men shouted to his NCOs. In the din of the struggle, his words should have been lost. But the Sergeant and Corporal knew the voice of their infantry officer and could pick it out in the roar of a landslide. Also, the squad leaders on the line knew and recognized their command staffs' voices.

"Assault through them," uttered the Centurion. Quickly his Optio and Tesserarius repeated the order. Almost as soon as it left the NCOs' mouths, the squad leaders repeated the command, as well as, the pivot men in each contubernium. Two heartbeats after Senior Centurion Publius signaled the Century's heavy infantrymen gathered the muscles in their shoulders and legs. As a single entity, they powered forward.

Alerio noted the change in attitude in the Century across from his. Almost as if witnessing a bull inhale before charging, the infantrymen rose, flexed, and lowered their shields.

"Brace, brace, brace," Corporal Sisera shouted.

Two of his squads repeated the order, but neither Optio Gustavi nor Centurion Megellus paid him any attention. As a result, two-thirds of the Century went from pushing to being knocked over and kicked as the opposing Century battered their way through Megellus Century. Only a two-squad huddle with Alerio fought off the advancing Century.

Unprepared, the twenty-four men in reserve were knocked off their feet as were the four men stationed for resupply. Then, the assaulting Century fell on the supply mules and when they left, the food, beverages, and extra weapons went with them.

The heavy infantrymen stopped to kick anyone on the ground, including the Optio and Centurion, as they filtered back to their original position.

The only men to avoid the violence of the winning Century were Corporal Sisera and his two squads. They stood behind a barricade of shields daring the assaulters to come at them.

"That was both sickening and embarrassing, Centurion Megellus," Publius stated looking down with disgust at the horizontal infantry officer. "Everyone of your ladies should consider going home to work on their weaving skills. Because it seems your Century has no cōleī for combat. Pull out of my skirmish line and move your sorry cūlī to the end position."

Fenoris Megellus rolled onto his hands and knees then shoved back and up. Holding his arms where a hobnailed boot's toe had kicked him, the infantry officer looked up at the Senior Centurion.

"I didn't know. We didn't get a warning the rules had changed," Megellus protested.

Publius raised his chin to look over the disheveled Century. On the other side of the line, the Legionaries were drinking the captured vino and eating the seized food.

"Centurion. Did the rules change?" Publius called to the other infantry officer.

The Centurion took a stream of vino, lowered the wineskin, and replied, "There is only one rule in the heavy infantry, Senior Centurion. Win at all costs."

"There you go Megellus. No new rule, just a total defeat on the shields of your betters," Publius described.

"Now, drag your sorry excuse of a Century out of my combat line before you infect any of my other Centuries."

Hisses and the word 'pests' followed the Century as they picked each other up, gathered their gear, and marched to the far end of the line. Alerio walked at the rear, his eyes downcast and his brain screaming in protest at the insults. And the shame he felt at his Centurion and Optio for allowing the assault to succeed.

When they reached the last position, they found themselves facing a bunch of recruits fresh out of Legionary training.

"They shouldn't be a problem," Caudini suggested.

"Why?" asked Alerio. "If we aren't acting like a unit, any Century with cohesion will dance right through us. Unbloodied or not."

"You really think so?" inquired the Lance Corporal from 5th Squad.

Alerio ignored the question and strolled to where Megellus and Gustavi stood talking.

"It was rough, but our plan worked," Gustavi said.

"What plan?" demanded Alerio.

"After studying the Legion attack line, I analyzed the best location for survival," Megellus replied. "In my opinion, I deduced the opportune position was at the end of the maniple."

"You do know, sir, they call the ends of the line the fifty percent solution?" questioned Alerio.

"Explain yourself and the meaning of that vague reference," demanded Megellus.

"It simple, Centurion. Command figures that a bad Century is held back by about fifty percent of the members," Alerio stated. "The Century at the end of the line faces not only infantry to the front but cavalry and skirmishers coming at them from the side. At the end of a battle, only fifty percent of the end Century will survive. Command assumes the worst half will die and thus provide a valid solution for a problem Century."

"And we are…?" stammered Megellus.

"The fifty percent solution, sir," Alerio assured him.

***

For the rest of the afternoon, they clashed with the new Century across the line. When the other units stopped for refreshments at midday, Megellus Century went without. Their supplies having been consumed by the assaulting Century. Word spread throughout the Century about the Optio and Centurion conspiring to downgrade the Century.

What hurt the most, they were now viewed as an embarrassment in the eyes of the Legion's command staff and in the opinion of the other heavy infantry Centuries.

Legionaries had armor, helmets, gladii, and javelins. But their single biggest asset, the one thing that pushed them through training and drove them to defeat the enemies of the Republic was pride. They could forgive going without food and drink, but they could never forgive their infantry officer and their Sergeant for trampling on their pride.

"Lance Corporal Dircium. Send me a body," ordered Alerio.

"Why?" Trax from 2nd Squad questioned.

"Because I asked for one," Alerio said while walking up to the squad leader. "Draw your gladius, Decanus. Do it. Let's see who has the bigger mentula."

121

Trax Dircium had crossed his Corporal several times, and in each instance, the Lance Corporal came away hurting. Under Sisera's glare, he shrugged and pointed to one of his infantrymen.

"Private Zelatus. Go with the Tesserarius," he ordered.

Alerio guided the Private away from his squad. As they walked, he called to 4th Squad, "Lance Corporal Enitui, give me a body."

"Ottone, go with the Corporal."

Acharis Enitui had watched with interest the exchange between Trax and Alerio. The Tesserarius seemed to be looking for a fight and as Trax had learned, a disagreement with Sisera almost always proved to be a painful experience.

Alerio took Privates Ottone and Zelatus far to the rear of the Century.

"I am holding you both responsible," Alerio warned. "You'll do your job, or you will lay down one night and never wake up. Am I clear?"

"But Tesserarius, we don't know what we're responsible for," they protested.

"You, Private Ottone are charged with protecting the Centurion," Alerio replied. "And you, Private Zelatus are to protect Optio Gustavi. If either of them stubs a toe, I am coming for you."

The Privates jogged back to the Century area, but they didn't return to their squads.

"Corporal Sisera. Why is Private Ottone following me around?" inquired Megellus.

"Because your incompetence has doomed half the Legionaries in this Century to death," Alerio whispered into the Centurion's ear. "Some of them might decide to return the favor."

"I don't see it that way," argued the infantry officer.

"We are going to war, not a construction site," Alerio replied. "Look around you, sir. This is a Legion formed to do one thing. Kill the enemy. It doesn't take much for a Legionary to decide there is an enemy within."

"But I was trying to save lives," pleaded Megellus. "Everything I've done was to save the lives of these Legionaries."

"But you broke the heavy infantry rule, sir," Alerio suggested. "You didn't win."

***

The Century staggered into their camp late in the afternoon. Exhausted and hungry, they longed for a bite to eat and a chance to get off their feet. Centurion Megellus vanished into his tent while the NCOs separated and began the job of overseeing the infantrymen.

"Report," ordered Optio Gustavi.

The four Legionaries who were left out of the days training, so they could guard the camp, marched to their Sergeant.

"All was quiet," one of the sentries replied. Then he glanced around at the dejected Legionaries who sulked to their tents. "Optio, what happened?"

"We've been assigned a unit designation," Gustavi informed the four. "We are Crassus Legion North, 25th Century."

"The left end of the battle line?" one asked in disbelief.

"We've trained hard," another complained. "How could we have failed so lavishly?"

The other two sentries grumbled under their breath. In response to the discontent, Private Zelatus, who had been a couple of paces behind the Optio, shuffled forward.

"I'll stand for no disrespect," announced Gustavi. "Get back to your contubernium."

Without another word to the senior NCO, the four sentries turned about and left him and his bodyguard standing in the center of the Century's area.

***

A Legion NCO leading a small caravan of mules came from the direction of supply tents.

"Tesserarius of 25th Century?" shouted an Optio as he came off the Legion road. Following him was two handlers guiding mules with bundles and sacks hanging against its flanks.

Alerio was at the other end of the camp speaking with Tescum, and 10th Squad.

"Make sure you have a guard rotation in place for the night," he said when the stranger entered the camp. Turning from the squad, Alerio responded. "I'm Corporal Sisera."

"Compliments of Senior Centurion Publius," the NCO declared.

"What is it?" inquired Alerio as he crossed the camp to meet the Optio.

"Replacement javelins," the supply Sergeant replied. Then holding up two pieces of parchment, he instructed. "Sign here for the weapons and here for the half rations."

"Half rations?" questioned Alerio as he signed both.

"As I said, compliments of Centurion Publius," the Sergeant added. "Handlers, drop the bundles and sacks and let's get back to the depot."

There was nothing to be done about the replacement javelins. The Century would have the expense deducted from their salaries on the next payday. But the half rations, that was purely retribution by the Senior Centurion. Unfortunately, the exchange between Alerio and the supply Optio had taken place deep in the Century's area. And within hearing distance of the Legionaries.

"Half rations?" a number of infantrymen grumbled. "Why?"

"Because of our leadership, we are perfututum," others ventured.

"It can't get any worse," another group of voices declared.

Alerio wanted to defend the Century's Centurion and Optio. But in his heart, he agreed with the men. Then, to everyone's surprise, the situation got worst.

Chapter 14 – A Bad Night for Pests

"Megellus, get your sorry excuse for an infantry officer's cūlus out here," a veteran Centurion bellowed as he and another Centurion marched into the camp.

"Who is that?" someone asked.

"Centurion Lichenis from 1st Century," replied Lance Corporal Italus from 3rd Squad.

The veteran infantry officer marched up to Italus and glared at the Decanus.

"Did you say my name, Pest?" demanded the Centurion.

"Yes, sir," admitted Italus. "Someone asked who…"

"You will not say my name," Lichenis threatened. "Pests don't have the right. Megellus! Don't make me come into your tent and drag you out of there."

Fenoris Megellus pushed aside the flap and emerged from his tent. Dressed in a tunic and stylish sandals, he seemed comfortable and ready to turn in for the night.

"I see Legionaries and NCOs sitting down to eat," Lichenis observed. "But I don't see a leader checking on the wellbeing of his men."

"I was just relaxing after..." Megellus started to explain.

"The Qart Hadasht Empire doesn't care. Their mercenary army doesn't care," Lichenis yelled into Megellus' face. "General Otacilius Crassus doesn't care. And I don't care what you were planning. Get on your armor and come with me."

Visibly trembling from the tongue lashing, Megellus vanished into his tent.

1st Centurion Lichenis turned to the other infantry officer and instructed, "You know the work details. Get the Pests to them."

"25th Century's Optio and Tesserarius, on me," the officer ordered.

Alerio and Gustavi jogged to the infantry officer, stopped, and saluted.

"My name is Quadantenus, Centurion for 8th Century," the officer stated.

7th and 8th Centuries' positions were the center of the battle line in the veteran's maniple. As such, they were the last line of defense before the 1st Century. Behind them, and surrounded by the 1st were the General, the Colonel, and the Legion's command staff. Plus, the 7th and 8th line Centuries, along with 1st Century, were sworn to die before breaking or retreating. In short, Centurion Quadantenus held an important command in the Legion and for him to be in the 25th's area, didn't bode well for the Fenoris Megellus' Century.

"While your Centurion converses with the 1st Centurion, I have assignments for your Century," Quadantenus explained. "And I expect each of the details to be inspected and supervised during the night. Am I clear?"

"Yes, sir," Alerio replied.

"And you, Optio, do you understand?"

"Look here, Centurion…"

Quadantenus' arm shot out and Gustavi's chest collapsed around the fist. When the officer pulled it back, the Optio staggered. Alerio reached out to steady his Sergeant.

"Get your paws off of him, Pest," Quadantenus growled. "He's a Sergeant of heavy infantry. He will stand on his own or fall by the wayside."

"Yes, sir," Alerio acknowledged. He pulled his arms back and stood straight in front of the no-nonsense officer. "Orders, Centurion."

"Two contuberniums to the watch positions on the hill," Quadantenus instructed while pointing at the tip of a high slice of land overlooking the sea. "Two contuberniums to dig latrines. The Senior Centurion wants them completed by morning. Two contuberniums to the animal pens. We seem to have a wealth of merda, and the Senior Centurion wants the excess shoveled into wagons and taken to a dump site. Two contuberniums for perimeter patrol. The Senior Centurion fears an attack by wolves so be sure the patrol ranges beyond the trench, picket poles, and fencing. And to help you get organized, the Senior Centurion will be here at daybreak for a Century inspection. Do not let him down."

Fenoris Megellus emerged from his tent in his armor, horse comb helmet, and wearing hobnailed boots.

"On me," ordered Lichenis who walked away leaving Megellus to run and catch up.

Alerio and Gustavi turned to look at their officer who was being ordered around like a recruit.

"That is none of your business," Quadantenus barked noting the NCOs' eyes were on their officer. "Don't you have assignments to pass out. Or do you need me to run down the list again?"

"No, sir. We have it," Alerio assured the Centurion.

Gustavi's mouth hung open and his eyes were glassy. Shocked at the reality of the situation, he was paralyzed at the brutality of life in a marching Legion.

"What about you, Sergeant, do you get it, yet?" inquired Quadantenus.

Gustavi blinked as awareness came to him.

"I believe so, Centurion," the Optio responded.

"Good, because the General has enough lawyers and Tribunes for strategizing on his staff," Quadantenus explained. "We don't need any in the ranks. Turn your people out and keep an eye on them. I'll see you in the morning."

8th Century's infantry officer turned about and marched away.

"He is rather intense," Gustavi observed. "At least we won't have to deal with him until morning."

"Optio. We have just met the Centurions for 1st and 8th Centuries," Alerio pointed out. "Do you think they're finished with us for the night?"

Gustavi creased his forehead in thought before replying.

"I believe we are a project for the Senior Centurion. And the veteran Centuries will be around to teach us lessons," the Sergeant ventured. "This could be a bad night."

"Only, if we don't win in every case," offered Alerio.

***

Ibis Gustavi strutted to the NCOs' tent, went in, and appeared a few moments later. In his hand, he carried a leather bag.

"Corporal Sisera. Get the remaining contuberniums started on cleaning gear for the inspection," Gustavi suggested. "If you'll handle the ocean watch and the patrol, I'll make sure the latrines and manure disposal go smoothly."

The distribution of supervisor duties matched the skills of the Corporal and the Sergeant.

"Optio, if this means you plan to start winning, I agree" Alerio declared.

"That's exactly what this means," Gustavi replied.

The Sergeant marched out of the camp heading for the Legion's latrine area.

***

When Optio Gustavi arrived, the sixteen Legionaries from the 25th were pacing off the location for the new facilities.

"Hold. Look at the drainage, the rocky soil, and the runoff," Gustavi announced as he pulled a stick from his bag. Looped around one end was a thick ball of string.

After marking off areas and analyzing the slope, the Optio shifted the proposed location, tapped in sticks to outline the latrines, and organized the line of men. Once they were digging the new and transporting the loose dirt to the old latrines for fill, the Sergeant left to check on the men moving the manure.

On the far side of the Legion camps at the stock pens, Ibis Gustavi located his contuberniums, huge piles of animal droppings, and two wagons.

"Put straw in the bed of the wagons," he advised. "The bedding will keep the merda from soiling the boards and make it easier to unload the wagons."

When they had both wagons lined with straw and one almost full, Gustavi jogged back to the latrines. As he approached, he noted the work had stopped. All of his men were lined up in front of a Centurion who was gesturing wildly.

"I told you where to put the new facilities," the infantry officer shouted. "And when I…"

"Sir. Is there a problem with my Legionaries?" Gustavi inquired as he slowed to a fast walk.

"Are you in charge of this detail, Optio?" the Centurion replied. "I explained before where I wanted them dug."

"Are you an engineer, sir," asked Gustavi. He positioned himself in front of the Centurion, so he stood between the officer and his Legionaries.

"No. But I was charged with digging new latrines and I made a field decision."

"Your decision, sir, will put any rain run-off from the latrines into a stream that will flow by the supply tents," Gustavi informed him. "We will dig them anywhere you want. But I'll need a release signed by you noting that you were advised of the health issues."

"Your location won't have a run-off problem?"

"No, sir. Downhill from here, any rainwater will run to a sandy area," Gustavi assured the officer. "The dirty water will disperse in the sandy soil."

"In that case, carry on," the Centurion said before walking away.

The officer marched to the first rows of tents and vanished down one. Once out of sight from the Optio and the contuberniums, he stopped beside 1st Centurion Lichenis.

"Your opinion of Optio Gustavi," inquired Lichenis.

"In his field, he's as tough and self-assured as any infantry NCO," the officer commented. "And he's protective of his men."

"That's the opinion shared by the other Centurions and Optios," Lichenis stated. "Gustavi's issue seems to be from a lack of leadership. I have a team working on Centurion Megellus tonight. They'll get his head right or scramble his brains. Are your men ready to test the Tesserarius?"

"About that. Is it safe to come up on Death Caller in the dark?" the Centurion inquired.

"Corporal Sisera may have a fun nickname but, despite his reputation, he is just a junior NCO," Lichenis assured the infantry officer. "Probe and push both the patrol and the lookouts. The lad with the cute moniker can't be in both places at once. Let's see if he taught the contuberniums any useful skills before the Century joined us."

***

Alerio took the trail on the side of the hill. It twisted and turned while climbing steeply to the plateau. As he trekked up the path, the view of the beach and along the shoreline improved.

"Corporal Sisera. This is the best duty ever," announced Lance Corporal Aternus when he saw his Tesserarius top the rise.

"This glorious assignment is about to go straight to Hades," Alerio replied. After locating the other squad leader, he called both of them to him. "Aternus, Enitui. Let's have a talk."

"What's up Corporal?" asked Enitui from 4th Squad.

"Sometime tonight, you will be tested," Alerio exclaimed. "I'd guess an attack from the trail and from your rear."

Both Lance Corporals glanced over their shoulders at the narrow spine of land that connected the flat area with the distant hills.

"Not much room for an attack," Aternus observed. "A couple of men from the 7th should be able to defend our rear."

"What if they come with a battering ram?" Alerio ventured. "They will blow your two Legionaries off the sides and follow up with a squad. Meanwhile, you can count on several more from the trail. You won't know they're coming until they reach the plateau."

"Should we stay at one hundred percent alert all evening?" suggested Enitui.

132

"You do that and your contuberniums will be exhausted by morning," Alerio offered. Then he pulled lengths of rope from a pouch. "Trip ropes. Tie lengths across the trail and spine and stay at fifty percent. When they come, the aggressors will trip and alert your sentries. And remember, the only rule in the heavy infantry is to win. Do not be gentle removing them from our hill."

They talked for a while before Alerio slipped down the trail and went in search of the squads assigned to the patrol route.

***

Corporal Sisera blurted out something about the squads being sacrificial meat. In the waning light, the Legionaries stopped and looked at the dark shape of their Tesserarius.

"Explain that," demanded Dircium from 2nd Squad.

The squads were lined up two abreast at an opening in the perimeter fence.

"Optio Gustavi and I believe that all of the assignments Centurion Quadantenus ordered are designed to test our Century," Alerio replied. "If that's the case, you may be ambushed by a superior force."

"But why?" asked Stulte from the 9th Squad.

"Harassment, toughening us up, or making us pay to fit in with the Legion, take your pick," suggested Alerio. "We were embarrassed on the line today. I don't want to be tonight."

"If what you say is true," Dircium challenged. "How do you plan to prevent it?"

"Unburden two of your men," described Alerio. "Let them roam around your formation. When they spot the aggressors, they can give you a few moments to get ready for the attack."

"And we'll be set before they hit us," guessed Stulte.

"If the Senior Centurion has been touched by Furor and embraces the Gods insanity enough to launch a night assault against us," urged Alerio. "make them hurt."

"They will," Dircium promised his Corporal.

***

Pink slashes marked the sky foretelling the coming sunrise. From one side of the Century's area, sixteen Legionaries marched into camp.

"Report," requested Optio Gustavi.

"They hit us early this morning," Aternus responded. "Once the first ones tripped on the ropes, we charged and tossed every one of them off the hill."

"They screamed all the way down," Enitui added.

"We've set up stations. You'll be shaved and have your hair cut while another contubernium cleans your gear," Corporal Sisera advised. "And congratulations on the win."

From the other side of the camp, 2nd and 9th Squads arrived out of the morning gloom.

"Report," ordered Optio Gustavi.

"They made a lot of noise when they rose out of the grass," described Stulte.

"It must have been painful when we advanced our shields," Dircium said with a laugh. "They ran right into them. You were right Tesserarius. It was insanity for them to try us in the dark."

"Shave and a haircut," Alerio advised. "Drop your gear with 1st and 10th, they'll clean it for you. One other thing, you surely proved you are craftsmen of war. Good work."

"Journeymen warriors," a few of the Legionaries added while unstrapping their armor.

***

By the time 1st Centurion Lichenis and Senior Centurion Publius marched into camp, all eighty heavy infantrymen stood in front of their tents dressed for battle. Alerio waited near the NCOs' while Gustavi positioned himself on the far end at the infantry officer's tent.

"Why isn't Megellus back?" questioned Publius.

"He had trouble navigating the night, Senior Centurion," replied Lichenis.

"The same kind of trouble your Centuries had?" commented Publius.

"Yes, sir. Can I suggest we get on with the inspection?"

"Optio Gustavi, walk with me," ordered Publius.

They started at 1st Squad and moved quickly down the line until they passed 9th.

"Corporal Sisera. Were the trip ropes your idea?" asked 1st Centurion Lichenis.

"Yes, sir. I hope none of your Legionaries were hurt," Alerio replied. "The 25th plays rough."

The four closest squads overheard the comment. They passed Alerio's remarks up the line to the rest of the Century.

"I heard reports to that effect from the men sent to harass your patrol," Senior Centurion Publius announced as he guided the inspection team away.

"Sir, if I might," Alerio requested loudly.

His voice carried all the way to 1st and 2nd Squads at the far end of the camp.

Publius stopped in mid-stride. Lichenis and Gustavi nearly bumped into the Senior Centurion as he turned to face the Corporal.

"Choose your next words carefully, Tesserarius," he warned.

"Your Centuries call that harassment?" Alerio bragged. "The 25th Century drilled harder, bled more, and climbed faster during our easy training days."

"What do you mean by that, Corporal Sisera?"

From the middle of the Century, four voices shouted into the early morning air, "Victoria Hill."

The mention of the steep slope and the brutal runs up the face brought laughter from the squads. Publius snapped his head around and pivoted his face while looking up both sides of the camp.

"You have a lot of faith in a Century that failed on the line yesterday," Publius challenged.

"Sir, that won't happen again," Alerio replied.

"We'll see about that," the Senior Centurion stated. Then he suggested to the 1st Centurion. "Lichenis. The inspection is over. Let's get back to the headquarters area."

The top infantry officers for the Legion left and a short while later Centurion Megellus staggered into camp.

"Sir, orders?" asked Gustavi.

Megellus peeled off his helmet and hung his head as if he was so exhausted, he couldn't stand straight. From what the Optio and the Tesserarius could see, their officer's nose had dried blood caked on his nostrils and he had fresh bruises on his cheeks.

"When the trumpets sound the form up, make sure I'm moving," Megellus said before staggering into his tent.

"The Centurion doesn't look well," Alerio remarked.

"I don't believe he won last night," Gustavi stated. "Make sure the men eat, Tesserarius. I have a feeling; it's going to be a long day."

Chapter 15 – The Victorious Part

The Century showed the effects of a short night and half rations. They kicked at the ground raising more dust which added to the cloud surrounding them. It only added to the clogging of their noses and coating on their equipment. Compounding the general misery, Centurion Megellus at the head of the column didn't inspire confidence. His feet scuffed the loose dirt and his shoulders drooped.

Ahead of the 25th Century, the twelve units of the veterans and eleven Centuries of other experienced units stomped the dirt into dust. Behind the 25th, twelve Centuries of the less experienced Legionaries followed. Far ahead, and waiting for the heavy infantry to arrive, was Colonel Bacaris, the battle commander, 1st Century, and the Legion's command staff.

As if the infantry units were a wagon caravan coming off the trail, the Senior Centurion indicated Centuries to the right and left as they arrived. When the ends of the twelve veteran Centuries were positioned, Publius nudged his horse to their front and began directing the experienced Centuries. The 14th and 15th marked one end. Keying off them, the Centuries fell out of the march and filled in the line.

"I trust the 25th is ready for a fun day," Publius called out as Megellus approached. "Cheer up Centurion. I have arranged for your Legionaries to redeem themselves."

Megellus was too exhausted and numb to care, however, Optio Gustavi and Tesserarius Sisera did care. From their positions on either side of the Century, they caught each other's eyes through the marching Legionaries. Both flexed their shoulders as if to assure themselves they didn't have targets plastered to their backs. Except they did, and the Senior Centurion had just verified it.

Corporal Sisera let loose a loud howl after noting the Senior Centurion's words drove the Century into deeper despair. The animal sound drew the Legionaries' attention and Alerio began a chant.

"What good is a steel blade without a firm fist to wield it?" Alerio sang out.

"What good is a steel blade?" the Century replied.

"What good is a Legion shield without a stout shoulder to brace it," Alerio called out.

"What good is a Legion shield?" the infantrymen responded.

"What good is an iron shaft without an ample arm to throw it?" Alerio asked.

"What good is an iron shaft," the 25th repeated.

"Or a hefty helmet without a hard head on which to stow it?" their Corporal inquired.

"Or a hefty helmet and a hard head?" reported the infantrymen.

"It's only flesh and bone without the spark," Alerio sang.

"It's only flesh and bone without the spark," eighty voices shouted. "Only rust and dust without the victorious part."

"Without the what?" demanded Corporal Sisera.

"Without the victorious part!" came back to him in a roar.

As the call and response continued, the men of the 25th Century lifted their heads higher and stomped the ground harder as they passed between the veterans and the forming lines of experienced Centuries. Of all the units in the Legion, only the men of the 25th chanted as they marched towards their position.

Alerio pitched his voice higher and sang.
"The warrior spirit that screams for blood
Driving you off your knees and out of the mud
To stand the line with shields intertwined
To face the ax, sword, and spear
To crush the horde as the barbarians draw near
What good are the tools without the heart
What good is the man without the victorious part."

"Without the what?" screamed the Century.

"Without the victorious part," Alerio cried back.

"The victorious part," the infantrymen responded.

"Century halt," Optio ordered as they reached their place at the end of the line.

"Thank the Goddess Algea," one Legionary whispered.

"It is painful when the Corporal sings," another added.

"You call that singing?" another suggested.

Alerio ignored the gossipers. He knew his singing was beautiful and the men spoke out of jealousy. Across

139

from his infantrymen, Corporal Sisera recognized the 24th Century. Experienced but not superior to the 25th, they shouldn't present much of a challenge.

The twelve least experienced Centuries formed their practice lines and once the three Legion battle maniples were in place, Senior Centurion Publius rode in front of the veteran Centuries. There he pulled the reins, stopped his mount, and studied the formations.

"19th, pull out and move to face the 2nd," he directed. It was an opportunity for an experienced center unit to test themselves against the end of the veteran's line. "Close the gap 24th. 10th Century, fill in where the 24th was positioned."

In the shuffling to fill in for the displaced Centuries, the veteran 10th Century stomped over and took the pace of the 24th across from the 25th. Alerio and the Sergeant walked to their officer to see if he had any suggestions.

"That's what the Senior Centurion considers an opportunity for redemption?" Gustavi complained. "It's more like additional punishment. Wouldn't you agree, sir?"

Fenoris Megellus didn't respond to the question. His eyes were locked on the Centurion of the 10th. Across the line, the other infantry officer glared back with a smug grin on his face.

"Him. Last night," Megellus ground his teeth as he talked.

"Are you making this personal, sir?" inquired Alerio.

"Very personal, Corporal Sisera," Megellus replied.

"In that case Centurion, I'm hungry," Alerio commented.

"What does your stomach, Tesserarius, have to do with our situation?" Gustavi demanded.

"There are full ration sacks over there," Alerio said while nodding at the supply mule behind the 10th. "All we have to do is walk over there and take them."

"That's the right-side center of the veteran line," Gustavi pointed out. "I would think they would have something to say about it."

"What are you thinking, Corporal Sisera?" Megellus asked.

"On the second rotation, we attack," Alerio explained.

"Can we beat them?" the Centurion questioned.

"Yes, sir. If you let me set it up."

The infantry officer searched his Optio's face for assurances that they could in fact successfully attack a veteran Century. He found none.

"I don't like it," Gustavi stated. "We could lose the few supplies we have left."

Megellus rubbed his forehead, hit a tender spot, and jerked his hand away from his face. Looking at his fingers, the Centurion seemed lost in thought. Then a smile crossed his face.

"Corporal Sisera. You have the lead on this," Megellus announced. "The Optio and I will follow your guidance."

"Thank you, sir," Alerio acknowledged. Then he called to the squads. "Lance Corporals Dircium, Caudini, and Tescum. On me."

Along with the squad leaders, Aternus from 7th Squad also broke from the ranks.

141

"That's the Century we pushed off the hill last night," the Lance Corporal offered. "What's up?"

"We are going to rout them," Alerio stated. "Now get back and spread the word. Any Legionary who doesn't follow directions will have a special gladius lesson with me."

"Those are painful," Aternus commented before walking back to the squads.

***

Sergeant Gustavi studied the three Lance Corporals. He understood the reason for two of them. Trax Dircium's arms were as big as most men's legs. And Telesia Caudini was rawboned and carried muscle evenly distributed from his legs to his shoulders. The man resembled a Greek statue. But the third Lance Corporal didn't fit in anyone's idea of an attack line. Lucius Tescum was easily the shortest and lightest Legionary in the Century.

"Tesserarius. Are you sure about the 10th Squad?" he asked.

"Absolutely, Optio," Alerio assured the Sergeant. "They are the right side of our front line."

The senior NCO shrugged and strolled over to speak with the other squads. Meanwhile, Alerio signaled for the three squad leaders to come in close so they could talk confidentially.

***

Along the three lines, Legionaries locked shields and pushed. Behind the front ranks, the second rank waved javelins in the air and shouted.

Junior Tribunes raced behind the opposing Centuries delivering messages. One jerked his horse to a stop and yelled at Megellus.

"Centurion, rotate the 25th," he bellowed before riding back towards Legion command to get another assignment.

"Rotate," Megellus ordered. Sisera and Gustavi repeated the instructions. All of the squad leaders and their pivot men echoed the directive.

The three squads on the attack line slammed their shields forward, turned them to the side, and stepped back. From between them, the members of the next three squads eased forward, centered their shields, and delivered another thrust. In the space of a single heartbeat, fresh Legionaries were on the shield wall.

The one's relieved filtered back between the Legionaries of 2nd, 5th, and 10th Squads. That ended the first rotation for the 25th Century.

***

The heavy infantry Centuries weren't the only units being drilled. On the other side of the command group, light infantrymen were dueling with short blades and small shields. They also had Tribunes delivering instructions. On the flanks, cavalrymen rode in sweeping rushes before reversing and sweeping back in the other direction.

At the center of the mayhem, battle commander Colonel Bacaris, Senior Tribune Nictavi, and Senior Centurion Publius shouted, strategized, and issued instructions.

"Tribune, rotate the 25th," Publius advised one of the junior staff officers. Then to Nictavi, he exclaimed. "My problem Century seems to be responding."

"How well?" the senior staff officer inquired.

"So far, they're keeping up," replied the Senior Centurion. "But I'd like to see more from them."

While the Senior Centurion offered his opinion, the junior staff officer with his message rode around the veteran Centuries and entered the space between the lines of combatants. He kneed his mount and raced for the 25th Century.

"Centurion, rotate the 25th," he shouted before spinning his horse and galloping away.

This time Megellus didn't order the movement. Instead, he lifted an arm and pointed at his Tesserarius.

Alerio nodded his understanding and looked to be sure Optio Gustavi caught the signal.

"Rotate and stand by," Corporal Sisera announced. The Sergeant and Centurion repeated the commands, and the orders were reiterated by the squad leaders and pivot men.

Trax Dircium and 2nd Squad, Telesia Caudini and 5th Squad, and the undersized Lucius Tescum's 10th Squad plus his right pivot man, Palinurus, sidestepped forward. The original twenty-four men faded back and away from the shield wall. The newly set forward rank hammered their shields forward as was expected by the 10th Century. Both sides seemed to settle into the ongoing shoving match. Then Alerio called out a second order.

"Half left, advance. Advance, Advance," he shouted.

The front twenty-four angled their shields forty-five degrees to the left, slammed forward, stepped up, and repeated the movements three times. On the second surge, the huge Private Palinurus caught the edge of the opposing Legionary's shield. The man stumbled back opening a space. With room to swing, Palinurus sent two more men of 10th Century to the ground. They tumbled to the dirt and collided with the legs of their squad mates and the rank behind them.

"Reserves, cover the ends," Alerio ordered.

The four Legionaries assigned to resupply, split apart and the pairs went to the ends of the 25th's line. As Palinurus moved left, a gap opened to his right. One pair jumped in sealing the hole.

"Half right, advance, advance, advance," Alerio instructed changing the angle of attack.

The standing Legionaries of the 10th Century had adjusted to the left angled attack. But their downed men presented a problem for the Legionaries their infantry officer rushed forward. Suddenly, the attack shifted and the 25th Century came at them with right-angled shields.

At the end of three more advances, the 10th was in disarray. Alerio smiled and turned the 25th loose.

"Assault through them," he ordered before the other Century could reset. "Go, go, go!"

Telesia Caudini waded into the opposing Legionaries. With 5th Squad trailing behind like a wake behind a boat, he separated the opposing Legionaries. After punching through, 5th Squad stripped wineskins, water bags, and food sacks from 10th Century's mule.

"What good is a steel blade without a firm fist to wield it?" Lance Corporal Tescum sang.

"What good is a steel blade?" the 25th Century replied.

"What good is a Legion shield without a stout shoulder to brace it," Tescum called out.

"What good is a Legion shield?" the infantrymen responded.

The heavy infantrymen from the 25th Century backed up. Keeping their shields tight, they protected the men carrying the captured food and drink.

"*What good is an iron shaft without an ample arm to throw it?*" Tescum yelled.

"*What good is an iron shaft,*" the 25th repeated.

"*Or a hefty helmet without a hard head on which to stow it?*" Tescum inquired.

"*Or a hefty helmet and a hard head?*" responded the infantrymen.

"*It's only flesh and bone without the spark,*" Tescum sang.

"*It's only flesh and bone without the spark,*" eighty-two voices shouted including Alerio and Gustavi. "*Only rust and dust without the victorious part.*"

"*Without the what?*" demanded Tescum.

"*Without the victorious part!*" a roar came back to him.

Wineskins were passed to their Centurion, Optio, and the Tesserarius.

"To our command staff," Trax Dircium declared as he bit into a big radish.

Across the line, the officer for the 10th Century glared at the 25th. But the sneer was gone, replaced by clenched teeth and tight lips.

Centurion Megellus lifted the wineskin, saluted the other officer, and took a long stream of stolen vino.

At the Legion command area, Senior Centurion Publius bowed his head.

"I didn't see that coming," he admitted. "Someone has drilled that Century hard and properly."

"I watched Sisera last year at Messina teach veterans," a Junior Tribune remarked. "His style is brutal."

"And as we just witnessed," Publius added. "very effective."

Chapter 16 – South to Rhégion

Late in the day, the 25th Century swaggered into their camp. Although it had been a long day of drills, the Legionaries' spirits were high and their steps lively. As the columns marched down the center, contuberniums fell out of the march at their tents. While the squads busied themselves with chores in their areas, Optio Gustavi and Tesserarius Sisera followed their officer to his tent.

"Do you think the Senior Centurion will reassign us?" Horatius Ostrei asked from where he squatted at the 1st Squad's campfire.

"A couple of days of us showing our muscle and he'll have to move us off the end," replied Hallus Italus from the adjacent 3rd Squad's area.

Before anyone could even unfold the leather-bags and cover their shields, a runner came off the road and jogged to Megellus. After delivering a letter to the Centurion, he ran off to deliver a message to the next Century.

"Decanus Ostrei, I'm afraid we're stuck with our unit designation," Megellus informed the squad leader. The infantry officer waved a piece of parchment in the air and added loudly. "The Legion is marching south to Rhégion in the morning. All assignments are fixed."

Groans from the Century greeted the news. They were the 25th Century and destined to anchor and defend the left end of the Legion line.

***

Before daybreak, and while Consul Valerius Mesalla's two Legions slept and Consul Otacilius Crassus' Southern Legion dozed, Crassus' Northern Legion strapped the final camp gear onto the backs of their mules. Once the pack animals were led away, the Legionaries hoisted their personal gear onto their shoulders and formed up on the road.

"Crassus' North, standby," voices passed on the words from the front of the column. They rolled over the 25th and continued on to the 37th Century and the mule handlers at the rear. Moments later, the order to move came from the front. "Forward march."

The Legionaries on Alerio's side of the Century burst out laughing.

"They always say march," one of the men offered. "It'll take half the morning for us to move."

As predicted, the 25th stood around until pink appeared in the sky. Then, the unit in front of them shuffled away. No one even tried to march. Just putting one foot in front of the other allowed them to keep up with the slow-moving columns of the Legion.

"Keep it tight," Gustavi instructed.

"Optio. At this rate, I could take a nap and jog a quarter of a mile to catch up and it would be considered tight," an infantryman pointed out.

"If you allow a quarter of a mile between the Centurion and you, I'll have Corporal Sisera give you a shield and gladius lesson," Gustavi warned.

To Alerio's delight, the threat brought a round of half-hearted complaints. The Century had begun to see themselves as infantrymen and the Optio and Centurion were doing their part to become line commanders.

It was long past sunup when the last of the Legion passed out of the camp. Stretched out on the road to Rhégion were the command staff, thirty-seven heavy infantry Centuries, ten Centuries of light infantry, three hundred cavalrymen, almost two hundred pack mules, and a long wagon train. They had two hundred miles to cover, and General Crassus wanted them at the port city in five days.

There would be no temporary camps with trenches and sharpened pole barriers. Other than breaks for midday meals and overnight rests periods, the Legionaries would march.

As the Senior Centurion stated when he rode down the columns, "The pack animals and supply wagons will catch up or not. But the infantrymen will be ready to board ships on the sixth day."

After delivering the order, Publius kneed his mount and rode back to inform the next Century. Based on the wishes of their General, the four thousand men of Crassus' Northern Legion put hobnailed boots on the ground or heels to flanks and moved southward.

***

The Legion threaded through the foothills stretching out so far, the lead elements had no idea where the tail, the middle, or back sections were located. Every unit received their guidance from the backs, elbows, and marching feet of the Century to their front. While the 25th reached the outskirts of Scilla, a small coastal town, the

Legion's command staff rode into Fort Rhégion some eleven miles away.

"We'll be sleeping on the beach tonight," Alerio announced.

"How do you know, Tesserarius?" asked Lance Corporal Umbria from 6th Squad.

"I was stationed with the Southern Legion before the Qart Hadasht Empire took over Messina," Alerio answered. "When you see Sicilia on the other side of the water, we'll turn southeast and, in a short while, march into Rhégion."

"This is dangerous," warned Lance Corporal Enitui. He indicated the gaps between Centuries and the distances where the hills and spaces caused most of the Legion to be out of sight.

"You're not wrong," Alerio admitted to the Decanus of 4th Squad. "If we were across the water and in enemy territory, we'd be in a defensive marching formation."

"I'll hold you to that," Enitui replied.

Despite the uneven ground, the 25th soon reached the Messina Strait. Following the toe of the Republic around in a southeasterly direction, they saw the tower at Fort Rhégion in the distance.

"Imposing structure," Gustavi called from the far side of the formation.

"It is that. And from the top, it commands a view of Sicilia from Messina and south along the coast to Giampilieri," Alerio shouted over. "Giampilieri has a deep channel and a broad beach. It's probably where we'll land."

"A sentry in the tower can see if a company is coming," the Optio ventured. "It'll make our landing safer."

"Yes, Optio," Alerio reported. "Unless we land in the dark."

"Would command have us do that?" inquired Lance Corporal Umbria. "I mean, land in the dark."

"It's not a generally acceptable tactic," Alerio informed him. "But it's been done."

"To what success?" Gustavi demanded.

"Sometimes it gives you the element of surprise," Alerio bellowed.

"And the other times?" someone inquired.

"Landing at night can have you fighting for your life in the dark."

***

They hiked into Rhégion, crossed the piers, and angled up into the heart of the city. Blocks later, the long string of exhausted Legionaries turned to the right and left the civilian area.

Once through the gates of the fort, duty NCOs stood in the drill field directing the column across the open area to the gates in the wall on the far side.

"I see the command staff has the luxury of indoor accommodations," Lance Corporal Frentani mentioned.

He referred to the Legion's Tribunes who were stripped down and lined up at the baths. It was obvious, their staff officers weren't headed for a bivouac on the beach as Corporal Sisera mentioned.

"You should have picked your father better," someone called out.

"Or he, his father," another Legionary suggested. "Then you could be a nobleman and have indoor plumbing."

"Stifle that talk," ordered Sergeant Gustavi. The last thing he needed was an officer to overhear the conversation and decide the Century required extra duty to tamp down the disrespectful thoughts. Changing the subject, he craned his neck back and noted. "The tower is a nice piece of engineering."

***

Standing at the western edge of the fort, the tower rose beside the water of the Messina Strait. In the afternoon sunlight, it cast a long, slim shadow back over Fort Rhégion. Three senior officers stood in the tower's shadow where it passed over the porch of the command building. Senior Tribune Nictavi, Senior Centurion Publius, and Tribune Velius from the Southern Legion watched the Centuries march across the drill field.

"The 25th?" Publius questioned.

"If that's the Century with Alerio Sisera," confirmed Velius.

"It is. But what difference will a Corporal make?" challenged Publius. "Why not use one of our veteran Centuries?"

"You saw what the 25th did to the veteran 10th Century," Nictavi pointed out.

"It's not the Century specifically. Although if Sisera trained them, I'd wager they are better than average," Velius ventured. "The reason I suggested him is Sisera knows the landscape and has done a number of successful missions for me on Sicilia."

"This is more than information gathering, spymaster," Nictavi stated.

"Most of Sisera's assignments became hands-on in one way or another," Velius responded. "Even if they didn't start that way."

"I still think ranks of heavy infantrymen is the best diplomacy," Nictavi insisted. "Let me line up the Legion outside their walls and then see if the rebels want to resist."

"Centuripe is one of the largest and most prosperous cities on Sicilia," Velius advised. "With an army second only to Syracuse and the Qart Hadasht Empire. If Centuripe can hold off both of those, your Legion wouldn't frighten them into submission. And they'll send our ambassador back over the wall one body part at a time."

"And you think the 25th can do what an entire Legion can't accomplish?" asked Senior Centurion Publius.

"A Century can sneak in close to the city in a shorter time than your Legion can cross the strait and march up the Symaethus valley," Velius offered. "And if Fortūna smiles on them, they will arrive at Centuripe without engaging in a glorious battle. One that is sure to lead to the death of Ambassador Octavius Sergius."

"Tribune Velius. We'll go with your recommendation. I'll clear it with Colonel Bacaris," Senior Tribune Nictavi declared. "Senior Centurion, pull the 25th off the march."

"Okay, but I still don't like it," Publius responded. He looked across the drill field to where the 25th Century was approaching the exit gate. "Centurion Megellus. Pull your Century out of the march and wait for me outside the wall."

Optio Gustavi's stomach twisted. Apparently, a senior officer had heard his Legionaries' comments about the Tribunes. He could only imagine the punishment duty his exhausted Century would be assigned. The thought hit him in the gut. If the Sergeant knew the real reason for pulling the Century to the side, his upset stomach might have escalated to vomiting.

***

"Have your Century drop their gear on the other side of these patrol boats," Velius instructed while pointing to an open space between overturned vessels.

"Tribune Velius. Why do I have a feeling the 25th being separated from the Legion isn't to award us an honor?" Alerio guessed.

"Corporal Sisera, you know me too well," the head of Southern Legion's planning and strategies section replied. "But this isn't my mission, so I'll leave it to the Senior Tribune to explain."

The eighty heavy infantrymen, their Optio, and Tesserarius dropped their equipment and personal belongings on the ground. Then the Legionaries sat and leaned against the stacked gear while the command staff remained standing.

"We have an issue," Nictavi stated. "The Senate sent an Ambassador to Centuripe to discuss a treaty. While Octavius Sergius met with the city council, their military revolted and took our diplomat and his party prisoners."

"We should march the Legion directly there," offered Megellus.

"My thoughts exactly," Nictavi replied. "Except, I was informed if the Legion showed up outside the city walls, Ambassador Sergius would be dismembered. He has a brother and two uncles in the Senate who would miss him dearly if we allowed that. Thus, the General has challenged us to find an alternate approach."

The Senior Tribune pointed to the spymaster from the Southern Legion.

"The militia has revolted and is holding our Ambassador. So, we are sending the 25th to Centuripe," Velius informed the Century. "You have one mission. Locate, secure, and protect Ambassador Sergius until the Legion arrives."

"Permission to speak freely, sir?" asked Alerio.

"Granted," the Tribune responded.

"If we succeed, the Legion claims a victory," Alerio described. "However, if the Ambassador and the 25th are killed, you can blame it on the failure of the Century. Did I miss anything, sir?"

"In a crude manner of speaking, you've summed it up," Velius admitted. "But the Centuripe city council wants peace and trade. So, it isn't as if you have to fight the entire population."

"Yes, sir. Only their military," added Optio Gustavi. "When do we leave, sir?"

"At moonrise," Velius told him. "The sailors need light to cross the strait."

"To Giampilieri," inquired Alerio.

"No, Corporal. The patrol boats will drop you at Catania."

"It'll take all night to row to that beach, sir."

"Then you better have some food and decide what equipment you'll be taking with you," suggested Senior Centurion Publius. "You don't want to hold the boats up."

Act 5

Chapter 17 – Simeto River

Rays from the morning sun broke over the far-off mountains and illuminated the path. In fact, the light truly only helped one man. He jogged at the head of the column. Behind him, the eighty Legionaries of the 25th Century and their command staff followed in a tight, twisting line. The formation resulted from a quick discussion when the eight patrol boats deposited them on the beach at Catania.

"Slow and steady?" inquired the infantry officer.

"No, sir. The Legion will hit this beach sometime tomorrow," Alerio offered. "They'll need another day to cover the thirty-two miles to Centuripe. If we haven't found the Ambassador and set a protective perimeter around him by then, we'll have failed."

"Two days isn't much time for the mission," Gustavi added. "We can do a Century march with flanking elements for security. We'll be slow until daylight. Or Corporal Sisera, did you have something else in mind?"

"The only hard navigation is the twelve miles west to the Simeto River," Alerio exclaimed. He looked at the stars in the sky and continued. "Give me a man blessed by the Goddess Theia to lead and I'll run second. We should make the river just after sunup."

"Then it's only a matter of moving upstream without being noticed by a patrol out of Centuripe," Centurion Megellus said.

"Who has the best night vision?" Gustavi called to the Legionaries gathered on the beach.

"Decanus Aternus. Theia had blessed him with eyes that can dance with Luna along moonbeams," a Legionary from 7th Squad advised. "If more game animals roamed the night, we'd never go hungry."

"Lance Corporal Aternus, lead us off," Alerio instructed the Lance Corporal with excellent night vision.

"In what direction?"

Alerio placed a hand on the squad leader's shoulder, turned him to face west, and announced to the men on the beach, "Grab a shoulder and keep up."

As if an uncoiling snake, the 25th Century unwound from ranks on the beach to a serpentine line heading for the Simeto River. With Alerio guiding and the Lance Corporal watching the ground as the trail twisted and turned up and downhill, they maneuvered through the night. Exhausted, they arrived at the riverbank of the Simeto shortly after sunrise. Thanks to the rapid movement, they avoided contact with locals and patrols.

From hyper-alert, the legs of the two men in the lead folded and they sank numbly to the grass. The Century flowed around them and fell into formation on the sand and gravel while the Legionaries at the tail end caught up.

"Ostrei. Push out with 1st Squad," instructed Gustavi. "We're a good way from Centuripe but I don't want to be caught off guard."

While the 1st moved upstream, the other squads straightened their ranks and began following them to the north. Alerio and Caricini Aternus climbed to their feet and fell into the center of the loose formation.

"Now I wish we had our armor and shields," Aternus complained. "I get it that we needed to move fast and appear to be a work crew. But come on, it's a stretch to believe we're anything except a Legion Century. Do you really think we'll fool the Centuripe military?"

"One Century against a militia that held off the Syracuse army," Alerio pointed out. "Not an open field match up I'd place coins on. However, a moment of hesitation on their part to allow us to react is worth not carrying shields."

I know, we're craftsmen of war," commented Lance Corporal Aternus. "I would still feel better if I had my armor and shield."

***

The Century moved rapidly throughout the day. By early afternoon, Lance Corporal Italus, whose 3rd Squad had the advanced position, sent back word that there were large hamlets and farms off the riverbank.

"I think it's time to head for the hills," suggested Megellus after the Legionary reported the sightings. "Have Lance Corporal Italus pull back. We'll let 4th Squad take the lead."

"Enitui. Break the trail," Gustavi instructed while pointing to the hills west of the river. "Get us off this exposed terrain."

"Just think of us as your mountain goats, Optio," Enitui exclaimed.

The squad climbed out of the river valley, reached the top of the hill some four hundred feet above the river, and dropped flat. Lance Corporal Enitui waved frantically from where he hugged the ground.

Centurion Megellus and Optio Gustavi scurried up to find out why the squad leader was panicked.

"What do you have?" Megellus inquired.

"Centuripe is maybe two miles away, sir," the Decanus of 4th Squad reported. "I can make out details of the guards on the wall. If I can see them, they can see me."

"Alright, stay below the crest of the hill and find a way to get us closer," Gustavi ordered. While the Legionaries, using their hands and knees, crawled by, the Sergeant pondered. "How are we supposed to get close to the city unnoticed? At least up north of the Capital, the hills have big trees."

Alerio climbed the rocky slope with the other squads. While they traversed the hill just below the crest, he fell out and sat next to the officer and NCO.

"I'll take two men into the city with me and find out where they're holding Ambassador Sergius," he offered. "Lance Corporal Lucius Tescum and Private Palinurus should make good cover."

"You're going to travel with the smallest and largest man in the Century?" quizzed Megellus. "According to Tribune Velius, you are an accomplished agent. Sneaking in with two men of opposite stature isn't exactly stealth."

"A woodworker and a stonemason," Alerio pointed out. "And yes, they do stand out."

"How are you going to search for the Ambassador with the brothers Centaurus and Lapithes following you around?" inquired the infantry officer.

"Sir, Private Palinurus is hardly half man, half horse," Alerio protested. "Even if he's almost the correct size. And I don't believe Tescum has any connection to the Greeks in the Thessaly mountains."

"I think the Centurion was teasing about them being the mythical twins," corrected Gustavi. "But he has a point. How are you going to secretly search with them in tow?"

"I'm not going to search," Alerio replied to the officer and NCO. "I'm going into Centuripe and ask."

"And no one will be suspicious of you asking for the whereabouts of a prisoner being held by their militia?" challenged Megellus.

"Not in the least, sir," Alerio assured him.

By then the Century had moved off the backside of the hill and started up a dry wash. The Centurion rolled forward onto his hands and feet and crab walked after them. Before Alerio moved, the Sergeant rested a hand on the arm of his Tesserarius.

"Sisera. This is going to get deadly really fast, isn't it?" suggested Gustavi without looking Alerio in the eyes. "Understand, I'm not looking forward to dying but I'm not afraid of having my strings cut."

"I understand, Optio. We need to get into the city where we can take advantage of the narrow streets," Alerio informed him. "If the Century is caught in an open field, the Centuripe militia will outflank our formation and cut us to pieces."

"What I am trying to say is that you have the wellbeing of the entire Century in your hands," Gustavi advised. He rolled forward into a stooped position and, this time, stared into the Corporal's eyes. "I know you have had issues with the Centurion and me and with a few of the Squad Leaders. I hope none of the past problems will keep you from doing your best."

"That's where you have miss interpreted the situations, Sergeant."

"What did I miss?"

"I never had a problem with any of you," Alerio related. "It was you, the Centurion, and the Squad Leaders that had problems with me. We should move, Optio."

***

Later, the Century dropped down into a dale running east-west. Out of sight from the walls of Centuripe, they moved closer to the city. While the slopes lacked the cover of trees and heavy growth, the landscape provided high rolling hills and interconnecting valleys. By staying in the low areas and avoiding farms and villages, they worked their way around to the western side of the city. Unobserved, the men settled into a gorge a couple of ridges from the western gate of Centuripe.

"It's late, Corporal Sisera," Megellus observed. "You'll probably want to wait for the morning before going into the city?"

"No, sir. The evening is perfect," Alerio replied. "The Century needs food beside the hard wheat cakes we packed. And we need to get a feel for the layout of the city."

"You're going to get us food?" questioned the Optio. "I thought the reason for sneaking around all day was to hide from the militia?"

"The purpose was to disguise our approach," Alerio informed the officer and NCO. "Now that we're here, we have a problem."

"Just one?" Megellus inquired. "How about we're camped outside a hostile city without our armor and shields? And the reason for our presence is to free a Republic Ambassador. That adds up to more than one problem."

162

"Lance Corporal Tescum and Private Palinurus, on me," Alerio ordered as he stood and pointed at 10th Squad. Then to the Centurion and NCO, he stated. "Actually, sir, our biggest issue is that our supply wagons are delayed."

"We have supply wagons?" questioned Gustavi.

"As would any crew of mining specialists, Optio," Alerio informed him. Standing, the Corporal motioned for the Lance Corporal and the Private to follow him up the hill and out of the gorge.

***

"Lance Corporal Tescum, how would you capture the gate?" Alerio asked.

The three Legionaries strolled up the road. Dressed in rough workmen's woolens and with their gladii hidden under the shirts and short robes, they appeared to be craftsmen heading into the city for the night. In the distance, two guards stood in the open gateway watching them.

"There's no cover for a surprise approach and the walls are built on top of steep slopes. Hades, the slopes are almost walls," Tescum replied. "Maybe we could sneak a few men over the wall, capture the gate, and control it until the rest of the Century arrives."

Alerio indicated the sentries on the walls where the high stone barrier angled away. Unlike the straight, squared walls of cities built on flat or slightly hilly ground, Centuripe's defensive barrier followed the couture of the terrain. On either side of the gate, the walls stretched to where the ground fell away. Then, the stonework rolled back following the ridge's elevation. The configuration allowed guards stationed on the wall to see the approach road and anyone heading for the gate.

"You'd need enough men to take down the guards on the walls," Alerio advised. "That adds up to about half the Century just to open the gate."

"If we come in under cover of darkness, we can scale the wall and gate," Tescum suggested. Then after a moment of hesitation, he added. "But we'd take a lot of casualties."

"And alert the reserve guards. It would hamper the mission if half the Century was caring for wounded while we fight our way across the city," Alerio described. "Forget locating and securing the Ambassador. We have nothing if we don't enter the city unobserved."

The three continued walking forward towards the gate. Alerio and Tescum's eyes scanned the walls looking for a way to get the Century into the city. No ideas came to them and there didn't appear to be a weakness in Centuripe's defenses.

"You never asked me, Tesserarius," commented the big Legionary.

"Ask you what, Private Palinurus?" questioned Alerio.

"How would I get the Century into the city."

Palinurus was an excellent stonemason and a solid Legionary. But he didn't have the reputation as being quick-witted or a deep thinker. It never occurred to the Corporal to ask the big man his opinion.

Alerio stopped, lifted an arm, and pointed to the north where the mining operations were visible. Palinurus and Tescum both halted and turned to face in the direction indicated by their Tesserarius.

164

"Which are we looking at?" inquired Tescum. "The sulfur or the salt mine compounds?"

"Palinurus, how would you get the Century into the city?" Alerio asked while ignoring the Lance Corporal's question.

"Around the right side of the gate, about hallway to the first guard position is a washout," Palinurus explained. "It must have eroded away during a heavy rain. Pooling water against a wall will do that."

"How would water pooling against a wall help us?" challenged Alerio.

"Not outside the wall, Tesserarius," Palinurus replied. "The water pooled on the other side of the wall."

"How do you know that?" inquired Alerio.

"From the hole under the wall."

"There's a hole under the wall?" gasped Tescum.

"They filled it in, but the stonemasons weren't very good at their job," Palinurus said in disgust. "The angry stones have shifted. It'll take me no time to dislodge the rocks and tunnel up inside the wall."

"Where would the tunnel come out?" inquired Alerio.

"Your guess is as good as mine, Tesserarius," Palinurus responded. "But that's why we're going into the city, isn't it?"

"It is now," Alerio agreed with the big man.

***

A hundred paces farther on, one of the guards stepped away from his partner and challenged the three strangers. The other sentry stepped deeper into the gateway ready to block any attempt by the trio to force their way through or to run for help.

"It's pretty late in the day to be entering the city," the soldier insisted while lowering his spear. "What's the purpose of your visit?"

Alerio pointed at the mines to the north, puffed up his chest, and replied, "We're an engineering crew here to locate and dig a new mineshaft. Our supply wagons got delayed. Most of our men are camped out not far from here."

"If three men arriving at your gate makes you nervous," Tescum suggested. "Imagine your panic if all thirty-five of our team had come with us."

Alerio ignored the lie. If the Lance Corporal had reported that eighty men were camped not far from the gate, the guards might have panicked.

"Your purpose?" the soldier repeated.

"Food and beverages for our people," Alerio replied. "Where's the best place to buy supplies?"

"There's a pub not far from the lower guard barracks," the sentry answered. "They treat the militia good, and their food is clean."

"Thank you," Alerio acknowledged as the soldier stepped to the side.

The Corporal and his Legionaries walked through the gate and Alerio breathed a sigh of relief. Then the stonemason offered an observation.

"I noticed you said the food was clean, not good," Palinurus commented to the sentry.

Alerio took the big man's arm and hurried him away from the portal.

"I'd like it better if they treated the militia clean and the food was good," Palinurus stated.

Alerio picked up the pace to prevent further dialogue with the guards. Once the three men were away from the gate, one of the soldiers turned to his companion.

"I thought we were supposed to double check anyone coming in," he advised.

"That's for the eastern gate," the other soldier replied. "The Republic's troops will come up the Simeto River and form up in the valley. If we report those three, Captain Cheir will increase the guard and keep us on duty all night."

His companion nodded in agreement and strolled to the other side of the gate.

"You're right," he acknowledged as he lowered the butt end of his spear to the road. "It's only three miners. Not anything for us to worry about."

Chapter 18 – The God Dolos

As if the gentle grade of the approach road along the spine of the ridge was a jest, once through the gate, the punchline burst on the travelers. A half a block from the walls, the Legionaries were forced to lift their forward foot to take a step. Doorways at boot level seemed mismatched with the adjacent store entrances just one building up the grade.

"I've hunted mountain rams," Tescum related. "And I don't remember the climb or the stalk being this difficult."

"It's as if Centuripe was built on a set of massive steps carved out by a titan," Palinurus offered. "The siege by the Legion is going to be bad. But the house to house fighting to secure the city is going to cost a lot of Legionaries their lives."

Before anyone could comment on the usually slow Legionary's remarks, Palinurus turned off the road and ducked down an alleyway. Alerio and Tescum, walking a couple of steps in front of him, had to turn back before hurrying to catch up with the Private.

"Where are you going?" Alerio asked.

The stone pavers in the alley stretched out flat and the two normal sized men found themselves jogging to keep pace with the long-legged stonemason.

"Palinurus. What's the rush?" Tescum demanded.

"I'm losing the light," Palinurus said without breaking stride.

They left the alley, crossed a road, and reentered the alleyway on the other side. A quick glance up the road showed the terrain continuing to climb. Four cross streets later, Palinurus hooked a right and rushed downhill. He reached the city wall, studied the stones on the street, turned, and passed Alerio and Tescum as he walked back to the mouth of the alley.

"I'm tempted to find a pub and have him come to us when he finds what he's looking for," suggested Tescum.

Alerio started to agree when the stonemason vanished off to the right. By the time the Corporal and Tescum reached the end of the alleyway, Palinurus was downhill and nearing the city's defensive wall.

The stonemason Legionary stomped his feet on the stones covering the street, then with a satisfying grin on his face, crossed his arms, and leaned against the rocks of the wall.

"The tunnel will come up here," Palinurus announced. "These pavers are larger than standard and roughly laid. The subsurface isn't properly compacted."

"What does that mean?" questioned Alerio.

"It means the repair crew from the city did a poor job repairing the storm damage," Tescum informed Alerio. "It'll be easy to dig our way up, but someone will have to pry loose the pavers and roll them out of the way."

"If not?"

"The pavers will fall down the hole and take out the squads doing the digging," Tescum replied. "Seeing as that includes me, Tesserarius, I'd appreciate a promise that you'll move the stones."

Alerio glanced around at the stone buildings bordering the wall. Most were the lower backs of structures, their entrances higher up and facing the alleyway. Only a few had doorways for root cellars or rear stairs. Few shops or businesses faced the narrow passageway between the defensive wall and the stone walls supporting the businesses higher up.

"The area is sparsely used," Alerio observed. "One man should be able to remove the stones and secure the area until the Century comes through."

"Wouldn't that depend on the militia patrols?" Tescum inquired while pointing up the street.

Four men carrying spears and shields and dressed in armor with tall helmets turned from the alleyway and marched up the road. As the patrol moved, one soldier stepped out of formation and checked the doorway of a store.

"What do you want to bet, once they've checked one side of the street, they'll check the other," remarked

Tescum. "Then, come down to the wall and walk the perimeter to the next street?"

"Have you had your physical training today?" inquired Alerio.

"You know we haven't, Tesserarius," Palinurus replied. "We've been on the march all day."

"Well, you are about to make up for it," Alerio said as he motioned them to a spot behind the corner building. "We need to be up the next street and through the alleyway before the patrol sees us."

"Sounds a lot like sprint drills," offered Tescum.

"Not a lot, Lance Corporal," Alerio corrected. "It is sprint drills. Now, run."

With robes flying, the Legionaries' hobnailed boots pounded the pavers. Their footwear being the only Legion attire they brought from Fort Rhégion. Even in rough workmen's clothing, they feared the mining crew description wouldn't hold up under scrutiny. To compensate for the lack of shields and armor and for security, every man in the Century carried his gladius and a knife under the woolens. Everyone except Corporal Sisera, who had on his dual gladius rig and the Ally of the Golden Valley dagger strapped to his lower back.

The one thing that gnawed at the Legionaries' pride was the cost of the clothing. Purchased in the city of Rhégion by the Legion's Tesserarius, the expense went against the Century's account. It was necessary as their pack animals and clothing were lost in the transport herd. Unfortunately, the expense would be deducted on the next payday.

"You can feel how solid the street stones are," Palinurus observed.

"Less talking, more running, Private," Alerio ordered.

"Absolutely, Tesserarius."

The three reached the adjacent street and turned uphill. They were halfway up the grade before the militia patrol reached the defensive wall and the unstable paver stones.

***

The trio of Legionaries huddled outside a pub. Long shadows draped one side of the street in darkness leaving the other side softly lit. They stood in the shadows.

"Take these coins. Buy meat and bread for the Century," Alerio said while handing Tescum a purse. Then to Palinurus, he instructed. "Wait for moonrise before digging out the tunnel."

"Aren't you coming in with us?" inquired Tescum.

"I'm going to find the Ambassador," Alerio replied.

Palinurus glanced around as if looking for a sign or a hint of where the Republic's representative was being held. Not seeing anything, he leaned in and spoke to Alerio.

"Don't forget to relocate the street stones, Tesserarius," the Private reminded him.

"They will be moved," Alerio assured the Legionary stonemason before he turned and walked away.

"Corporal Sisera seems to have the second sight," Palinurus observed while watching Alerio fade into the darkness. "Do you think he'll stroll around the city until the Ambassador's location comes to him?"

"You've seen how his gladius' blade is always ahead of his opponent's. It's almost as if the Goddess Nenia does direct his arm. And why did command choose the 25th

171

Century for this mission? Because of him, and certainly not because of Centurion Megellus," Tescum said listing the martial skill of their junior NCO and the circumstances of their Century being selected for this mission. A job that rightly should have gone to a veteran unit. "Things happen around Death Caller. I'm just not sure it's healthy to be too close to him."

"Do you think he's dangerous?" the big Legionary questioned.

"Of that, there is no argument," Tescum responded. "I'm just not always sure to whom. Come on, we'll have a mug of vino while we wait for the cook to fill our order."

"A fine idea," Palinurus acknowledged. "But this doesn't look like the pub recommended by the gate guard."

"How do you know?" Tescum questioned.

"There are no soldiers, and I don't see a barracks."

The two Legionaries crossed the street and entered the pub. Two blocks away, Alerio ducked into a shop. A few heartbeats later, he appeared back on the street. While Tescum and Palinurus took seats and placed their orders, the Legion Corporal quick-stepped up the road and followed it around to the next level of the city. When mugs of vino splashed down on the tabletop and were lifted to thirsty lips, Alerio walked the last fifty paces and arrived at his destination.

***

In the dark, Alerio ran his fingertips over the face of one of the support columns for the gates. On it, he identified an indention where a craftsman had chiseled the shape of a single bee. Once satisfied he had located the

172

proper compound, Alerio rapped on the gates using the pommel of the Ally of the Golden Valley dagger.

"We're closed for the day," a voice stated from the other side of the gates. "Come back in the morning. We look forward to doing business with you in the daylight."

Alerio flipped the dagger, caught it by the blade, and passed it, hilt first, through the gap between the gates. The Legionary felt the presence of two people at the top of the wall. He didn't bother glancing up to confirm. Drawn bowstrings made distinctive noises as the wood creaked and the shafts scraped against the bows. Without a doubt, the bows were loaded with steel-tipped arrows and targeting him.

"Some business is best conducted in the dark," he whispered.

The weight of the dagger lifted from his hand. A few breaths later, the clicking of the gate unlatching followed by the squawking of the hinges announced the opening of one gate.

"Special orders are always given priority," a man exclaimed. "But let's not talk here. My office, if you please."

The flash of a body against the emerging stars showed a form vaulting off the wall and landing lightly in the courtyard. Once on solid ground, the person gestured for Alerio to follow. Before they reached the building, a lantern flared to life, and a door opened.

'Three adults and an apprentice,' Alerio thought as he entered a room filled with luxury goods. On the far side at another doorway, the man from the yard and the lad with the light signaled for Alerio to come their way.

'If the manager was at the gate and had placed two additional assassins on the wall, something wasn't right. Since when does a Golden Valley compound need overt defenses?'

***

The assassin and apprentice guided Alerio down a corridor to an office. They continued onward while he stepped through a doorway they indicated. Another man entered from a different door, settled in behind a desk, and motioned for the Legionary to come into the room.

Out of habit, Alerio glanced around looking for hidden bodies. In his experience, the trading houses liked to use strangers to demonstrate tactics and he wanted to be ready.

"I am Heteros. And you, Corporal Sisera, are a long way from home," the manager of the trading house suggested as he studied Alerio's Ally of the Golden Valley dagger. "Yet Dolos smiles on your arrival. Please, sit."

At every Golden Valley facility he visited, the managers always knew details about him. For a period, Alerio believed the managers were mind readers or magicians. But he learned recently, they read information about him from markings on the dagger. There was no mystery to their knowledge but, the reference to the Greek God of deception, craftiness, and treachery did present a riddle.

"I would think Dolos applies to your other line of commerce," Alerio commented hinting at the assassins-for-hire part of the Golden Valley's enterprise. "But I must confess, I don't see the God's connection to the duties of a Corporal of the Legion."

"It's true we hold the God's blessings in high esteem," Heteros replied while placing the dagger on the desktop. Using two fingers, he slid it across the desk to Alerio. "Your skills and sudden arrival fit nicely with a need. Although, the Legion was expected. You are a bonus."

"I came to you for information," Alerio stated. "Not for an assignment."

"As is your right, Ally of the Golden Valley," Heteros agreed. "The information is yours for the asking. The assignment, as you call it, is a favor."

Alerio wanted to get the location of the Ambassador and leave. He was tired, hungry, thirsty, and had a busy evening ahead of him. Getting involved with a sect of assassins beyond acquiring information didn't sit well with him. That logic was sound, and it's why he surprised himself when he opened his mouth.

"What forces a trading house of the Golden Valley into a defensive posture?" Alerio inquired. "Two archers above the gate for one visitor. And, the apprentice kept behind the walls. I expected the youth to be on lookout duty across from the compound."

"Captain Cheir of the city militia is the reason," Heteros explained. "He is the son of a Centuripe councilman, the nephew of a priest, and his other uncle owns a trading house. In short, Captain Cheir is a powerful enemy of the Golden Valley. And when this crisis is resolved, he'll be promoted to General of Centuripe."

"Most enemies of the Golden Valley just fail to wake up one morning," offered Alerio. "What's different about the Captain?"

"It's rare for Golden Valley trading houses to involve themselves in local politics," Heteros advised. "With his family's connections, if Cheir's strings are cut in the middle of the night, his death would enrage the locals for a generation."

"And hurt the Valley's business," suggested Alerio. "I assume you want the Captain removed publicly."

"You seem very willing to kill without hesitation," Heteros questioned while reaching out and retrieving the dagger. He studied it carefully. "Why is that?"

"The answer isn't in my history," Alerio offered. "The militia has taken an Ambassador of the Republic prisoner. That act has sentenced all of the militia's officers, including Captain Cheir, to death. I've just agreed to carry out the judgment personally."

"Ambassador Octavius Sergius has accommodations in the upper barracks," Heteros described while placing the dagger in front of Alerio. "It's across the street from the Agora. Surrounded by a wall with gates and steps to the upper watch hill. You'll find about two hundred fifty soldiers along with Captain Cheir stationed there. Unfortunately, the current General is not there. He is out checking on his defensive positions."

The two talked about details and locations for a while longer. Finally, Alerio picked up the dagger and slid it into the sheath on the small of his back.

"One more question, Master Heteros," inquired Alerio as he pushed out of his chair. "What does the God Dolos have to do with this?"

"Don't you find it deceptive and crafty for an assassination to be carried out legally and in view of witnesses?"

176

"You've been away from the Golden Valley for a long time, haven't you?"

"That I have Corporal Sisera," Heteros confessed. "I recommend you leave the back way. Cheir has agents watching the front. On the lower road, you'll find a pub on the other side of the lower militia barracks. The food is…"

"The food is clean," Alerio commented while crossing the room to where the young apprentice stood waiting. Just before going through the doorway, the Legionary glanced back at Heteros and added. "I've heard of the pub."

Chapter 19 – Her Blue Scarf

Corporal Sisera tightened the rope and slowed the descent. When Heteros mentioned the back way, Alerio assumed he meant a doorway and stairs. Rappelling from the rear roof of the Golden Valley trading house's building was the last thing he expected. His feet touched the roof of the building on the lower street, and he released the rope. Following the lad's directions lead to a staircase on the side of the building. Several steps later, he walked away from the building and onto a dark road.

Lights glowing from a three-story building created the brightest spot on the street. Between the lanterns hanging from the porch and Alerio was a structure of tall dark walls with sentries manning the gates. On the other side of the guard barracks, a pub occupied the lower level of the three-story building. Alerio didn't care what the upper floors were used for, hunger pains tapped at his belly and guided his legs in the direction of the pub.

Pushing through the doorway, Alerio entered a noisy, crowded great room. Some locals were sequestered at tables against the walls. Their choice of seating necessary because the rest of the room was claimed by a large group of men. They were young and fit, brash, loud, and looking for a challenge. To feed the aggression, they gambled, shouted lies, pushed, and shoved, and screamed in each other's faces. Vino mixed with idle young men often led to fighting. The room felt as if it only required a single incident to set off a brawl. The group, obviously, was composed of off duty soldiers from the Centuripe militia.

Given a choice, Alerio would have taken his appetite and business to another establishment. But he was a stranger in the city and the only other pub he knew was where Tescum and Palinurus had gone to buy supplies. But that pub was on the other side of Centuripe. With no good alternative, the Legionary started across the floor. In order to stay out of the soldiers' focus, Alerio kept the cowl over his head. After threading carefully through the crowd, he arrived at the wall and selected an empty seat.

"Vino and lamb," Alerio ordered from the serving lass.

"It'll take a few," she stated with a tip of her chin at the milling crowd.

"I'll wait," he assured her.

The waitress stepped back, whirled around, and danced across the room. It wasn't a dance of joy. Her moves were dodges and ducks to evade groping hands and lunging arms.

People had bad jobs, Alerio thought while watching her out of the corner of his eye. Being a serving lass in a warm pub with bad nights had nothing on a slave who spent his short life melting, pouring, and hammering lead. Or moving manure and trying to keep the swarms of flies out of their eyes, noses, and mouths while shoveling the blessed of Sterculius. Although, the God of Poo might appreciate the merda manners displayed by the rowdy soldiers.

When the food arrived, the lamb was cold and the vino room temperature. Seeing as Alerio hadn't eaten since midday, and that consisted of a few wheat cakes washed down with water, he didn't complain. Cutting off a slice, the Legionary used his teeth to pull the meat off the end of his knife. Out in the middle of the room, a soldier raised his voice and started to sing.

Ignore the babblings of old women
Her reputation they would blacken
By pointing to events of fabrication

Groans and laughter from all sides came at the crooner. Some were negative but most encouraged the soldier. With their backing, he continued the song while Alerio chewed.

There's a rumor of indiscretion
With a Landowner of persuasion
Crops to market sold for profits
Profits to spend for any occasion
It was innocent I submit
My beautiful blue wildflower
Is no hypocrite

There's a rumor of impropriety
With a mine manager of notoriety
Big salty chunks from the mine

Earn him top coins undeniably
It was innocent I opine
My beautiful blue wildflower
Is no concubine

Her blue scarf's knotted around my heart
Since the day we met in the park
And her blue eyes hit me like a dart
Her blue paint stained my cheek
I washed it not for over a week
And her blue skirt offered a peak
But it was her simple purity
Even if I saw way above her knee
And her winning personality
That drew my coins and heart from me

A few soldiers cried out that the song was poking fun at their girlfriends. Alerio never understood when Legionaries took lyrics personally and assumed the singer had singled out two or three of them for ridicule. The protesters were shouted down by the rest and the singer belted out the next verse.

Ignore the babblings of old women
Her reputation they would blacken
By pointing to events of fabrication

There's a rumor of an expletive
With a brimstone executive
Medicines and incense for pleasure
From ground sulfur to curative
It was innocent I plea
My beautiful blue wildflower
Is no harpy

There's a rumor of a bawdy thing
With a boss at a pottery building
Sticky mud and sand from the Simeto
Shaped into ceramic gold earrings
It was innocent I spew
My beautiful blue wildflower
Is no shrew

Her blue scarf's knotted around my heart
Since the day we met in the park
And her blue eyes hit me like a dart
Her blue paint stained my cheek
I washed it not for over a week
And her blue skirt offered a peak
But it was her simple purity
Even if I saw way above the knee
And her winning personality
That drew my coins and heart from me

Ignore the babblings of old women
Her reputation they would blacken
By pointing to events of fabrication

One of the offended soldiers drew back his fist and smashed the singer in the nose. A friend of the song stylist retaliated and, as Alerio suspected when he walked in, a riot began. Wine mugs sailed over battling men's heads before crashing into the unwary.

A man stumbled backward, bumped into Alerio's table, and sprawled on the platter of lamb. To add to the offense, his arm knocked the mug of vino off the tabletop spilling it on the floor.

Corporal Sisera forgot he was alone in a sea of fighting enemy soldiers. The ruined meal swept away his caution, and he hammered the man with his elbow. Four of the soldier's friends saw the elbow sink into their comrade's neck and they rushed to his defense.

***

There were problems with getting involved in a barroom brawl. At the top of the list was Alerio's job of getting the Century into the city and guiding them to where Ambassador Sergius was being held. To accomplish the task, he needed to be healthy, not beaten up, uninjured, and not in jail. He was under no illusion that when the militia came to break up the fight, civilians would be blamed and arrested for starting the melee. Confirming the idea wasn't just his alone, a quick glance around showed the other non-military patrons had already fled.

Second, on the problem list, was standing out in the crowd by creating a spectacle. This meant he couldn't pull the dual gladii from the sheaths on his back and simply hack his way out of the pub. Leaving a trail of dead and wounded soldiers was a sure way to alert the city guard and have them call out the reserves. That left Alerio with one option, run away.

The Legionary hooked the leg of the table with his foot and flipped it over. With the table legs outward, he fended off the four soldiers while looking for an escape route. In one direction was a counter holding large barrels of vino. There was a door behind the counter, but it was closed. Probably bolted shut from the other side, he guessed.

A stairway to the upper levels was three tables away in the other direction. Stepping away from the wall, Corporal Sisera entangled three of his assaulters in the table legs, twisted the tabletop, and swung it to the side. Happily, the three men flew back and into the brawling mass. Alerio kicked the last soldier to the floor of the pub and using the chaos, ran for the bottom of the stairs.

***

On the second floor, Alerio had to make a decision. He could move to the front of the building, climb out a window, drop to the street, and try to get away. But the militia would form up at street level before coming in to stop the brawl. Chances were, duty soldiers from the lower guard barracks had already staged there. Taking a chance, he ran up the stairs to the third floor.

At the end of a long corridor, the Legionary gripped a door and slung it open. In a small closet with a ladder mounted on one wall, stood a lad with a lantern.

"Master Heteros asked me to keep an eye on you and offer help," stated the apprentice assassin. "Do you require help?"

After a glance over his shoulder, Alerio replied, "Yes, little Golden Valley assassin, I do require help."

"Then I will lead you out of the building," announced the apprentice killer.

"That will help but I need one more thing," Alerio informed him as they started up the ladder to the roof. "I also need a pickax."

Chapter 20 – Shadows of Death

Another session of hanging from a rope while traversing the back of a structure ended at the roof of a building on a lower street. Moving stealthily from the rooftop to the street allowed Alerio and his young guide to jog away from that section of Centuripe unseen and unchallenged.

Somewhere during the trip across the city, while shifting to streets heading downhill, two things occurred. The little assassin in training vanished in the dark and the moon rose. One didn't bother the Legion Corporal. Moonlight, on the other hand, forced him to move faster. His Century would be exposed on the slope while they climbed to the weak part of the city's defensive wall. While he couldn't protect them on the approach, he could get them safely into the city by preparing and defending the entrance.

***

Alone, hungry, and a little tired, Alerio reached the moon shadowed area near the wall. After stomping on the pavers covering the road, he located the stones identified by Palinurus. With his dagger grasped in his fist, Alerio got down on his hands and knees and began scraping the dirt and mortar from around each of the chosen stones.

"What are you doing, citizen?" a voice called from up the street.

Alerio twisted his head, caught sight of the bottom edges of four shields and four boots coming towards him. With no excuse for his position or for the line of dirt he'd dug from between the stones, the Legionary searched his mind for an excuse. He sorted through options, but none sounded convincing. Then he realized the only reason for a man to be on his hands and knees in the middle of a public street.

"Ignore the babblings of old women. Her reputation they would blacken," Alerio sang softly. *"By pointing to events of fabrication."*

The four-man patrol got close enough to hear what the man on his knees was saying.

"He's drunk," one announced.

"And there must be something wrong with his throat," another tossed out.

"There's a rumor of indiscretion, with a Landowner of persuasion," Alerio sang, raising his voice so it echoed off the wall. *"Crops to market sold for profits, profits to spend for any occasion."*

"Get him up," the patrol NCO ordered. "Before he wakes the whole district."

As soon as he felt the hands of two militiamen on his arms, Alerio gathered his legs under him and sprang off the ground.

"It was innocent I submit," he sang. Gripping the dagger in an underhanded fashion, he plunged the blade into the groin of the soldier on his left. *"My beautiful blue wildflower is no hypocrite."*

The wounded man crumpled to his side and Alerio faded in that direction. Assuming his partner had lost his footing, the second soldier pulled harder on Alerio's arm. Allowing the yank to guide him, Alerio came the rest of the way up. He lurched sideways while clipping the soldier's chin with his elbow.

"There's a rumor of impropriety, with a mine manager of notoriety," the Legionary sang while driving the soldier sideways. The man tripped and Alerio appeared to

stumble. Following the soldier to the ground, Alerio slammed his head into the road pavers. Pushing to his feet, Sisera stepped over the body and staggered towards the last two soldiers. *"Big salty chunks from the mine, earn him top coins undeniably."*

"It was innocent I opine," Alerio belted out. Grabbing the closest shield, the Legionary twisted it, throwing the man to the side and out of the way. *"My beautiful blue wildflower is no concubine."*

"Her blue scarf's knotted around my heart," Alerio sang while rushing for the last standing soldier.

Unfortunately, the NCO was a combat veteran and noticed the takedowns weren't accidents. Before Alerio could reach him, the man dropped into a defensive stance, braced his shield, and lowered his spear.

"Since the day we met in the park. And her blue eyes hit me like a dart."

Alerio slid to a stop on the pavers. He and the soldier were half in the moon shadow and half in the weak moon glow.

"Her blue paint stained my cheek. I washed it not for over a week," Alerio sang while throwing off his robe. Reaching over his shoulders, he sank both hands into the back of the shirt. *"And her blue skirt offered a peak."*

"But it was her simple purity. Even if I saw way above her knee. And her winning personality," Alerio drew out two gladii as he sang. He crossed the blades and edged forward. *"That drew my coins and heart from me."*

The spear slashed from the light and vanished into the dark. Before it reappeared, Alerio rushed forward. One gladius blocked the spear shaft keeping it off to the side. The other stabbed directly onto the soldier's lower belly.

"Ignore the babblings of old women. Her reputation they would blacken," Alerio sang while twisting the blade before withdrawing it. *"By pointing to events…"*

Something impacted Alerio's left shoulder driving him to the right. He'd forgotten about the third soldier who was only thrown off to the side. Dropping his center of gravity, the Legionary spun to face the deep moon shadow.

Then the soldier's face appeared briefly as he fell forward into the moonlight. Once the body was stretched out on the pavers, Alerio noticed a wooden handle sticking up from the man's back.

"By pointing to events of fabrication," the young Golden Valley assassin sang as he stepped into the moon glow. He reached down, grabbed the wooden handle, and pulled it from the soldier's back. Offering it to Alerio, he questioned. "You asked for a pickax?"

***

Alerio rolled the flagstones to the side and rested them against the defensive wall. Moments later, the sand and gravel under the paving stones flowed away and a hole developed. It enlarged until a Legionary's head popped up.

"Tesserarius. Good evening," Private Zelatus exclaimed. His eyes sparkled through the dirt on his smiling face. "Where are the dancing girls?"

"Get up here," Alerio instructed. "And keep your voice down."

"Sorry. I seem to have sand in my ears."

Alerio gripped his shoulders. Between the clawing of Zelatus' arms and help from his Corporal, the Legionary crawled out of the hole and onto the street.

"Help the next man through," Alerio ordered.

Once Lance Corporal Trax Dircium and four more men from 2nd Squad crawled under the wall, traversed the narrow tunnel, and entered Centuripe, Alerio pointed out the four dead soldiers.

"Armor and spears," he advised. "Put them on."

"And the tall helmets?" Dircium inquired.

"Yes. I want them to look like a city patrol. Any militia we run into will take a pause before recognizing that our men aren't."

"Can we really pull this off, Tesserarius?"

Alerio looked up the moonlit street and back to the Legionaries crawling out of the hole in the road.

"We will or we'll die trying," he reflected. "It's up to you and her."

"Her, Corporal Sisera?"

"The Goddess Fortūna. Now get your men geared up and go watch the street."

***

As complete squads arrived, Alerio sent them off in all directions. They were ordered to watch for militia patrols or civilians that might stumble upon the insertion operation. Another reason to disperse the Century, eighty men milling around the defensive wall looked suspicious.

"This is dangerous," warned Lance Corporal Enitui as soon as he came through. "We are exposed here."

"Sorry Lance Corporal, it's the best I can do at the moment," Alerio informed him. "Collect 4th Squad and stage them on the street to your left."

Centurion Megellus arrived right before 5th Squad. While Optio Gustavi coordinated the feeding of men into the access tunnel and guarded the tail end, the officer came through early.

"What's our situation, Tesserarius," Megellus inquired while scraping sand from his ears with his little fingers.

"So far, no contact, sir," Alerio reported. "Other than a patrol earlier."

"Let's hope it stays that way."

***

After what seemed to be ages for every man in the 25th Century, the last Legionary climbed from the hole. And finally, their senior NCO, the last men crawled through the tunnel.

"Good evening, Optio," Alerio greeted Gustavi. "I trust you had a pleasant journey."

"Save your platitudes, Corporal," growled the Sergeant. "If you have the directions, move us off the street. We're exposed here."

"Have you been consulting with Lance Corporal Enitui, Sergeant?"

"What did you say, Tesserarius?" the NCO asked while clearing the sand and dirt from his ears.

"I said, we're ready to move, Optio." Alerio lied.

***

Private Palinurus and 10th Squad set the stones to cover the hole.

"It won't fool anybody for long," the stonemason advised. "One heavy wagon will expose the instability of the pavers."

"We won't be here when that happens," Alerio assured him.

Three blocks from the covered hole, Alerio directed the Legionaries in the Centuripe militia gear to take the lead. He had the rest of the 2nd tucked in behind the armored men.

"Step off so there's a gap," Alerio instructed.

"Where are we going?" inquired Centurion Megellus.

"Near the top of the city, the streets circle the terrain. The locals call it The Serpent. It's four levels of streets high above each other and far apart. The last street is where we'll find the militia's main compound, their upper barracks," Alerio reported.

"And we are searching for a barracks full of soldiers, why?"

"Because, sir, it's where they are keeping Ambassador Sergius."

"Above the final street is an observation hill. It's the best defensive position in Centuripe," Alerio informed the infantry officer. "We'll need to take down the watchers and clear the barracks."

"Define clearing?" demanded the Optio.

"Two hundred and fifty soldiers and officers."

"We're going to attack a compound defended by twice our number?" Lance Corporal Aternus inquired. "Without our Legion war gear."

"Decanus Aternus. Clothing does not define the journeymen warrior," offered Alerio. "Infantrymen are, if nothing else, craftsmen of war. We can do the job naked and with only our gladii if necessary."

"That's the infantry," Aternus sneered. Then to the squad behind him, he commented. "Corporal Sisera says we are craftsmen, skilled at war. And woolen clothing is as good as armor if you paid attention during the training."

***

A militia patrol came around a corner and stopped when their leader noted the patrol of disguised Legionaries.

"You are off your route," he challenged from up the street.

"Tesserarius. Orders?" Caricini Aternus from 7th Squad asked.

"We need to back up 2nd Squad. Take two squads and single file up the dark sides of the street."

Not realizing reinforcements were moving up, Lance Corporal Trax Dircium reached out and placed his hands on the backs of his armored Legionaries.

"Don't reply to him or say anything," he urged. "Keep walking."

Behind the Lance Corporal and the armored members of his squad, two squads moved up the sides of the street.

"I asked you a question," the NCO from the militia called. "Who is in charge of your patrol?"

Trax watched between the shields until he was comfortable with the distance. The 2nd Squad was ready and in another few paces, the Decanus would order the assault. He knew they had to put the patrol down quickly to prevent any of them from sounding the alarm.

"Attack," Dircium ordered. "Go, go, go."

The four-man militia patrol sensed something wasn't right. When the four coming up the street began running

191

at them, they lowered their spears, centered their shields, and prepared to fight the rebellious patrol.

Dircium's fist clenched, and he swore at himself. He'd ordered the assault too soon. The militia patrol had time to prepare, and the situation could go bad rapidly.

Then, his seven Legionaries were joined by sixteen others coming out of the dark. The militia NCO shouted once before he and the patrol were swarmed off their feet. The four soldiers died without another cry of alarm.

"8th Squad, strip their armor and gear up," Gustavi ordered. The armor came off and soon, four more Legionaries were dressed for war. "All of those in armor move to the front."

***

The Century topped the final steep road and entered The Serpent. From a steep hike, the street wrapped around and up the grade as it climbed to the next higher level. Alerio jogged to the front when the lead squads stopped.

"Decani Frentani and Dircium, push it out and increase your pace," Alerio ordered the squad leaders with armored men. "If you run into any patrols, don't wait. Put them down."

"What about civilians?" questioned Trax Dircium.

"We are about to attack a fortified location holding more than twice our number," Alerio replied. "Surprise is our only tactical advantage. Use your discretion."

Following the squads up the narrow twisting street, the other sixty-four Legionaries of the 25th moved silently. Thankfully for them, no patrols appeared on the circuitous route. And luckily for the citizens, no civilians came out for a moonlight stroll.

Chapter 21 – Hostile Pursuit

The broad Agora area where the people of Centuripe gathered was dark and empty. Across the street, lanterns illuminated the gates to the militia compound. Soldiers stood in the light. Other lanterns lit a courtyard beyond the entrance. A few militiamen could be seen resting on benches eating or talking.

2nd and 8th Squads knelt on the side of the road four storefronts from the barracks.

"We'll attack through the gate and sweep the compound," instructed Centurion Megellus. "If we're quick enough, we'll take control before the sleeping troops know what hit them."

"Give me two squads, sir. I'll seal off the gate on the other side of the barracks," Alerio offered.

"Good idea. We don't want any more soldiers escaping into the city. There are enough out there as it is," ventured Optio Gustavi. "Take Enitui and Aternus' squads, Tesserarius."

***

The 4th and 7th Squads followed their Corporal off the road. In a single file, they crossed the Agora and, on the far side, staged behind the closed vendor stalls. When a voice screamed out from the far side of the barracks compound, the sixteen Legionaries charged forward and closed in on the barrack's east gate.

Before they reached the opening, a group broke from the compound. Seeing men brandishing swords, ten militiamen peeled off from the group and intercepted the Legionaries. One thing saved the unarmored infantrymen from being massacred. In the dark, the soldiers assumed they faced armored warriors. As taught by their officers, the soldiers set a shield wall and lowered their spears. Had they attacked; the outcome would have been different.

Ten Legionaries ran up to just shy of the jabbing spear tips, stopped, then swatted and hacked at the shafts. The remaining six Legionaries separated. Three ran around one side of the Centuripe line while the other three attacked the opposite side. In short order, the defensive formation began collapsing.

Alerio hung back waiting to see if his two gladii were required. The squads overwhelmed the hastily set formation with little trouble, so Alerio remained away from the cries of battle. It's why he was able to hear the shouted warning.

"It's the Republic, Captain Cheir," a voice from behind the enemy line shouted. "Run, sir. We'll hold them."

Three men sprinted from behind the shield wall. Two wore the tall helmets of militiamen. The third man's helmet was heightened by a spike and feathers. They sprinted down the road and away from the compound.

Rushing forward, Alerio grabbed two Legionaries and yanked them away from where his men were finishing off the soldiers.

"Their officer is escaping," he shouted. "Come with me."

Private Ottone from 4th Squad and Private Tatis from the 7th looked in the direction indicated. When their Corporal raced after the Centuripe officer, the Legionaries followed.

Behind them, the Lance Corporals adjusted their squads as the last of the soldiers fell. After collecting the shields and spears, they moved the squads to block the east gate. No one noticed the disappearance of the Tesserarius and the two Legionaries.

***

Captain Cheir's helmet reflected the moonlight, and the feathers identified the officer. Both allowed Alerio to home in on the glow and track him. Legionaries run in training and for exercise. As a result, they began closing the distance.

Hobnailed boots clicking loudly on the stone road alerted the militia Captain. Realizing the pursuers were close, Cheir turned off the street and vanished into a large building.

Corporal Sisera reached the doorway a moment later. He paused for a heartbeat before kicking the door off the hinges and charging into the structure.

Inside, Alerio noted the air smelled of wet clay. When his Legionaries caught up, the three stood at the entrance gazing over rows of long tables with pottery on the tabletops. Silently, the Corporal positioned his two Legionaries at different rows. Once set, the three moved deeper into the building searching around and under the tables for the militiamen.

They were halfway along the length of the tables when the sounds of wood striking wood came from a distance. Rushing forward, the Legionaries spied a hole in the floor at the end of the rows. As they neared the opening, they saw light drifting up from a lower level. Fearing an arrow in the chest, the two Privates hesitated at the top of a ramp. But Corporal Sisera didn't. He shoved between them and raced down to the ground floor.

At the bottom of the ramp, Alerio glanced around until he located the Centuripe officer. Cheir stood to the side of a barred door while his two soldiers hammered at it with wooden planks.

"Captain Cheir. I am Corporal Sisera of the Legion," announced Alerio. "You have taken an Ambassador of the Republic captive. For that, I sentence you to death."

"You can have the cheap, coward back. He is useless," Cheir responded. "As far as a death sentence. It is you attempting to make the fruit from the sheep into woolen armor."

The soldiers dropped the planks, drew their swords, and charged at Alerio. Armor against woolen cloth was a bad mismatch. The two should have easily gutted the Legion NCO. But, even without a breastplate, two expertly handled gladii kept them at bay. Then it became four blades when the Legionnaires joined in the fight.

"We've got this Corporal," Tatis told Alerio.

He caught one solder's sword and parried it off to the side.

"Two on two," Ottone described. "It's a fair fight."

Alerio dropped below the level of dueling blades, hacked one soldier's leg out from under the man and, as he fell, the Corporal rolled away and came up on his feet.

"There is no fair in a battle," Alerio explained. "The only justification for a fight is to win."

While his two Legionaries attacked the last militiaman, Alerio stalked towards the officer.

"Captain Cheir. If you'll walk over to me, we can duel like men," proposed the Legion NCO.

As much as Alerio wanted to offer Cheir a chance to surrender, the favor requested by the Golden Valley assassin didn't allow for the alternative. The organization really didn't ask for favors. Requesting the death of Cheir was a polite way to soften the reality of ordering a public murder.

By offering to fight one on one, Alerio gave the illusion that the officer had a chance. In reality, Corporal Sisera harbored no doubt that he could easily execute the Captain.

"I have coins and influence," Cheir suggested. "Let me walk out and when this is over, you'll be a very rich man."

And become another rich man to die in his sleep with the help of a Golden Valley assassin, Alerio thought.

"Sorry, sir. Your choices are blades and a stroll over my dead body. Or dying. Those are the only way you're leaving this warehouse," Alerio replied. "And no amount of coins or influence can change your path."

Rather than be trapped against a barred door, Cheir ran around a stack of vases. Using other piles of pottery to slow down the Legionary, the militia officer raced between the ceramic stacks trying to find a route to the ramp.

While he ran, voices of men working an evening shift cried out.

"Be careful," they shouted. "Leave now. Please. Stop this madness."

Alerio heard them and assumed they were attempting to beg for the Centuripe officer's freedom. Ignoring their pleas, he vaulted onto a tabletop. His feet kicked vases off as he slid to the other side. Jumping down, he landed on a heap of splintered pottery.

"Stop you maniac," the workmen cried.

But Alerio refused to give up and let the Captain go. Seeing Cheir push through the workmen, the Legion NCO raced after him. The men reared back when Alerio waved the gladii as he threaded between them.

"Enough! For the love of Athena, stop this barbaric act," the workmen pleaded.

Alerio caught up with the Captain in a corner of the building. On the other side of a tall pile of vases, Cheir stood with his sword extended.

"If I throw down my sword, what can I expect?" he demanded.

"You will be put down, immediately," Alerio informed him. "We're outmanned until the Legion arrives. I've no men to spare to guard a prisoner."

"But if I kill you, I can walk away and join my men in defending the city."

Without replying, Corporal Sisera swung both gladii at the barricade of vases. The decorative and thin sided ceramics exploded, the mound of vases shattered, and Alerio stepped through the broken clay containers. Kicking the ruined pieces away, he shuffled towards Captain Cheir.

Their blades clashed and the ringing of steel drowned out the weeping and howling of the workmen.

Alerio carved a deep gash in the officer's chest plate. Cheir attempted to back away to give him room to duel but the Legion NCO crowded forward. Slashing with both gladii, Alerio beat down the sword and once it was out of place, he drew the tip of a gladius across Cheir's neck. The

Centuripe Captain fell back and crashed into a stack of pottery. Ceramics shattered as the blood and life drained from the officer.

The workmen took Cheir's death hard. Their wailing reached an epic volume.

***

"We should get out of here," Alerio suggested to Private Ottone.

Ottone was wrapping a piece of cloth around Tatis' arm as their Corporal approached. Alerio pointed to the bloody arm.

"How bad?"

"It'll heal, Tesserarius," Tatis stated. "Orders?"

"We're five blocks and downhill from the barracks," Alerio replied. "It shouldn't be a problem if the Centuripe military is still in the lower city."

"And if they're not?" Ottone asked.

"Then we have a problem," Alerio informed the Legionary. "Come on. We won't know until we look outside."

Corporal Sisera took the lead and guided the infantrymen up the ramp. Behind them, the craftsmen and workers collapsed to the floor and, in the midst of the broken pieces of vase, they cried and moaned the loss of Captain Cheir. The Legionaries ignored the lamentations of the workmen while they crossed to the front of the pottery factory.

***

Tatis stumbled and the Corporal caught him around the waist. Then, Alerio's hand felt moisture on the man's clothing.

199

"Go check the street," Alerio directed Ottone. He rested the injured Private against one of the long tables to stabilize him. "Let me check your wound."

"It's bandaged," Tatis assured his Corporal. He waved his arm in front of Alerio's face.

"I'm talking about your side, not your forearm," Alerio said as he untied the woolen trousers. Then, while probing the Legionary's side, his fingers dipped into a gash.

"Hades, Tesserarius," Tatis protested. "that hurts."

A mystery to all Legionaries was why a cut on a finger hurt more than being cleaved open like a slab of meat. But here was proof, Tatis' more severe injury sat unannounced while his arm was wrapped.

"You've been opened up like a sacrificial goat."

"I didn't feel it before. But now, I'm receiving the attention of Algea."

"You know what they say about the Goddess of Pain?"

"Yes, Corporal. If you can feel her touch, you're alive."

"Maybe not for long," Ottone offered as he walked back from the front of the factory. "The militia is staging men right in front of the building. I wouldn't be surprised if we didn't have visitors soon."

"We might be able to sneak through if we leave now," Tatis recommended. "But it'll require a sprint to the barracks if we're spotted."

"Private Tatis, you are in no shape for an uphill jog," Alerio advised. "Let alone a foot race."

***

After knotting a piece of his robe around Tatis' waist, Corporal Sisera rushed to the east wall of the factory. There he located a ladder and an opening in the roof.

"Ottone, help Tatis up. You two take to the roofs and make your way towards the barracks," Alerio ordered. "I'll stay here and keep the soldiers busy. Hopefully, they won't realize we're escaping that way."

"What do you mean we?" questioned Ottone. "It seems like Tatis, and I are escaping while you're still here, Tesserarius."

"I'll be along shortly," Alerio assured him. "I don't plan on dying on the gritty floor in a factory that smells of clay."

Tatis struggled up the ladder. Under him, Ottone gave the wounded man support with a push of a hand. When they vanished through the opening, Alerio moved to the front of the factory and peered through the shutters. On the street, armored soldiers were forming ranks.

Alerio expected a couple of squads or less to assault the building. When forty men turned to face the façade, he realized that the odds of dying in the clay dust was closer than he suggested to Ottone. With the threat of facing overwhelming odds, the Legion NCO put away his gladii, spun away from the shutters, and ran for the ladder.

***

On his knees, Alerio leaned through the opening and hacked at the top rungs. It wouldn't slow the soldiers down for long, but it would delay them until they found a replacement ladder. Once he inflicted as much damage on the wood as he could from the awkward position, he pushed the rails with the broken rungs over. The ladder toppled over and crashed onto a tableful of pottery.

Moving the short distance to the end of the roof, Alerio faced the shoulder-high wall of the neighboring building. Thankfully, there was no sign of Ottone or Tatis. Gripping the top of the wall, he pulled up while swinging his legs to the side. Once a foot had purchase, Alerio vaulted to the roof of the next building.

He was up on his feet and two steps from the wall when ladders tapped against the edge of the hole in the factory's roof. Soon militiamen climbed up, clustered together, and began seeking an enemy. Unfortunately, the Legion Corporal didn't drop below the line of sight before he was seen, and cries of discovery went out. With no chance of stealth, Alerio sprinted across the roof, reached the next building, and climbed up. Then his heart sank. Across the expanse, he spotted Ottone hoisting an almost limp Tatis over the next wall.

With soldiers closing from behind and his men struggling to stay ahead, Corporal Sisera reached over his shoulders, gripped the hilts, and drew his gladii. Then he ran to the wall, climbed up, and turned to face the lower building.

"Tesserarius, you made it," Ottone called from over his shoulder.

The infantryman had an arm around the waist of his companion. Together, they struggled across the roof heading for the next wall.

"Not yet," Alerio replied. "Keep moving."

Ten Centuripe helmets appeared over the far wall, then ten soldiers climbed up on the lower building's roof. A glance back revealed that Ottone and Tatis were close to the next building. Alerio moved back from the edge and squatted down, so he wasn't visible from the lower roof.

When the ten helmets approached the drop-off, Alerio leaped forward, leaned over, and hacked at two necks before the threat of Centuripe spears drove him back. Twisting away, the Corporal rose up and ran hard for the next wall.

He didn't see the two Legionaries. Free of having to defend them on this level, Alerio jumped, flew through the air, and impacted the top of the next wall with his stomach. A flip of his legs rolled him onto the roof. Another kick and he leaped to his feet, then froze.

Twenty sets of Centuripe armor, helmets, shields, and the tips of spears were lined up facing him. Not sure or caring how the soldiers got in front of him, Alerio sank into a fighting stance and positioned his blades.

"You want to move out of our way, Tesserarius?" Lance Corporal Stulte inquired.

It took a heartbeat before Alerio recognized the voice of the squad leader from the 9th Squad.

"How did you get here?"

"5th and 7th Squads have archery duty on the roof of the barracks," Stulte replied. "Thanks to Caricini Aternus' gift from Theia, he saw Ottone, Tatis, and you crossing the roofs. Optio Gustavi sent us over to see if you needed help."

"I believe I do, Lance Corporal Stulte."

"In that case, Corporal Sisera, step aside," Stulte directed. Then he ordered. "Squads, attack formation."

Alerio jumped to the side and the first eight Legionaries leaped off the edge. Following closely behind them, the next squad hopped down and formed a second line. While the Legionaries advanced into the Centuripe soldiers, Alerio went to find Ottone and help him get Tatis down to street level and across to the barracks.

Chapter 22 – An Honorable Day

"We have five men with minor wounds and ten more with serious injuries, sir," Gustavi reported.

A pained expression passed over Centurion Megellus' face. He hid the look by lifting a mug to his lips and taking a sip of wine.

"Very good, Optio. Have we removed the lookouts from the hill?" asked the officer.

"No, sir. Our squads are just securing the last rooms in the barracks," the Sergeant replied.

As if to emphasize the statement, four young Latians rushed into the room and ran to a man in a gold trimmed robe. Each had visible bruises and ripped and soiled clothing.

"Ambassador, you're safe?" one of the young men exclaimed.

"I am now that the Legion has arrived," Octavius Sergius stated. Then, the Ambassador informed Megellus. "My staff is here. We are ready to leave Centuripe."

The expression of tension passed over the infantry officer's face again and he concentrated on replacing it with a blank look.

"Master Sergius, as I've explained before, we are only a heavy infantry Century," Megellus started to say but the Ambassador cut him off.

"I don't care about your problems, Centurion," Octavius Sergius barked. "I have been an unwelcome and unwilling guest here for three weeks. It's high time I returned to the Capital and made my report to the Senate. Assign my personal bodyguards and let's get on the road."

"Sir, I have fifteen wounded Legionaries," Megellus began to explain but he was interrupted by the arrival of his Tesserarius.

Alerio strutted in and, without context, responded to his officer's words, "Plus, Private Tatis, sir. He's cut up pretty bad."

"Corporal Sisera, where have you been?" the Centurion demanded.

"I saw a Centuripe officer run away from the barracks and chased him down, sir," Alerio reported.

"His name?" Sergius questioned.

Alerio noted the rich clothing, the stiff mannerisms of the man, and his Centurion's braced posture. Just to be safe, he answered with an honorific.

"Captain Cheir, sir," Alerio said.

"And where is Cheir?" Sergius inquired.

"He is dead, sir."

"That puts things in a different light," Sergius announced to the room. "Send a runner for Councilman Grapho. We must meet as soon as possible."

"Ambassador. As I've been trying to explain, we are an advance unit sent to free and protect you," Megellus related. "It's late at night, my men are exhausted, and the Centuripe military is staging for an attack. Might I suggest you rest, and we'll take up the conversation in the morning?"

The Centurion wanted to add, if we're alive and still in control of the barracks in the morning. But he didn't.

Sergius crossed his arms and glanced around at his scruffy staff. After several heartbeats, he indicated a collection of couches in the corner of the room.

"Come, we'll talk about your experiences of captivity," the Ambassador suggested. "Then you can go, clean up, and make yourselves presentable."

Megellus followed them to the seating area. Once the diplomat and his staff were positioned on sofas, the Centurion asked, "Ambassador. Before the news about the Captain's death, you seemed to be in a rush to leave. Now you're planning meetings. What changed?"

"I do not like explaining my decisions to mere infantry officers, Megellus. But this one time, I will. Captain Cheir and General Periander of the militia are the leaders of the rebellion," Sergius answered. "With the Captain dead, it negates his political and economic influence. I believe from here on, Centuripe and the Republic can reach accords."

Across the room, the Sergeant turned to Alerio.

"Sisera. The compound is taken. All that remains is the Centuripe military watchers on the hill," Gustavi stated. "Take a squad and remove them."

"Yes, Optio," Alerio stated.

At the mention of the barracks being under the control of his men, Centurion Megellus allowed a smile to grace his face. Even if the Ambassador didn't appreciate the work of his Squads, or respect his leadership qualities, the 25th Century had successfully completed a tough mission. Unexpectedly, for the construction professional, Fenoris Megellus felt a sense of military pride in the accomplishment.

***

"I miss my own armor," Pentri Umbria complained in a muffled voice.

"We all do, Lance Corporal," Alerio added, also speaking in hushed tones.

High above them, a small structure reflected the moonlight while the Legionaries on the path sweated in the unfamiliar armor. It wasn't the armor or the climb causing the nervous responses. The anxiety came from the arrows shot at them from the top of the mammoth hill. Their voices muted because their faces were buried in the backs of the militia shields.

The 6th Squad had made it halfway up the serpentine trail before the Centuripe soldiers unleashed a barrage. Two Legionaries went down with arrow wounds. After checking on the seriousness of their injuries, Corporal Sisera ordered them left behind. He couldn't spare the men to carry the wounded down to the barracks. They would be uncomfortable, but both would live. By firing of the arrows, the militia archers sealed the fate of every soldier in the lookout bunker.

Nearer the summit, Alerio's shield picked up two arrows. Using his blade, he hacked off most of the arrows leaving two stubby shafts jutting from the face. A few steps later, he tossed away the shield and drew both gladii.

"Give me a four-shield front," he directed. "Everyone else, tuck in and stay tight."

Behind the overlapping shields, the Tesserarius and the remaining six members of 6th Squad attacked up the final rise.

***

From the platform, Alerio peered down into the Symaethus Valley. The landscape was dark except for the fires in the Centuripe military camp. Counting campfires and guessing, the Legion Corporal estimated the army fielded about two thousand men. The Crassus Legion North had more in heavy infantrymen.

He sat on the brickwork until the sky lightened and his view of the valley extended beyond the campfires. A dark line appeared against the lighter colored sand and gravel of the riverbank. Studying the moving line as the sun rose, Corporal Sisera finally made out individual shapes. Looking the other way, he peered down at Centuripe. From the heights, he could see the twisting and turning upper roads and movement behind the buildings on either side of the barracks.

"Lance Corporal Umbria. I'm going to report to the Optio," Alerio declared as he hopped off the wall. "Get your wounded to the medical area and report to him for orders."

Alerio rushed as much as was safe while descending the steep slope. His only stopped twice. One was to grab the shield he had discarded. It stopped two arrows from reaching his body and Alerio held great affection for the shield. He also checked on his wounded Legionaries. After a few words, and assurances they weren't bleeding out, he continued to the barracks.

Crassus Legion North was still a long way off. Between the march, and setting up the defensive camp, the 25th Century wouldn't get relieved until sometime tomorrow or the day after.

Even so, Centurion Megellus would want the news about the Legion as soon as possible. And there was the defense of the compound. Optio Gustavi needed to know the militia was massing for an assault.

***

"Ambassador Sergius, the Legion is in sight," Megellus reported after consulting with Corporal Sisera.

While the Tesserarius rushed off to take charge of the east gate and the barracks defenses on that side of the compound, the officer crossed the room while speaking with the diplomat.

"Excellent, send a runner for Councilman Grapho, immediately," the diplomat responded.

"Sir, we are preparing to defend against an attack by the Centuripe militia."

"A competent military man would have secured the surrounding area," Octavius Sergius accused. "But I shouldn't expect that level of professionalism from you. And if the Legion hasn't arrived, and I am not safe, why did you tell me the Legion was here?"

"I thought you wanted to know they were in sight, Ambassador," Megellus replied. He walked away biting his tongue. The infantry officer almost added. 'In sight, you pompous cūlus. Not here.' But he didn't.

While the Centurion lost a verbal fight with the Ambassador, at the east and west entrances to the barracks, shields clashed, spears jabbed seeking flesh, and arrows filled the sky.

***

Scores of arrows flew from buildings along the street. They fell among the Legionaries at the gates and into the shields of those in reserve. Answering the flights of arrows, 5th and 7th Squads launched twice as many from the barracks rooftop. The aggressive response suppressed

209

the militia's air assault, and the archery war was soon reduced to individuals against a mass of Legionary launched retaliation.

"If only the training Optio could see me now," a Legionary for 5th Squad boasted. He drew the bow, launched an arrow at a window of a building far down the street. Snatching up another, he notched it, drew back, aimed, and released. "Reserve your arrows, he used to say, save your inventory, make every shot count. It's good to control your enemy's armory. Isn't it, Decanus?"

"I expect you to expend as much of Centuripe's arrow inventory as possible," Lance Corporal Caudini replied. "At least they won't have them to use on the Legion. Besides, based on that last shot, you need the practice."

In some part of their brains, the Legionaries at ground level appreciated the Legion's mandatory archery training. But they were too busy at the moment to give it conscious thought.

Two Legionaries from 8th Squad caught spear tips in their sides. As they fell, soldiers crowded forward attempting to breach the east gate.

"Palinurus, fill that gap," Alerio shouted.

The big Private shouldered aside his squad mates and stepped into the forward rank. Hands reached down and pulled the injured men back and out from under his feet.

Alerio watched the large man's bulk stabilize the front rank for a heartbeat. However, the militiamen seeing the opening, stacked, and surged towards where the two men had fallen. Only Palinurus' strength held back the wave. And as with all waves, if stopped, it attempted to flow around the barrier. One side was the immovable frame of the ten-shield wide east gate. On the other side, men of normal stature fought to hold back the rushing militiamen. None were as massive as Private Palinurus, and the Legion ranks bent.

Fearing his defensive line would collapse, Corporal Sisera adjusted his grip on the Centuripe shield, drew his gladius and, with a roar, charged forward.

A soldier shoved forward by the weight of the men behind him, glanced to his left and his mouth fell open. Beside him was a huge Legionary. If he had known he would be this far forward, he would have led with his spear and gutted the big man. Unfortunately, the shaft of his spear was in use pounding on the shields in front of him.

He turned his head. Over his shoulder, he shouted to be heard above the noise of battle, "Kill the giant Latian."

The spearman behind pulled back his spear, adjust the direction of the tip, and…

After directing the death of the large Legionary, the soldier looked back to the front. Suddenly, a rising shield connected with his and the soldier was lifted into the air before being thrown back into the spearman trying to stab Palinurus.

Having driven the soldier back into the men massed behind him, Alerio stepped up beside Palinurus. There the Legion NCO rose to his full height and began smashing with his shield and stabbing with the short Legion blade.

"Palinurus. Together," Alerio instructed. And the big Legionary began to match his Tesserarius' strikes and bashes. "9th Squad, stand by."

To the Corporal's left, Squad Leader Stulte repeated the warning. His pivot men called out the phrase and the eight men of the 9th readied themselves for the next set of commands.

"Squad, brace, step back, step back, advance, advance, advance," Alerio ordered.

Bowed and bent offline, the members of the 9th went from fighting as individuals against the soldiers in front of them to a motionless, solid line of shields. The unmoving Legionaries paused for three heartbeats. During the time of inactivity, the militiamen increased the intensity of their attack and the pressure on the shield wall.

The brace gave each Legionary a few moments to gather his strength and get his mind focused. Then the brace ended. As a unit, the eight men of the squad stepped back two measured paces.

When the pushback against their shields suddenly lifted, the soldiers in the front rank stumbled forward into the newly formed gap. Before the militiamen had a chance to right themselves, the next command released the craftsmen of war to ply their trade.

"Advance, advance, advance."

Shields smacked into the off-balanced militiamen throwing them into the soldiers behind them. Almost instantly, the shields withdrew, and the gladii lashed out. Not once, but three times and by the third, the front three ranks of the soldiers were bleeding, dead, or in the process of being stomped to death.

"Straighten your line and hold," Alerio commanded.

He wanted to release the Legionaries to chase the retreating militiamen. But with the limited number of men under his command, they couldn't safely go beyond the walls of the compound.

"You fight good," Palinurus stated, indicating the bodies piled up in front of them.

"As do you, big man," Alerio said returning the compliment. "You know you are covered in blood, right?"

"Ah, Tesserarius. You look like a priest after a sacrifice," offered Palinurus.

"She'll take it," Alerio remarked while stepping back and allowing men from the 10th Squad to fill the space.

"Think they'll be back, Corporal?" Lance Corporal Frentani inquired.

"For more punishment by the 25th?" Alerio asked loudly. "Not unless they are sadistic and enjoy getting thrashed by good Republic steel."

Alerio assumed after a rest, the militia would attack again. In order to keep everyone in place, he only allowed for water and snacking on hardtack or biscuits. Dirty, coated in streaks of blood, and sweat, the Legionaries waited for the soldiers to return.

Unseen by Corporal Sisera and his squads, the situation at the west gate was the same. Until it wasn't.

***

Optio Megellus also held his squads at their post waiting for the next assault. Then the soldiers far down the street parted and a group of men in robes strolled through the opening.

As they approached the west gate, Megellus could see they were six older men.

"I am Chairman Grapho, and this is the Centuripe City Council," one exclaimed indicating the other five. "You will escort us to Ambassador Sergius."

213

Sergeant Gustavi along with six guards escorted the city Councilmen into the barracks. While walking the stairs to the chamber commandeered by Ambassador Sergius, trumpets blared.

"Is this a trick?" Gustavi demanded.

"Calm yourself," instructed Grapho. "It's only a signal for the soldiers to fall back. Had you injured any of the council, our militia would have revenged us."

The Centuripe units pulled back from the west gate. On the other side of the compound, Alerio watched them fall back from the east gate.

"I guess they've had enough," commented Lance Corporal Tescum.

"It appears that way," Palinurus remarked.

"Let's wait and see," Alerio advised.

***

"There is a Legion of the Republic at your gates and a heavy infantry Century holding your main barracks," Sergius exclaimed when the civilian leaders of Centuripe shuffled into the room. "I will accept your surrender, your offer of tribute, and trade terms. There is nothing more to discuss."

Octavius Sergius folded his arms over his chest and looked down his nose at the representatives.

"Ambassador Sergius. There is one issue that must be resolved before we can move forward," one Councilman declared while stepping in front of the other five.

"And what issue is that, Councilman Grapho?"

"Last night, three of your men attacked the pottery factory," Grapho replied. "A fortune in Kentoripa vases were destroyed. We've lost months of work and precious

214

inventory. Our traders have orders that cannot be filled. What do you propose to do about our loss?"

Sergius looked over the Councilmen's heads to where the officer for the 25th Century stood.

"Centurion. What do you know about the destruction of those valuable commodities?"

"We didn't engage in any area other than the barracks, sir," Megellus responded. "I don't know anything about a factory."

Optio Gustavi leaned in, tugged on the officer's arm, and whispered close to his ear.

With a sour look on his face, the infantry officer corrected his statement, "We did have a pursuit of a hostile force during the assault. However, I'm not familiar with the details."

"Then who is familiar with the details?" demanded Sergius. He placed his fists on his hips and glared at the officer.

"Corporal Sisera, Ambassador."

"Is he here?" Sergius questioned. He craned his neck and glanced around the room.

"No, Ambassador," Megellus informed the diplomat. Turning to one of the Legionaries he assigned to guard the Republic's envoy, he ordered. "Find Sisera and tell him to get here right away."

"As swiftly as if Mercury himself carried the Tesserarius," the Legionary assured Megellus.

The Private rushed out of the room and before the dust raised by his boots settled, the Ambassador began to complain.

"Where is he?" insisted Sergius. Then he raised his voice. "I want the Corporal here, in front of me, to explain his actions."

The Centurion meant to say Corporal Sisera was being sent for but, in light of the rude treatment by the Ambassador, his brain fumbled the clarification.

"The God Mercury is bringing him, sir," Megellus blurted out.

"You invoke the name of a God? You'll add blasphemy to your incompetence?" charged Sergius.

Centurion Fenoris Megellus began to shake at the insolent treatment and the accusation. His Century had completed their mission, rescued the Ambassador, and kept the ungrateful diplomat safe throughout the night and against attacks this morning. Not just safe. They had restored Octavius Sergius to a position of power.

"I asked you a question," berated the diplomat as if his impatient questioning deserved answers.

Before Centurion Megellus ruined his career with a biting retort, the doors on the eastern end of the chamber swung open and crashed against the walls. Shocked at the disturbance from the lightly used entrance, the Ambassador, the Councilmen, the Centurion, and the Legionaries on guard duty jerked their heads in that direction.

The God of War, obviously fresh from battle based on the dents and stubs of arrow shafts in his shield, strutted over the threshold. Blood stains and gore covered his armor. The room reverberated as if a thunderclap when the warrior slammed one filthy hobnailed boot on the floor. Then, he saluted.

"Centurion Megellus. I apologize for the doors. I didn't realize they were so well oiled. You sent for me, sir?"

Chapter 23 – Kentoripa Pottery

"What is the meaning of this?" Sergius uttered in disgust.

The Centurion picked up on the reason and added his voice to the complaint.

"You could have cleaned up before presenting yourself, Tesserarius," Megellus scolded.

"I apologize, sir. I was informed that the matter was urgent," Alerio replied. "If you'll excuse me, I'll go wash."

He was half twisted to the door when Megellus continued, "No, Corporal Sisera, you're already here. Tell us about the vase factory?"

"Sir, I'm not clear on what you're looking for," protested Alerio turning back to face the room. He thought for a heartbeat and offered. "Are you asking about the death of Captain Cheir?"

"The death of a Centuripe officer is unimportant," announced Ambassador Sergius.

Centurion Megellus hid his grin with a hand. Last night, the diplomat wanted out of the city until he heard about the death of Cheir. Now, he was full of bluster, thanks to the Legionaries defending him.

Sergius got to the heart of his concern by asking, "Corporal Sisera, I want to know why you destroyed the Kentoripa vases?"

"Ambassador, I don't know what Kentoripa vases are," Alerio pleaded. "I was in pursuit of Captain Cheir, and he ran into a clay manufacturing facility. I followed him, we fought, and he died. It's that simple, sir."

"There is nothing simple about your actions. I am disgusted and at a loss for words," Sergius professed. The Ambassador turned his back on the chamber, strolled to a chair, turned, and sat as if exhausted. To accent his fatigue, he buried his face in the palms of his hands. Then he looked up and asked. "Councilman Grapho, please enlighten the ignorant Legionary."

Centurion Megellus made fists with his hands, willed his feet to remain rooted to the floor, and worked to keep his lips sealed. Shifting his eyes over to Corporal Sisera, he recognized the same struggle to maintain control.

The Councilman rubbed his eyes with the tips of his fingers while walking to shelving on a wall. Placed on the gilded shelves were vases. Each was thin sided and covered in colored pictures on layers of tinted clay that overlaid the vessel.

Grapho reached up, lifted one of the vases off the shelf, and held it up lovingly in both hands.

"Kentoripa pottery is sought after by people of taste in every city in the civilized world. It is so exquisite; we describe each piece as if it was alive," he proclaimed. He guided a finger just off the fine clay surface and explained. "The opening of the vase, we call the mouth; the stem is the neck; the slope from the neck to the body resembles and is denoted as the shoulder, and the base is known as the foot."

He carefully placed the vase back on the shelf. Then he dropped his arms and lowered his head.

"Our craftsmen start with the smoothest of clays and the finest of sand to form the shapes," Grapho described by cupping his hand as if holding a substance. "But the secret to the strength of Kentoripa ceramic is the baking process. Initially, the clay shapes are cooked in vented kilns. At this point, the entire vase turns red in color. But then, our craftsmen seal the vents and allow the heat to increase. At this point, the vases turn black, and the areas painted with the colored clay transforms into a glassy substance. Finally, the vents are reopened. The unpainted zones of the vessel became red again while the painted areas retained a glossy black hue."

The Councilman walked in a circle shaking his head. Bending at the waist, he pointed to the floor as if showing different piles.

"Only a few craftsmen hold the secrets to our process. But understand, it takes weeks to create a perfect piece of Kentoripa ceramic," he said while spreading his fingers and indicating different areas of the floor. "But you, Legionary, marched into the factory and swept newly formed clay vases off the workbenches where they crashed to the ground. And you crushed vessels in the process of being painted. However, your cruelest act was using your sword's blade to smash stacks of finished vases. My heart hurts at the willful destruction and the loss of product worth thousands and thousands in gold coins."

Lifting his head and standing straighter, the Councilman looked towards the Ambassador.

"You talk of tribute and trade terms," Grapho stated. "I ask, how are we to be compensated for our losses?"

Octavius Sergius peered at the ceiling as if seeking divine guidance. After a few moments, he bit his lip, nodded his head as if having received an answer, and lowered his eyes.

"The Republic will wave two years of tribute payments," The Ambassador proposed. "But I expect below market rates in trade for the products from your sulfur mines and your salt mines. And a fair price for your grain and, of course, Kentoripa vases."

"We can work with those terns," Grapho responded. "And now to finalize the proceedings. Ambassador Octavius Sergius, the independent city of Centuripe, formally requests a treaty with your Republic."

"As a representative of the Senate of the Republic, I offer a treaty for the mutual benefits of our city-states," Sergius vowed.

***

Moments later after setting a day for further negotiations, the six councilmen filed out of the room. One of Sergius' staff rushed over with a ceramic mug of vino.

"An excellent solution, as always, Ambassador," the assistant gushed.

Hearing the word solution, Centurion Megellus marched across the room and stopped in front of the diplomat.

"Sir. If you are ready, we'll join the Legion," the infantry officer suggested. "I assume you'll want to inform the General of the progress."

"Centurion. I'm not going anywhere," Sergius declared. "Send a messenger to the Legion and have the Senior Tribune attend me. I want to inform him of your incompetence and the barbaric behavior of your Legionaries. Dismissed."

Act 6

Chapter 24 – Abandoned in a Sea of Plenty

Alerio stood on the roof eyeing the street as it twisted downhill and vanished behind the buildings on the lower level of Centuripe. While his head was turned to the west and his eyes stared in that direction, his brain wasn't enjoying the view. Other matters occupied his imagination and demanded his concentration.

"I can't say I'll miss this place," Caricini Aternus said breaking into the Corporal's thoughts.

"I'm sorry Lance Corporal. What did you say?"

From the location of the lower buildings, two Centuries of Legionaries marched into view. Disciplined and precise, they came around the bend and up the road.

"I said, it will be good to get off the roof and out of this inhospitable city," replied the Decanus of 7th Squad. He wiped the back of his neck with a cloth and pointed at the approaching Legionaries. "Among other things, this archery duty has drawbacks. Chief among them, there's no shade on the high ground."

Around the roof, Legionaries from the 5th and 7th Squads sat under makeshift covers. Those on watch stood in the hot afternoon sun holding pieces of cloth up with one hand while gripping their bows in the other.

"How are Private Tatis' wounds?" Alerio inquired.

"He's healing but any more than a stroll to and back from the latrine and he's exhausted," Aternus reported. "He'll need transportation."

"As will eleven others," Alerio added. It was the transportation of the injured men of the 25th that occupied his mind. Looking around, he noted the condemnation and accusation in the faces of the Legionaries on the roof. "Now that reinforcements have finally been sent, I'm going to see about a wagon or two."

"Tesserarius. No one except those wrapped in the arms of Coalemus thinks this is your fault," Aternus offered.

"Decanus. That's nice of you to say," Alerio responded as he started for the stairs. Before descending, he stopped and smiled at the Lance Corporal. "However, for that to be true, over half of the Century would need to be making offerings to the God of Stupid. Including the Optio, Centurion, and the Ambassador. And I don't believe that to be true."

When Alerio dropped below roof level and out of sight, one of the Legionaries from the 5th Squad spit on the deck.

"There's a pub just downhill. Will they serve us? No," he complained. "There's a wealth of fresh meat, bread, and vegetables in the market. Will they sell to us? No. And all because of…"

"Don't say it, Private. Don't even think it," challenged Decanus Caudini. "Because if you do, I'll throw you off this roof. Then, I'll jump down and kick the merda out of you for good measure."

"Ah, Lance Corporal Caudini, why are you defending the Tesserarius?"

"We snuck an entire Century into a hostile city," Telesia Caudini explained. "And although we have some badly hurt, we took a barracks compound from almost two hundred soldiers. And because of Corporal Sisera's planning and tactics, we are all sitting here waiting to be relieved. So shut your mouth. Or have you suddenly grown wings?"

"I'm good right where I am, Decanus."

***

On the second floor of the barracks, Alerio turned down a long hallway and marched towards the doorway to a meeting chamber. Ambassador Sergius had taken over the large room and declared it and the entire barracks as the temporary property of the Republic. With a Legion of heavy and light infantry camped just outside the gates of the city, and infantrymen guarding the walls of the compound, the Ambassador could do just about anything he wanted.

Unfortunately, his largesse didn't extend to the men of the 25th Century. And despite the snide remarks and harsh language directed at the Century's officer, Octavius Sergius insisted Centurion Megellus stay at his side during conferences with the locals. As a result, any meetings with the infantry officer took place in full view and within hearing distance of the Ambassador.

Alerio entered the room, marched to the end of the conference table, and saluted.

"Centurion Megellus. A word, sir," he requested.

The Centurion stood off to the left of the Ambassador's chair. Alerio intentionally stared at the officer and didn't make eye contact with the diplomat.

"Corporal Sisera, the man who cost the Republic a fortune," Sergius sneered when he noticed the Legion NCO. "What is it now? Have you collapsed one of Centuripe's salt mineshafts?"

Alerio bit his tongue, remained silent, and stood rigid at the end of the long table. A blank expression graced his face while waiting for directions from his officer. When the Ambassador lowered his head and began reading a piece of parchment, Megellus lifted a hand and made an out-with-it motion.

"Sir. There are two Centuries coming up the road. They are more than likely our replacements," Alerio reported. "I'd like permission to leave the compound and procure transportation for our wounded."

Centurion Megellus' lips parted, he inhaled preparing to speak but Octavius Sergius spoke first.

"Want to go carousing, get drunk, and brag about your exploits in Centuripe?" suggested the Ambassador. "Maybe challenge a few locals so you can add notches to your blade? After you've sated your taste for blood, I imagine you'll steal a couple of wagons and teams of horses?"

Megellus stiffened as did the Ambassador's staff and the four Centuripe businessmen at the table. The 25th Century had problems and no doubt Corporal Sisera was about to offer a solution. But the diplomat's petty outburst stifled the exchange and the infantry officer waited for Sisera to reply harshly and end his career and maybe his life.

"Ambassador Octavius Sergius, your estimate of the Century's transportation needs is correct," Alerio responded. "I'd like to point out that we have a shortage of food and beverage for the Century. As you are aware, we can't purchase supplies because our Century's funds are with Crassus Legion North. And the few coins we have will not pay the inflated prices. We are forced to survive on the barracks' stores of salted swine, sir."

Alerio paused waiting for the Ambassador or his Centurion to add something or correct him. He prayed that the Goddess Concordia would drop in and put everyone in an agreeable frame of mind. When no light of fellowship brightened their eyes, he continued.

"Three days ago, the Century expected to be relieved. When that didn't happen, the Legionaries did the best they could," Alerio restated things the two men already knew. "But, as I've said, we have eleven wounded men who, not only require transportation but require better medical care. I am simply requesting permission to go into the city and procure two wagons for men injured while pulling the Ambassador's tiny, raisin-like cōleī out of the fire, sir."

Centurion Megellus swallowed hard at the indelicate version of the diplomat's rescue. When Sergius didn't say anything, the infantry officer relaxed. Then, one of his staff members leaned in and whispered in the Ambassador's ear.

"What did you say about me?" Sergius demanded, his tan face turning a deeper shade. "I'll have you charged, punished, and crucified."

"That Ambassador is your prerogative," Alerio replied. "But not until I do my job and get transportation for eleven wounded Legionaries. After they are out of this city and under the care of the Legion doctors, you can do what you must."

"Centurion Megellus. I demand that you arrest this insufferable reprobate, at once," Sergius shouted. "It will be done now and not later."

"What should be done now?" inquired a Senior Centurion from the doorway.

225

"Who are you?" questioned Sergius.

"Centurion Edidi, Senior Centurion of Mesalla Legion East," the officer replied. "And I am not in the habit of repeating myself."

"I want this NCO arrested, Senior Centurion," Sergius commanded.

The Senior infantry officer cocked his head to the side as if he was puzzled by the situation.

"I'm Centurion Megellus of the 25th Century. The Ambassador wants my Corporal Sisera placed under guard and punished."

The senior infantry officer for the Legion shifted his focus to Alerio.

"And why Corporal Sisera, are you to be arrested?" Edidi questioned.

"Senior Centurion. I broke some valuable possessions and offended a lot of locals. And apparently, the Ambassador as well, sir," Alerio reported. "I'm not disputing the charges. But we have eleven seriously wounded that require transportation."

Edidi stomped fully into the room, edged by Alerio, and power walked the length of the table. While ignoring the Ambassador, the Senior Centurion stopped nose to nose with Fenoris Megellus.

"You have eleven seriously injured infantrymen rotting in this prison?" he barked. "What kind of officer doesn't provide the best treatment available for his Legionaries?"

"Well, Senior Centurion, the Ambassador said…"

"The Ambassador is a representative of the Senate," Edidi explained. "We are the Legion. We enforce the will of the Senate. Part of that is protecting Ambassadors and trade delegations. But we do not take orders from them."

"Now see here, Centurion," Sergius protested. Edidi stepped away from Megellus and jammed a finger into the Ambassador's chest.

"That's Senior Centurion Edidi, Octavius Sergius. If you cross me, I will pull all of my Centuries from this city. Let's see how much respect you get sitting at this table alone," warned the Senior Centurion. Then, over his shoulder, he asked. "Tesserarius Sisera. Don't you have a job to do?"

"Yes, sir."

"Then get your swinging mentula out of here and do it," Edidi ordered. "And don't come back until you have a plan to transports the wounded infantrymen."

"Yes, Senior Centurion."

***

Considering the animosity towards the Legion, and especially Alerio by the citizens of Centuripe, Optio Gustavi wasn't surprised when his Corporal strolled back empty-handed.

"That didn't take long," observed the Sergeant. "It must be rough out there. And the prices? They must be sky high if you can get someone to do business with a Legionary."

"It wasn't too difficult, Optio," Alerio informed the NCO. "The wagons and ponies will be here in the morning."

Alerio and Gustavi walked into the part of the barracks claimed by the 25th. The newly arrived Centuries, having assumed guard duty on the roof and walls, were spread throughout the rest of the barracks.

Even Centurion Megellus had been replaced as company for the Ambassador by two Centurions.

The wounded were being attended to in the corner of one large room. Several squads occupied the rest of the room and the other contuberniums slept in adjacent spaces. After checking on the injured, Alerio and his Optio walked to a courtyard and settled in around a pot of steaming salted pork. For two days, the meat had been a treat. At the end of day three, they missed grain, vegetables, and vino.

"Where did you find the wagons?" inquired Gustavi. He used a finger to dislodge a piece of gristle. Once free, he spit the offending tissue into the campfire.

"An independent trading house," Alerio replied.

"It didn't take you long," observed Gustavi. "It seemed like you left and returned almost immediately."

"It's nice to know I dazzled you with my brilliance," suggested Alerio. "To be truthful, the negotiations took longer than you could imagine."

"An impressive job, Tesserarius," proclaimed the Optio. He pushed off the ground and excused himself. "I'm going to report to the Centurion and inform him that transportation has been arranged."

"Ask him why the Ambassador treats the Century like merda?" remarked Alerio.

"I'll do nothing of the kind," Gustavi said as he walked off.

Alerio leaned back and allowed himself to relax. When he left the barracks, he didn't go in search of a stable. Rather, he wrote a note and tied it to a stone. His trip out of the compound consisted of a stroll down the road and a single pass in front of the Golden Valley

Trading House. Once he dropped the stone and note on the side of the road, he marched back uphill and directly into the barracks compound.

The apprentice would retrieve the message and deliver it to Heteros. It was up to the sect of assassins to decide how to fill the request without bringing down the ire of the citizens.

Captain Cheir died publicly and, as it turned out, at a great personal cost to Alerio and his Century. Three wagons and horses in payment for the killing wasn't too high a price to ask.

***

Late in the afternoon, another Century marched up the road. Larger than a standard Century and more solemn, they were veterans who projected an aura of menace. When they came through the west gate, without a single command, squads broke ranks and took over strategic positions around and inside the barrack. No one voiced a complaint or lodged a protest because the 1st Century's single responsibility was the protection of the Legion's General and the battle commander.

Consul/General Valerius Mesalla commanded his western Legion in southern Sicilia. Without Mesalla in attendance at Centuripe, 1st Century focused all of their attention on guarding Colonel Ruscus, the battle commander of Mesalla Legion East.

"I'm going to inspect the security, Colonel," 1st Centurion Irrisus informed the battle commander.

"Very good. I don't expect my meeting with the Ambassador will take long," Ruscus offered.

"We'll be ready to leave when you are, sir."

Ruscus marched into the main structure leaving Irrisus glancing around at the exterior of the compound. His eyes caught something suspicious in a courtyard just off the entrance. As far as he knew, a detached Century had taken the barracks and were still here despite two Centuries from the Legion sent to relieve them.

He spotted men around a campfire who appeared to be Samnites, not Latians. Curiosity and caution guided his feet, and he moved in their direction. It wasn't the men specifically, it was the stacked Centuripe militia armor, helmets, shields, and spears behind each man that drew his attention.

"What's in the pot?" Irrisus asked the men.

"Salted pork, 1st Centurion," replied one of them. "It's all they had in the militia stores."

"And who are you?"

"Lance Corporal Frentani, 8th Squad, 25th Century, Crassus Legion North," one of the men at the campfire replied.

"You took this compound using militia equipment?" Irrisus inquired.

"No, sir. We took the war gear later," Frentani described. He stood, drew a gladius, and caught a bunch of the woolen cloth in his other hand. Pulling and stretching the material out of shape, he explained. "We attacked with a blade and what we were wearing. According to Corporal Sisera, clothing doesn't define the journeymen warrior. And infantrymen, if nothing else are craftsmen of war. So, we went to work with what we had."

"An interesting thought, Decanus Frentani. Don't let me keep you from your dinner."

"It's alright, sir. We're all sick of salted pork. We eat it because it's all we have."

Before Irrisus could question the diet, Centurion Megellus marched from the building.

"1st Centurion, can I help you?"

"Legionaries have ration requirements," Irrisus informed him.

"We are a long way from home and without Century funds," Megellus began to explain. "Plus…"

A Legionary stepped from the main entrance, spied Irrisus, and shouted. "1st Centurion, Colonel Ruscus would like to see you."

"I've got to go. But here, buy your Legionaries some grain and vegetables," Irrisus instructed while handing Megellus a sack of coins.

Then he jogged to the entrance and went inside.

"What is that, sir?" inquired the squad leader from the 8th.

"It's an addition to the Century's food fund, Lance Corporal Frentani," Megellus replied while holding up the pouch.

"Doesn't he know no one in this city will sell us grain?"

"I didn't have time to tell the 1st Centurion," the infantry officer explained while stuffing the coins under his militia armor.

***

"Halt," challenged the sentry.

In the shadows before dawn, the Legionary looked through the west gate at three approaching wagons. Joined by his Sergeant of the Guard, they walked out and inspected the empty wagons. After completing a circuit of the transports, the NCO marched back to the gate and raised an arm.

"Alright, bring them in," he shouted.

But the horses stood unmoving except for two that pawed the ground.

"Drivers, bring them in," the NCO repeated with more force.

Curiously, the wagons sat unmoving. In response to the nonactivity, the sentry walked from the gate and approached the first wagon.

"Optio. The drivers have left," the Legionary reported.

Peering at the empty seat of the first wagon, he noticed a piece of parchment. After plucking it from the bench, the guard walked it back to the gate.

"What have you got there?"

"It seems to be a message of some kind," the Legionary replied as he held the missive up to a lantern and read the writing. "These wagons belong to a Corporal Sisera. Whoever he is."

"He's the Tesserarius for the 25th Century," the NCO replied.

"The special unit they sent over from Crassus Legion North?" the Private ventured.

"Why do you say special?"

"They infiltrated an enemy city and fought the militia without armor. Captured the main barracks and freed an Ambassador of the Republic," offered the Legionary. "They were selected and sent over specially for the mission. If that's not special, I don't know what is."

"Spare me the hero worship," the Optio scolded. "I'm going to find Corporal Sisera and have him get his wagons off my approach road."

Chapter 25 – Break Out and Insolvent

"Optio. Why is the Centuripe army still camped outside the walls? We have two Centuries in control of their main barracks and the high ground," Horatius Ostrei stated. He pointed over a single-story house to the valley far below. "If they attack, they'll have no fallback position in the city."

"Lance Corporal Ostrei, if I knew the answer to that I'd be a Greek commander," Gustavi replied to the Decanus of 1st Squad. "I can only imagine General Periander is maintaining a show of force."

The wagons with the wounded slowed the Century's descent. They left the barracks at sunup and were just reaching the lower section of The Serpent. Once they made another complete circle of the city, the caravan could drop down the final streets and exit through the eastern gate.

"Optio, there's activity in the Centuripe camp," Lance Corporal Italus reported.

"It's morning," Gustavi responded. "Usually there is movement in a military camp once the sun comes up."

"No Sergeant. I'm talking ranks, armor, and spears," the Decanus of 3rd Squad corrected.

"Century halt," the Optio shouted.

The Legionaries assigned as drivers reined in the horses and tossed blocks to the men marching beside the wagons. Once the wheels were chocked, they let the lines go slack and looked over the low structures.

Down where the Symaethus Valley started, armored soldiers and Centuripe cavalry lined up between their tents and the city's defensive wall. While the movement was obvious from the heights of Centuripe, down in the valley and closer to the Simeto river, the Legion's sentries were oblivious.

Most of Mesalla Legion East was behind the trenches and spikes of the marching camp. However, early morning work parties on the way to collect water from upriver, foragers after wild fodder for the pack animals, and wood harvesters going to cut fuel for the fires ranged far from the camp. Plus, contuberniums patrolled out in the open as did several cavalry units. None of the exposed Legionaries realized the Centuripe army was up, awake, and dressed for war.

***

A single man in gold-edged armor kicked his horse into motion. He trotted through the Centuripe tents and out onto the plane of the valley. Partway to the Legion camp, the lone officer reined in his horse. He sat still until a couple of patrols noticed the Centuripe officer.

Whether out of curiosity or military courtesy, two Legion squads and a cavalry unit adjusted and headed for him. As they neared, the officer raised an arm, and it appeared as if he was greeting the Legionaries. Then, he raised the arm higher and swung it in a circle. To the squads nearing the officer, it seemed to be a strange but harmless motion.

Alerio recognized the arm movement as a signal and anything except harmless. His fear came to fruition when the ranks of soldiers sprinted away from the wall, ran through the tents, and charged towards the Legionaries.

"25th Century. Form a defensive formation," he shouted.

Centurion Megellus and Optio Gustavi stood where they had stopped. While their commanders seemed shocked at the command, the squads drew inwards, stacked in two ranks, and shuffled together until their shoulders touched, forming an oval around the wagons.

"What's the meaning of this?" questioned Megellus.

"Sir, Tesserarius Sisera has recognized a danger. As such, he has wisely called the Century into a defensive posture," stated Lance Corporal Enitui. "It is recommended that you and the Optio step inside our circle for your own protection."

"It would be more impressive if we had javelins and our Legion shields," added Lance Corporal Italus.

Enitui glanced over his unarmored 4th Squad, smiled, and said, "The Goddess Bia gave you strength. Let that be enough."

"I'd still prefer a shield," Italus complained while looking around at his 3rd Squad.

"We should have kept the Centuripe gear," someone whined.

"Stow it and watch your sectors," Alerio instructed. "Sir. If you and the Optio would step into the circle, I'd feel better about your security."

***

Down in the valley, the two squads of Legionaries formed a shield wall, but the mass of soldiers rolled over them. Centuripe horsemen ran down the work details after unhorsing the outnumbered cavalry. The wave of militiaman rolled beyond the Legion camp leaving the bodies of butchered Legionaries scattered across the field.

By then the camp was awake and Centuries were forming up while still strapping on their armor. Trumpets blared and as the herd of Centuripe soldiers splashed across the Simeto river, angry Legionaries jogged out of the gate. The heavy infantry units remained compacted to present a solid front for when the soldiers turned and headed back to Centuripe.

Close behind, the Velites, in their light armor, chased after the soldiers. Their job was to report on the distribution when the enemy turned back towards their city. But the Centuripe army didn't turn. Following General Periander, they continued down the valley and crossed the river. Then, they hiked up the steep slope, approached a line of high stone walls, and marched into the city of Adrano.

***

Down in the valley, the soldiers who didn't accompany their General ran for the gates of Centuripe.

"Steady," ordered Centurion Megellus. "It looks like they're coming to take back their city."

"Sir, I don't think they are planning on attacking," Gustavi offered. "You'll note, they've forgotten to put on their armor and helmets. And neglected to take their spears."

"You're suggesting those men are deserting?"

"Just the opposite, sir," the Optio offered. "I believe the men who ran up the valley are the deserters."

"Corporal Sisera, stand down the Century," the Centurion ordered. "Get them moving and let's get out of this city."

"Yes, sir. Century, break formation and resume the march," Alerio called out.

***

Smoke billowed from the Centuripe camp causing a haze to fill the upper valley. Most of the tents and equipment blazed and those not yet on fire would soon be in flames.

"Someone has a case of the red cūlus," suggested Decanus Umbria.

"Can you blame the Legion for burning it?" a member of his 6th Squad asked. "They lost a lot of men."

"No. They have a valid reason. But it's a waste of good equipment."

The 25th Century came through the city gates and marched by the burning camp. None of the skirmishers with torches paid any attention to them as they set fire to anything not yet ablaze. Four squads of heavy infantry did pay attention to the three wagons and the men in woolen workmen's clothing.

"Halt. State your business," an Optio challenged.

"I am Centurion Megellus of the 25th Century, Crassus Legion North," the officer replied.

"Sir, you and your Century are a long way from home."

"Where is the Crassus Legion?"

"The last we heard, they marched west to take Enna, sir."

"Open your ranks, we have wounded," Megellus instructed. With a wave of his hand, he dismissed the Sergeant and signaled the wagons forward.

The infantrymen separated and the 25th marched to the Legion camp.

"State your business," challenged the sentry at the gate.

"I am Centurion Megellus of the 25th Century, Crassus Legion North," Megellus spit out. "Lift the barrier or I will have my men break it down."

"Yes, sir," the guard acknowledged.

Once he lifted the pole, the Century entered the Legion camp. At the medical tent, they unloaded the wounded, then stood around the empty wagons.

"Where to, sir?" Gustavi inquired.

"Hold here and I'll see about getting us an assigned space and equipment," replied the officer.

From far down the street, a Centurion in bright armor with a scowl on his face stormed in their direction.

"Who are you and why are you blocking my street?" demanded the officer.

"Centurion Fenoris Megellus of the 25th Century, Crassus Legion North. And I'm getting sick of having to explain that to everyone I meet," Megellus shot back. "We attacked a city unarmored, saved the Ambassador, and have been treated like your impoverished cousin's orphan children. At this rate, we'll need to adopt the Goddess Orbona as the Century's deity. If you are in charge, fine. If not, point me to someone who is and get out of my way."

Alerio stood a little straighter as pride flooded his chest. Centurion Megellus had displayed the type of aggression Legionaries required of their infantry officers. Then, the officer in the new armor bristled, answered, and Alerio deflated.

"My name is Osvaldo and, I am the Tesserarius of Mesalla Legion East."

Alerio's stomach soured. As the Century's Tesserarius, he had to deal with Osvaldo's staff for pay, armor, and equipment. And Centurion Osvaldo had to approve and sign off on all of it. No one wanted a demotivated Legion Tesserarius dragging his feet before allowing supplies to be released.

The one thing that saved Corporal Sisera from dropping to his knees and begging the Legion's Tesserarius forgiveness was the 25th would be leaving in a day or so. No matter how angry the officer, the Century could live with it until they left to return to Crassus Legion North.

Unfortunately, it wasn't only Centurion Osvaldo that held a grudge against the Century. The animosity towards the 25th came from high up on Centuripe in the chambers of a Republic's diplomat.

"Well, then Centurion Osvaldo. We require a Century square, tents, food rations, and cooking utensils," Megellus ordered.

"Can't do it."

"And why not?" questioned Megellus.

"Because the Legion is breaking camp and moving across the river," Osvaldo informed him. "We will attack Adrano and put General Periander up on the wood for what he did."

"What do you suggest we do in the meanwhile?"

"You have three wagons and healthy men," observed Osvaldo. "Help move the wounded and the medical equipment to the other side of the river."

Alerio felt good about the assignment. The Century would earn esteem from the Legion staff by working with the medical personnel and respect from the other Centuries. He wouldn't realize until days later, that the debt of gratitude would be repaid to so few men.

Chapter 26 – The Price of Bonuses

Thirty-four infantry officers of heavy infantry and the officer for 25th Crassus stood in ranks receiving information and assignments for the coming assault.

"Centurion Megellus. I have two Centuries on duty in Centuripe. Your Century doesn't make up for them, but I need your infantrymen. Have them draw armor and weapons," the Senior Tribune informed him. "We'll figure out the compensation later."

"But, sir. We haven't been issued tents or cooking equipment," Megellus protested. "My men are sleeping in the open next to the animal pens."

"Then how have they been eating their rations for the last four days?"

"We haven't been issued food either, sir."

Senior Tribune Istac stopped talking, pressed his lips together, and turned his head. Behind him, Senior Centurion Edidi gritted his teeth and stared a hole in Centurion Osvaldo's chest.

"I can't send infantrymen weak from hunger up a thirteen-hundred-foot slope. All I could expect of them at the top is to die in front of the walls at Adrano," Istac related. "Edidi?"

"I'm on it, Senior Tribune," the Senior Centurion responded. "25th Crassus will be bedded, fed, and equipped today, sir."

Before Istac had a chance to say more, the flap of the commander's tent flew back, and the Legion's Colonel strutted from the tent. While walking to the assembly, he nodded to the ranks of officers in greeting.

"It's a mile and a half to the walls of Adrano, uphill all the way," announced battle commander Ruscus. "As always, but especially tomorrow, the job of breaching those walls falls to my heavy infantry. Are you ready?"

The voices of thirty-four proud and motivated Centurions cried back.

"Mesalla Legion East, standing by," they replied while stomping their right feet.

"That's what I want to hear," Ruscus declared. "Where is Centurion Megellus?"

"Here, sir," the infantry officer responded.

"Your 25th Century has the honor of front rank, center position during the assault," Ruscus informed Megellus. Then the battle commander shifted and scanned the faces of the Centurion. "At daybreak, there will be sacrifices to the great God Mars for the opportunity and the Goddess Victoria for the outcome. Make sure your Legionaries are fed, watered, and ready to fight. Good afternoon, Centurions."

Colonel Ruscus walked away with cheers ringing in his ears. The enthusiasm of the Centurions should have bolstered his confidence. But the reality that an assault on Adrano held the possibility of a tragic outcome, gnawed at his gut.

Despite his bravado in front of his infantry officers, the reality of climbing a steep grade then his Legionaries being filtered to a narrow area at the city's gates, presented a difficult tactical situation.

If only the council at Adrano had turned over General Periander, Ruscus could have backed away claiming justice was served. But after four days of negotiations, the Centuripe General and his thirteen hundred infantrymen remained behind the walls.

Consul/General Valerius Mesalla ordered, "Get a treaty from every city along the east coast of Sicilia or bleed the noncompliant cities and take slaves. Then, get the Legion down to Syracuse." Centuripe signed as did eighteen others. Only Adrano had opted to fight by harboring General Periander.

***

"What have you got there, Tesserarius?" inquired Apulia Frentani.

"Radishes to go with the salted pork," Alerio replied.

He stopped at the 8th Squad's campfire and slung the sack of vegetables off his shoulder. Reaching in, he pulled out handfuls of radishes and distributed them to the Legionaries. Then, he twisted the sack closed and started to walk away.

"Corporal Sisera. If not for you, we would have starved," one of the squad members said.

"I doubt that but thanks," Alerio replied. "I'd be a poor Tesserarius if I let the Century go hungry before I had the opportunity to charge you for lost or broken equipment."

"I'd settle for equipment to break," Quiris Stulte from the 9th Squad offered.

"Lance Corporal, we should be moving out in a day or so," Alerio suggested while setting down the bag in front of the campfire of the 9th. "All of this will be forgotten once we're on the road."

He handed out more radishes, hoisted the bag to his shoulder, and walked to where the 10th squad camped. A little beyond the area rested the fence of the animal pens.

The offended Centurion Osvaldo provided a location for the Century. But that was the extent of his allowances. Despite two a day visits from Corporal Sisera to the supply area, no other supplies had been issued.

"Corporal Sisera. You've finally done it," Lucius Tescum announced.

"Done what?" questioned Alerio.

"Broken through Centurion Osvaldo's resistance," the Decanus replied.

The Legion camp was composed of neat squares of Century areas. Eight-man tents defined the squares, except the block controlled by the hapless and tentless 25th Century. Now supply wagons began arriving and it seemed the Century's fortune had changed.

Ten wagons rolled into the center of the Century area and supply personnel climbed down. They began unloading tents, sacks of grain, bags of wine, amphorae of olive oil, and a variety of dried meats. Almost as if all the missed rations were being delivered at once.

Alerio began walking towards the wagons. Taking his time, the frustrated Tesserarius ogled the much-needed rations. Then, helmets, armor, shields, and javelins appeared. Panic struck Corporal Sisera, and he broke into a run.

"Hold on there, Optio," he called out to a supply Sergeant. "That gear can't be for the 25th. We're leaving to rejoin our Legion in a day or so."

"Corporal Sisera? I have documents for you to sign," the NCO told him. Picking up a handful of parchments, the Optio jumped from the wagon to the ground and held out the forms. Then he assured Alerio. "There's no mistake, Tesserarius. Sign these."

***

That evening, with the aromas of camp stew boiling in pots and bread baking in hastily assembled brick ovens, the men of the 25th Century relaxed, nibbled on vegetables, and passed around wineskins.

"As much as I hate tents, tonight I'm looking forward to sleeping in one," mentioned Lance Corporal Dircium.

The comment drew laughter from the men of 2nd Squad. With guylines taut, the edges of each tent in perfect alignment, and food cooking, outbursts of laughter erupted regularly around the Century's area. Bliss reigned at every tent on the block, except in the officer's tent.

***

"Sir, that's suicide," observed Alerio. "We don't know the Centuries on either side of us or the adjacent squads. Their strengths or weaknesses, or if they'll stand and not break."

"I would tend to agree with you, Corporal Sisera," asserted Centurion Megellus. "But the honor came directly from the battle commander's lips."

"If you want, you can go to the headquarters' tent and inform Colonel Ruscus of his mistake," suggested Optio Gustavi. "Not a bad strategy if you want out. You'll miss the battle but have a nice view of the sunset from a cross."

"Sergeant. I have no intention of talking to the Colonel," Alerio assured him. "I was merely pointing out the issue with putting a strange unit in the center of an attack line."

Megellus pulled over a new camp table and unrolled a piece of goatskin.

"I took notes during the briefing and drew this map," the infantry officer explained. "There is one benefit to leading a construction division for three years. You learn to visualize and draw your ideas."

"Sir. I'd like to learn how to draw those details," Alerio remarked.

"When this is over, we'll see if you have any talent for Cartography. Okay, see this approach…"

At the top of the long, steep approach, a three-thousand-foot-wide flat area gradually narrowed as it advanced towards the city. At the gates of Adrano, the flat ground was only two hundred feet wide. Any attacking force would be bunched up in the tight space and vulnerable to arrows and spears from the city's defensive walls. The Legion would take heavy casualties before breaching the three-portal entrance.

On either side of the entrance gates, the defensive wall consisted of a double wall filled with pebbles, dirt, and volcanic rock from Mount Etna. The flat top provided a stable platform for slingers, spearmen, and archers. In short, the area in front of the gates to Adrano was a kill zone.

"How many men can we shelter in the gateways?" Gustavi asked in the form of a sick joke. "Because anywhere in front of that wall, our Legionaries will need coins for the ferryman."

"What's this space beyond the gates, sir?" inquired Alerio while running his finger over the entrances and into an area behind the gate wall

"Inside Adrano's gates is an amphitheater-shaped depression," Megellus described. "The sides are high but scalable with ramps to the tops of the walls on either side. Straight ahead is the real problem."

"Why's that, sir?" Gustavi questioned.

"At the end of the bowl-shaped area, is where the bulk of their infantry will be waiting for us," Megellus stated while tapping a finger on the map.

"We're supposed to climb a mountain, pass under projectiles, and breach three gates?" Sergeant Gustavi said listing the challenges. "Survive more iron rain, form up, and then confront their infantry?"

"And, all while moving and fighting beside units we know nothing about," Alerio added.

"I believe Corporal Sisera, that's where this conversation began," the infantry officer pointed out. While rolling up the map, he suggested. "Let's go tell the men."

"Sir, I recommend we wait for later," Gustavi submitted. "Let them eat and relax. Then we can ruin their night."

"An excellent idea, Optio."

"Sir. If I may be excused?" inquired Alerio.

"In a rush to eat some of the extra rations?" questioned Gustavi.

"No Optio. I'm going to speak to the Legion engineers about a battering ram."

"Battering ram?" questioned Megellus. "Isn't getting a battering ram to the gates the job of the Legion engineers?"

"Actually sir, three battering rams and harnesses for hauling them into combat," Alerio explained. "From your map, there's not a lot of recreational area around the gates. I think we should have our own key to the city."

"You want us to have our own battering ram, so we don't have to wait for the Legion engineers," guessed Centurion Megellus. "Go on Tesserarius, see what you can scrounge up."

"Yes, sir," Alerio replied while saluting.

He left the officer's tent and went in search of an engineer, a woodcutter, and a harness maker.

Act 7

Chapter 27 - The Slope

"This morning's sacrifices went well, sir," Istac remarked.

"That they did. The bulls died satisfactorily," Colonel Ruscus said agreeing with the Senior Tribune. "Let's hope the Gods appreciate it. I know the priests did. All that blood exchanged for blessings and sacrificial coins. And all for nothing."

"You don't seem too concerned about the attack, sir."

"Attacking this mountain hovel is so low on my list of priorities, I wouldn't waste a day on it. But General Periander's parting gifts to the Fields of Elysium require a response," explained the Colonel. "Our men need to see blood. Unfortunately, I don't have days to spill it. We'll have a go at their walls, and after the retreat, I'll offer Adrano's council Periander's weight in gold."

"You can't see the walls of the city from down here," observed the Senior Turbine. "How will you know when to sound the retreat?"

"I won't have to. According to Ambassador Sergius, the Centurion for 25th Crassus is incompetent," Ruscus replied while fishing a pile of messages out of a box. "As long as his Century holds the center, the line will move forward. When it gets bad and he withdraws, the attack line will fold. I'll fine Fenoris Megellus a hefty amount of coins and send him back to the Capital in disgrace. Our junior Centurions will be chastised but excused as falling victim to a rout. Afterward, we'll send the 25th Century back to Crassus Legion North and let Colonel Bacaris assign them a new officer."

"I heard what the Ambassador said about Centurion Megellus and the 25th. But they did infiltrate the city, take the barracks against odds, and secure the Ambassador," Istac mentioned. "That doesn't sound like inept leadership or a failed mission to me, sir. In fact, I'd say it was a well-executed operation."

"Executed like the bulls except the Century got lucky. Everybody gets lucky occasionally," the Colonel offered as he selected a message. Before reading it, he looked around, judged the landscape, and shouted. "First Centurion Irrisus. Stagger your Century uphill from here and protect me from projectiles. I'm making this my command position."

"Very good, sir," responded the infantry officer for the Legion's 1st Century.

***

On either side of the 25th Century, the first maniple, composed of inexperienced Legionaries, struggled against the steep grade. Behind them, the second and third maniples moved up, keeping pace. Far ahead and almost at the crest, the Velites, in their lighter armor and smaller shields hunched down waiting on the heavy infantry. This fight involved attacking into ranged weapons across a killing zone; something more suited to heavy infantrymen and their big shields rather than skirmishers. Wisely, the Velites ducked as they reached the top and didn't expose themselves to the projectiles from the Adrano defenders.

"Second and third maniples, hold here," instructed Istac to a group of waiting Tribunes. "The first maniple is to maintain their pace."

The Tribunes sprinted off, heading for the infantry officers at each Century. A mile to the rear, the Legion's ballista crews sat on their wagons, the bolt throwers still packed in their crates. Milling around, the cavalry also watched. Both divisions of the Legion were out of place and relegated to observer status by the steep slope. They weren't the only unit out of place.

***

"Why are we assigned to the first maniple?" complained the squad leader from 1st Squad.

"What, Lance Corporal Ostrei, doesn't it make you feel special?" shot back Optio Gustavi. "You should be honored to be leading the young in their first taste of blood."

Although he mocked the contubernium's Decanus, the Sergeant of 25th Crassus asked himself the same question. Based on the Centuries hiking up the slope on both sides, the center made sense as they were more experienced. But why an experienced unit moved online with rookie Legionaries in the first place, couldn't be deciphered.

On the other side of the Century, Corporal Sisera was also communicating with his four squads.

"Keep your shields tight and the rows straight," Alerio shouted.

"We aren't at the top yet," noted Aternus from 7th Squad. "You can't even see the wall from here."

"When you see the walls of Adrano, it'll be too late," Alerio replied. "Tighten it up."

The movement up the slope continued. Keeping the eight hundred Legionaries of the first maniple inline were directions and corrections from their NCOs and Centurions.

In order to fit the wide area at the top and provide a solid wall of shields, the infantrymen were stacked in two rows. This allowed for a barrier of shields up front with another held overhead to protect against arrows, pebbles, and spears. Earlier scouting and intelligence reported the presences of oxybeles, lithobolois, and onagers manned by Syracusan engineers. These range weapons were the reason the approach in front of the gates was dubbed the killing zone.

***

"I'm going to move closer to the top and have a look, Colonel," Istac informed his battle commander.

"Don't do that Senior Tribune," advised Ruscus. He finished reading a note, placed it in the box, and pulled out another. "I expect a stampede to come off the summit after the first volley. Besides, if they have bolt throwers on platforms, the projectiles will travel over the open ground, fly downhill, and tumble before stopping. You don't want to be in the way of those."

"I can't imagine anybody wanting to be in front of giant arrows," Istac stated. "or trying to dodge big flying stones."

"You have summed up the situation nicely, Senior Tribune," the Colonel responded. "Keep an eye on the crest and let's see who comes back first. Care to put a few coins on Centurion Megellus?"

"No, sir. I'll trust your judgment."

Chapter 28 – The Trip to the Summit

"Palinurus, duck down and slow up," suggested Tescum from 10th Squad. "You're beginning to drag your partner along with the log. Besides, your head is as tall as a goose on a pole. You'll tip off the soldiers at Adrano that we're coming."

"But I want to see where I'm going, Decanus," the big Legionary offered. "Tesserarius?"

"I think they already know we're coming, Lance Corporal. But do slow down a little, Palinurus. At least for the sake of your partner," Alerio replied from behind the assault line. Then he shouted, not only to his four squads but to the rookie Century on his right. "Tighten the gaps in your shields and keep pace. Straighten the line, people, straighten the line."

The 10th, 9th, 8th, and 7th Squads responded to their Corporal's voice and Palinurus shortened his stride, allowing the other Legionary harnessed to the battering ram to keep up with the large man. To the Corporal's left, Centurion Megellus encouraged the 5th and 6th Squads.

Just as the 10th did, the 6th Squad hauled a long, straight log up the slope. It was yoked to a pair of men by straps across their chests. During the climb, the pulling duty had been rotated. Now, as they drew close to the top, the final teams with the battering rams would haul them over the crest, across the killing ground, and up to the gates of Adrano.

"Lance Corporal Umbria, how is the 6th doing with Corporal Sisera's log?" Megellus inquired using the running joke about the battering rams.

"Sir, I can report that the Corporal's log is straight, firm, and coming along nicely," Umbria called back after checking on the two Legionaries struggling uphill with the battering ram.

"Well, praise Sterculius. At least something is going smoothly," Centurion Megellus responded. His reference to the God of Merda brought a chuckle from the squads in the center of the attack line. "Tighten the gaps in your shields and keep pace. Straighten the line, people, straighten the line."

On the officer's left, Optio Gustavi herded the 1st, 2nd, 3rd, and 4th Squads uphill and as Alerio had done, he shouted loud enough to benefit the inexperienced Century adjacent to his end squad. 4th Squad had another of Corporal Sisera's logs.

***

The first maniple stretched out two ranks deep for a thousand feet across the slope. Because of the infantry officer and the NCOs of 25th Crassus, the center of the attack line remained uniform and together even in the rough terrain. As a final maneuver before the Legion helmets popped up revealing them to the enemy, the heavy infantrymen opened gaps to allow them to march around the Velites.

"Cap the testudo," Centurion Megellus instructed once the maniple moved beyond the crouching skirmishers.

In response, the second rank flattened and lowered their shields forming a roof over them and the first rank. The tortoise formed just as the top of the steep grade reached eye level.

While the Legionaries huddled behind and under their shields, and the Optios and Tesserarii tucked their shields tightly against their bodies, the infantry officers marched without personal defenses.

Along the thousand-foot attack line, the infantry officers hiked forward unguarded to face the enemy. Each identifiable by the bright horsehair combs on their helmets and their lack of javelins and shields. Every officer was acutely aware that the Legionaries in their Centuries drew courage and strength for the valor of their Centurions. The infantry officers were a pillar of the Republic's Legions.

The Centurions knew it. The Legionaries, Decani, Tesserarii, and Optios knew it. But this one time, a distracted battle commander, Ruscus, failed to appreciate and take into account the pride and stubbornness of his infantry officers. One in particular.

Centurion Fenoris Megellus no longer considered himself a construction supervisor. He was a leader of warriors and his Century had been given a position of trust. As he and his Optio and Tesserarius had discussed in the morning before starting the climb, there would be no retreat from Adrano.

***

On platforms behind the wide walls of the city, mercenary engineers from Syracuse had placed oxybeles and lithobolois. Both were tension weapons resembling huge crossbows. Each oxybele had grooves for double bolts. The lithoboloi, while rated for large wall demolishing rocks, was supplied with smaller stones.

"I could take down a wall with this weapon," bragged one of the engineers while patting the center section. "But the Republic didn't bring walls. That's why I've selected stones as today's ammunition."

"Isn't bigger better for knocking them down?" questioned a Captain of the Adrano militia.

"Everything hit by the lithoboloi goes down. But at this range, the smaller stones will travel fast enough to cut a tree trunk in half," the engineer assured the officer. He picked up a stone the size of two fists and bounced it on the palm of his hand. "Be assured, this little pebble launched from my weapon is a man killer."

Despite the deadliness of the tension weapons, neither the oxybeles nor lithobolois fired first. When the Legion helmets appeared over the rise, the distinction of being the first to rain down rocks on them were the torsion weapons. Each capable of slinging large stones higher and farther than the lithobolois.

"Release the onagers," ordered the commander of Adrano's defenses.

The order was passed to the four weapon stations. From the ground, mostly because of the size and weight of the war machines and the ammunition, the onagers launched.

Shortly after, the oxybeles and lithobolois received the same order. Across At the crest of the hill and before they reached deeply into the kill zone, the Legionaries were suddenly on the receiving end of deadly rocks, stones, and shaped bolts.

Chapter 29 - Rocks and Heads Roll Downhill

"Aternus. The 7th is falling behind," shouted Alerio.

Caricini Aternus glanced back and noted the pair hauling the battering ram were struggling.

255

"You and you, help out with Corporal Sisera's log," the squad leader ordered adding two Legionaries to the team pulling the ram. "Help them keep up with the line."

The Privates of the 7th lowered their shields. Stepping close to the men pulling, they bent over, grabbed straps, and wrapped them around their wrists.

"Let's get the ram up the hill. Put your backs into it, and..."

It was bigger than three Legionaries' helmets and dropped from high in the sky. Upon impact, the rock from an onager drove one end of the battering ram into the soil. As the log's end was slammed into the dirt, the four Legionaries on the straps were pulled down so hard they bounced off the log and the rocky ground. Then they bounced up again before being jerked back down by the straps. Two suffered dislocated shoulders. Ones back was crushed, and the fourth Legionary's neck snapped from the collision with the log.

Before they realized the extent of their injuries, the other end of the log, which rose high into the air on the initial impact, reached the limit of its bounce. When the tail end crashed back down, it lifted the other end and the Legionaries into the air.

The Velites craned their necks to look up at the sight of four infantrymen dangling for a moment from the top of a pole. Then the battering ram tipped over, smacked into the slope, and flipped over end after end.

In hindsight, Senior Tribune Istac should have taken Colonel Ruscus' bet. Centurion Megellus wasn't the first one down. That dubious honor went to four infantrymen flopping around as the battering ram hit, bounced, and tumbled downhill. It finally stopped at the front rank of the 1st Century's shields. The shaken and broken Legionaries weren't the last to be violently removed from the top of the slope.

***

Decanus Aternus shrieked in horror as four of his contubernium pinwheeled downhill. Then something crashed into 5th Squad off to his left. He spun in that direction and saw Legionaries with crushed chests and legs from another large rock. Although their mouths were open, he couldn't hear their shrieks. His own screaming drowned them out.

"Aternus, get it together and keep your people moving," Corporal Sisera shouted.

Lance Corporal Aternus, he who was blessed by the Goddess Theia with excellent vision, stood with a blank expression on his face and stared back at his Tesserarius.

"Move your…"

As if a leaf snatched away by a strong gust of wind, Aternus was swept off his feet. It might have been difficult following his flying body if the bolt from one of the oxybele didn't also pierce a second Legionary.

The two bodies appeared to be locked in an embrace as they hurdled off the top of the slope. Their plunge, however, wasn't voluntary as the skirmishers might have thought. They were pinned together by a long iron barb protruding through their stomachs.

***

Lance Corporal Telesia Caudini attempted to stand but his right ankle refused to stop flopping around. Finally, by using his shield, the squad leader climbed to one leg. Confused at first, he fought off the pain and surveyed the injuries to his 5th Squad.

257

"Sir. What happened?" questioned Caudini in a voice so soft it didn't carry beyond his helmet.

Centurion Megellus didn't know which way to dodge. There had been two loud crashes and men began screaming. Then two swooshes as if giant birds of prey flapped their wings one thunderous time.

Caudini hopped on one foot and the Centurion started to yell for the squad leader to sit down and wait for a medic. Before the words reached the officer's throat, the Lance Corporal's body buckled backward. His heels and head touched as the energy from a large stone carried his body over the crest of the hill. Someone grabbed Megellus' arm and pulled him to the ground.

"We need to get out of here, sir," Pentri Umbria stammered. "This is not a defensible position."

"It's not a position at all, Lance Corporal," shot back the infantry officer. "Get 6th Squad up and moving."

"Downhill, sir?" Umbria questioned.

There must be a name for the sound of a mountain dropping from the sky, thought the Centurion. It would need to be a short name as the sound didn't last long. He pondered this as he wiped Lance Corporal Umbria's blood from his face.

Pentri Umbria's helmet, head, and one shoulder were under a large rock. Gray matter, pieces of forehead bone, and blood covered his face. Only one eye was visible, the other lost under the crushed skull.

"Sir. Are you injured?" asked Optio Gustavi.

The NCO stood over the Centurion holding out an arm. Megellus locked wrists with his Optio and pulled himself off the ground.

The birds of prey flapped their wings again and the oxybele bolts plucked three more Legionaries off the summit.

"Orders, sir," inquired Gustavi.

"Tighten them up and move the maniple forward," Megellus growled. Then the infantry officer looked to his right and called out. "Corporal Sisera. Pull them in, tighten this line, and get them moving."

"Yes, sir," Alerio shouted back. "Moving."

***

The center of the 25th Century was devastated. 5th, 6th, and 7th Squads reduced to individual Legionaries wandering around in shock. They weren't the only units to suffer from the tension and torsion weapons. All along the first maniple, some squads closed up to fill in positions left by lost comrades. Others folded under the pressure and ran downhill.

"Lance Corporal Frentani. Collect the strays and get them in line with the 8th," Alerio ordered. Then to the end of his Century, he directed. "Lance Corporal Tescum. Pull that rookie Century in and give them guidance."

Alerio roamed back and forth behind the line as the smallest man in the Century bullied and convinced strange squads to close in with the 10th. Their Optio had fallen on the second barrage, and they almost broke and ran. Then Decanus Tescum walked their ranks and jumped up into each squad leader's face with a challenge.

"Your body's bigger than mine," he defied the decani from the adjacent Century. "But my heart is twice the size. Run if you want, cowards. Or close the gap and join me in Hades."

259

To Alerio's surprise, while four of the squads broke and ran, the other six braced their shields and followed the little man's directions.

"The longer we stand here the more the engineers have time to target us," Alerio bellowed. "Shift left, move it, close it, and shield it."

With the center filled, Centurion Megellus lifted an arm and just as he dropped it, he cried out, "Double time, march."

The maniple began at eight hundred strong. When the Centurion of 25th Crassus ordered the run, only two hundred and ten Legionaries made the mad dash for the gates of Adrano. The rest were dead, injured, or had retreated down the hill and out of the rain of rocks, stones, and iron bolts.

***

Ruscus watched as groups of Legionaries picked their way down the slope.

"Is that it?" inquired the battle commander.

"Sir, I don't know about that," Istac corrected. "One of the skirmisher Centurions is signaling."

The command staff watched as the Velites officer flashed hand signs. When the messaging ended, the Centurion gave one last sign.

"It appears two hundred plus Legionaries charged the gates," Senior Centurion Edidi reported. "And the Centurion requests permission to advance his skirmishers."

"He wants to add to the Adrano body count," demanded Ruscus. "As it is, I am speculating how many men I will have to sacrifice to extract the ones at the gate?"

"I don't know, sir. But it's Centurion Megellus' 25th Crassus leading the assault," Edidi replied. "And they still have two battering rams with them."

"What do you suggest I do?" asked the battle commander.

"Colonel, if I may make a suggestion," Irrisus spoke up.

"Highly unusual, but please tell me, 1st Centurion."

"Send up the second maniple," Irrisus advised. "Because if you don't, Megellus and the 25th Century will break down the gates and claim all the glory."

"Why do you say that?" questioned Ruscus.

The 1st Centurion pointed to the lead rank of his 1st Century and swept his hand across a broad swath of land.

"Because I watched Legionaries from that Century die gruesomely on this slope all morning," Irrisus explained. "And while Centuries with fewer casualties have retreated, not one, even slightly wounded Legionary from the 25th has voluntarily come off the field of battle."

The Colonel closed the lid on his correspondence box, peered up at the top of the slope, then spit on the ground.

"Senior Tribune, forward the second maniple," Ruscus instructed. "And stand by the third. We have a city to take."

"Yes, sir," Istac replied before sprinting to the knot of Tribunes.

"Irrisus, I'm going up to the kill zone. I can't direct a Legion in combat from down here," Ruscus stated. "I hope you're ready to protect me."

"Absolutely Colonel," the 1st Centurion assured him. "Although you won't see much from inside a one-hundred-man testudo, sir."

Chapter 30 – Infectious Courage

Various thoughts invaded Alerio's mind as he ran across the kill zone. Every time an archer or a slinger knocked a Legionary out of the run, he thanked the Goddess Bia for the strength of his body.

When boulders fell and crippled pairs of men, he offered a different prayer. This time to Fortūna for the luck of not having a huge rock fall on him from out of the sky.

But when the sinew and hair strings on the enormous crossbows twanged and stones or bolts knocked runners back and to the ground, his oath took on a more personal tone.

"Goddess Nenia. If it's my time and my strings are to be cut, come for me quickly," he prayed to his personal deity, the Goddess of Death.

Out of the corner of his eyes, he saw an arrow jutting from Optio Gustavi's shoulder. The NCO staggered and would have fallen if not for the big arm of Lance Corporal Dircium. The two slowed a little and that worried Alerio.

Then an odd clarity came over him, and Alerio's senses slowed. Suddenly, the enemy spearmen, archers, and slingers vanished. And the running Legionaries faded away leaving him an unobstructed view of the gates to Adrano.

Encased in a granite and brick framework, the three gates were taller and thinner than the defensive walls. So tall in fact, there were no soldiers above the gates. And for a half circle in front of the portals, the ground was bare of spent arrows, bolts, rocks, and stones. Artistically, the gate wall served to impress visitors. For an attacking Legion NCO, it impressed Alerio in a different way.

A giant bird of prey batted its wings next to Alerio's ears and he came back to the battlefield. Beside him, a bolt pulverized a Legionary's head. It shot through so quickly, the faceless body took two more steps before falling.

"Thank you for the vision, Nenia," Alerio exclaimed. Whether it was a combat veteran's instinct or an actual gift from the Goddess, didn't matter. Alerio had a plan on how to get into the city while protecting the Legionaries breaching the gates. "Crowd the center gate. Close in on the center of the gate wall."

Somehow, Centurion Megellus ended up running beside him.

"Sisera. Is this for any reason other than getting good men killed?" the officer asked.

"We still have a battering ram," Alerio replied. "And there is a blind spot in front of the center gate."

"What does that mean?"

"We have a protected space. We can ram the gate unmolested."

"Is this more of your, Legionaries are craftsmen?"

"Journeymen of war, sir."

But Megellus had fallen out of the run and lay sprawled on his face with an arrow shaft sticking out of his thigh. Alerio veered to his left, spun around, and ran back for the officer.

"No, you don't," Alerio shouted while hoisting the injured officer to his right shoulder. With the shield held up to defend Megellus, Corporal Sisera raced towards the gates bellowing. "No, he's finally become a leader. Don't do this."

"What are you talking about, Corporal Sisera?" requested the weakened Centurion.

"Sorry, sir," Alerio answered. "This is between her and me"

"Who?" Megellus asked before going limp on the Corporal's shoulder.

***

The fleetest of foot made it through the arrows shot and spears thrown from on top of Adrano's walls. Slower runners needed to dodge, duck, and depend on Fortūna's luck. Those simply jogging across the kill zone required answers to heartfelt prayers. In all cases, whether injured or not, the Legionaries who reached the center gate discovered a sanctuary from the missiles.

"Tesserarius. Where do you want this?"

At the end of jogging across the zone, Alerio heard the question and looked up into the smiling face of 10th Squad's right pivot. Glancing down, he noted the big man's feet straddling the battering ram.

"We saved your log, Corporal Sisera," Lance Corporal Tescum added from beside the pivot.

As near as Alerio could figure, there were almost two hundred Legionaries crowded against the gate wall. If veterans or experienced men from the second maniple, it would be a major force. But most of the faces, other than the survivors of the 25th Century, were young with fear in their eyes.

"Put a contubernium on it and knock on the door," Alerio responded. "Let the soldiers of Adrano know, the Legion has come calling."

Tescum and Palinurus bent down and grabbed the straps wrapped around the log.

264

"Not the 10th. I have a different job for you," instructed Alerio. Peering around, he nodded to an unfamiliar Lance Corporal. "Decanus. Pick eight men, put them on the ram, and bust a hole in that gate."

A scream from the outer edge of the cluster drew everyone's attention. A bolt from one of the oxybeles had pinned a Legionary to the ground. As he lay squirming like a bug and his screams faded to sobs, those around the fringes pushed inward smashing the men on the inside up against the gate wall.

"Private Palinurus. I want you at the wall and Legionaries on either side of you," Alerio ordered. "Lance Corporal Tescum. Put two more men on their shoulders, then you climb up. I want to know what's waiting for us on the other side of the gate."

It took Palinurus' big hands to shove clear a circle. Once a space opened, members of the 10th Squad formed a human pyramid. During the shuffle, a couple of infantrymen lifted the unconscious Centurion Megellus from Alerio's shoulder.

"We'll take care of him, Tesserarius," one assured him.

Then from the other side of the center door, the battering ram connected with the planks of the gate. Thrum! The wood rocked and the men on the ram guided it to the rear for another swing forward. Thrum!

"Tescum. What are we facing?"

From the stack of bodies, the squad leader looked away from the top of the gate door and reported, "There are a few gate minders. Most of their infantry is on the hill to the front. Archers and spearmen on steep hills on both sides."

Thrum!

"Please tell me when we get through," suggested Alerio. "that we can fight them off and open all three gates."

"Corporal Sisera. Have you ever walked away from a fight?" the petite Lance Corporal asked.

Thrum!

"Not since just before I joined the infantry," Alerio replied. He shoved his way into the tightly packed Legionaries calling out. "Optio Gustavi. Optio Gustavi, where are you?"

From behind a gaggle of men, the Sergeant's voice answered, "Tesserarius Sisera. Back here."

Thrum!

After shoving a pair of Legionaries aside, Alerio stuck his head through the gap. Gustavi sat next to the Centurion. Both men had broken off arrow shafts protruding from bandaged wounds.

"Optio. We are short of experience and very soon, it's going to get intense."

"That may be an understatement, Corporal Sisera," the NCO stammered. Obviously, he was hurting and a bit groggy. "We die if we go back and die if we go forward. As you can see, I'm not much good to you."

Thrum!

"You stay seated," Alerio informed the Sergeant. "What I need is a song to inspire the rookies."

"If I today?" asked the Optio.

"Perfect. Count to thirty and start the song," Alerio requested.

Thrum! Crack!

"Make that to fifteen."

266

As if swimming through mud, Alerio needed both arms to part the sea of tightly packed bodies while migrating towards the battering ram. As he progressed, he called to the surrounding infantrymen.

"When we go through, form five ranks in front of the gates," he shouted. "Testudo formation."

Thrum! Crack! Crack!

Near the center of the gate where the men were swinging the ram, he called up, "Lance Corporal Tescum. Any change?"

"They haven't sent forward reinforcements for the gate guards."

"That's an opportunity," Alerio assured the men around him.

Thrum! Crack! Crack! Crack!

A section of the gate fractured, and a few infantrymen sang softly. Almost as if unsure if they should be singing.

If I today, if I today
Don't enter the Fray

Optio Gustavi had started a tune from Legionary training. A song only advanced recruits were allowed to sing. Alerio smiled and joined in with them.

Fail to shoulder my shield and disobey
Duck my orders and pull away

The survivors of the inexperienced first maniple stood straighter and accompanying the full-throated rendition of the song, a light of pride and confidence returned to their eyes.

If I today
My comrades betray

Their funeral fires will blaze away
And I will be damned
For I am a Legion man
Yesterday, Tomorrow, and Today

The planks on the gate below the center locking bar cracked and light streamed through. A spearman jabbed an iron head into the gap and a Legionary with a powerful chop cut the shaft in half. Seeing the strength of the young Lance Corporal, Alerio stepped up behind him.

"Drop your javelins," he directed. "Keep your gladius and stand by."

"I don't understand, Corporal," he questioned.

"What's your name Decanus?"

"Messoris. What am I standing by for?"

The battering ram rocked back then shot forward splintering wood and vibrating the entire door.

If I today, if I today
See it my Optio's way
Stab the javelin and bring on doomsday
Stomp the field where my enemy lay

"We're going to assault the gate," Alerio informed the Lance Corporal.

"I thought we already did that," Messoris protested.

If I today
My orders obey
Barbarians hordes I will slay
And they will be damned
For I am a Legion man
Yesterday, Tomorrow, and Today

On the next collision between the log and the gate, the log won. A section of the wooden planks broke off and fell inward. Alerio shoved the Lance Corporal down, forward, and through the mini doorway. He followed directly behind the Legionary and the two emerged in the midst of the Adrano gate guards.

The sounds of the infantrymen singing on the other side of the gate were muffled.

If I today, if I today

Hear my Centurion say

Alerio bellowed as he swung his shield in front of Messoris. The move cleared the soldiers' spears allowing the young infantryman a moment to collect himself and set his own shield.

Ply your trade their attack is underway

Spinning away from the gate, Alerio slammed his shield into a guard while slashing down on another's arm with the gladius.

Make our enemies wail and pray

If I today

A spear jabbed forward forcing Alerio to cock his head sideways. The move put him off balance and he stepped to the left to maintain his stance. That's when four Adrano gate guards rushed him. Using the shield to cover up, he backpedaled until his back hit what he thought was the gate.

Stab away

To earn my Republic pay

A big, muscular arm dropped over his shoulder and a javelin tip slashed one of the guards. Then six Legionaries leaped forward driving the soldiers back and finally to the ground.

"Can't let you have all the fun, Corporal Sisera," Trax Dircium from 2nd Squad informed him.

And my foes be damned

For I am a Legion man
Yesterday, Tomorrow, and Today

With more Legionaries coming through the opening, the guards were soon lying dead in the street. That's when the spearmen and the archers on the sides of the bowl-shaped area showered down their missiles.

"Testudo formation," Alerio ordered. He rushed through the middle of the newly arrived infantrymen. After searching, he found four of his squad leaders. "Lance Corporals Enitui and Italus, get those gates open. Lance Corporals Frentani and Stulte, organize a defensives shield wall."

In the distance and far down the hill beyond Adrano's defensive walls, trumpets blared. The call signaled the advance of the second maniple. Alerio grabbed the Decanus of 2nd Squad and pulled him close.

"Lance Corporal Dircium. Come with me."

"Where are we going?" asked the squad leader.

"I'm grabbing a contubernium and taking out the oxybeles and the lithobolois on the weapons platform to our left," Alerio informed him. "You are going to do the same to the platform on the right."

"What about their infantry, Corporal?"

"They can't afford to break too many units away from their ranks or our infantry will chew them up when they arrive," Alerio replied. "I'm counting on them staying mostly in formation. Even so, they may attack the gate or send units around and try to stop us on the walls. Anything they do takes their soldiers off the high ground. But I'm not worried about the Adrano infantry. I just don't want another Legionary to die from those mounted weapons."

"Let's go cut some strings," Trax Dircium advised.

Then four lightly armored Legionaries popped through the broken gate.

"Who's in charge?" one asked. Someone pointed to Alerio, and the four skirmishers rushed over to the Tesserarius. "What do you need Corporal?"

"Those spearmen and the archers swept off the defensive walls," Alerio replied without looking. "That will isolate the soldiers on our flanks, and we can stop the spears and arrows."

"Give us a squad of heavy infantrymen then consider it done," the Veles replied before hopping back to the opening where he directed the skirmishers coming through the break.

"That was interesting, Corporal," commented Trax Dircium.

"What?" questioned Alerio.

"He is a Centurion of Velites, and he took orders from you."

"Must be my fine singing voice," Alerio suggested. "I've been told it's captivating."

"I have no comment, but I do feel the urge to go and kill someone," Dircium offered.

"That's the heavy infantry spirit," Alerio assured him.

The squad leader left to round up the 2nd and Alerio went in search of the Legionary with the powerful arm he'd shoved through the gate. He hoped Messoris survived the hurried assault after they were separated.

Chapter 31 – The Walls of Adrano

"Lance Corporal Messoris, collect your squad," Alerio instructed while shaking the shield off his left arm.

The young squad leader from the first maniple looked at the aggressive Tesserarius who had pushed him through the hole in the gate. He wasn't sure he trusted the crazy NCO after the man forced the fight with the gate guards. Especially now that the Corporal exchanged the protection of an infantry shield for a second gladius.

"What are you doing, Corporal?" Messoris inquired.

At the gates, two contuberniums worked at removing the locking bars from the three gateways. To the front, Legionaries fought off soldiers sent to attack the shield wall. Others, not involved with the gates or the defensive line, held shields overhead to block arrows and spears. It worked for the small shafts but many of the spears powered aside the shields and struck within the formation. It's where Corporal Sisera got the second gladius and why the number of their wounded grew with every new wave of thrown spears.

"We are going to clear the walls then remove the mounted weapons on those platforms," Alerio informed him. He nodded to the left although neither man could see through the roof of shields. "I have another squad forming up to do the same on the right."

"I'd rather stay here and defend the gates," Messoris insisted. "I'm needed and it's where the real fight is taking place."

Alerio lowered and twisted his head sideways as if he could see around the bodies pushing and stabbing over the Legionaries' shields wall.

"I believe squads from the 25th Century have that covered. But, while we stand here discussing the matter, the second maniple is about to come up the mountain. Unless we act, they will catch all of the stones and bolts from the mounted weapons."

Age lines attempted to crease the smooth face of Lance Corporal Messoris. He was young and the attempt to appear contemplative while forming a logical argument to resist the NCO failed badly. He opened his mouth to reply but he was drowned out.

Roars came from the edges of the tortoise formation and daylight filtered in from the sides. Two squads charged out of the cluster and attacked up the hills on both sides. The spears and arrows stopped falling on the testudo in the bowl. Instead, the spearmen and archers focused on the Legionaries scrambling up to engage them.

***

Lance Corporals Tescum and Ostrei from the 10th and 1st had talked. Centurion Megellus and Optio Gustavi were out of the fight and Tesserarius Sisera had his hands full organizing the defenses and getting the gates open.

"I'm going to stop those spearmen," Ostrei exclaimed when a man next to him fell to the ground with a shaft protruding from the back of his neck. "I'd rather face the spear that takes my life."

"The 10th will clear the right side," offered Tescum.

"Then the 1st will do our killing on the left," Ostrei stated.

The Decani clamped wrists. One tall and arrogant and the other short and almost frail, the two squad leaders couldn't have been more dissimilar. They locked eyes, nodded goodbye, and went to collect their contuberniums. In their commitment to clearing the hills and stopping the rain of arrows and spears, they were exactly alike. They were heavy infantry squad leaders.

***

"No, not yet. Oh, Gods, we are perfututum," Alerio screamed when he realized the two squads were attacking early. He grabbed Messoris' armor, pulled him in close, and threatened. "Do not argue with me. Good men will die because you hesitated. Get your squad or I will cripple you right here, right now, and find another squad leader."

When Trax Dircium saw Ostrei and 1st Squad break from the cover and scramble up the slope, he also swore.

"2nd Squad, form up," he yelled.

It seemed to take forever but his contubernium finally gathered. Stacking them in two rows, he ordered the squad forward.

They marched out from under the tortoiseshell of shields, up the twisting ramp beside the gate wall, and onto the top of Adrano's defensive wall. There, they faced spearman, archers, and slingers. But as the militiamen soon discovered, Legionaries below the wall and down range were different from Legionaries in an attack formation. One situation presented targets; the other brought infantrymen hunting prey. And the spearmen, archers, and slingers soon realized the lockstep, tight shields, and narrow space between the helmets and top of the shields created an almost impenetrable barrier.

Trax Dircium glanced to his left and his stomach soured. 1st Squad had made it out of the bowl-shaped area and almost to the top of the hill. And, while their javelins had thinned the number of spearmen and archers, there were still enough soldiers to have brought down three of the Legionaries. By attacking early, Horatius Ostrei and

274

his squad drew arrows, bolts, and spears from the soldiers on the wall and the oxybeles. The result was, as the 1st Squad cleared the hill it left the Legionaries exposed to the missiles from the wall and platform.

"Launch," Dircium ordered while drawing back his own javelin.

Eight shafts arched into the sky, tilted over, dropped, and swept archers and slingers from the wall. The spearmen ducked behind their shields and, while they didn't die, the incoming javelins stopped them from launching spears.

2nd Squad marched forward stomping downed soldiers, kneeing others, and stabbing any not laying on the dirt and stone fill of the wall. Dircium looked towards the hill again. Only two Legionaries from the 1st showed signs of life.

"Stay down and get off the hill," Trax Dircium whispered.

But the Legionaries pushed to their feet, both bleeding from arrows wounds, and near misses from spears. They didn't retreat; they surged forward, swinging gladii, and clearing the remaining soldiers from the hill. Then, one took an arrow in the face and the other seemed to leap off the hill when a bolt snatched him from the crest.

The rain of steel and iron on the right side of the testudo ended. Now half the Legionaries defending the gates were safe from enemy spears dropping in among them. But the 1st Squad paid dearly for the relief.

The 2nd squad moved along stabbing, parring, and clearing the wall of defenders. By the time they came abreast of the first weapons platform, Trax Dircium's anger had built, his eyes glowed red, and the veins in his neck throbbed.

"Left pivot section, continue killing the limp mentulas on the wall," he cried out. "Right pivot section, on me. We're going to rip the throats out of every engineer we can find."

All seven Legionaries of the 2nd Squad responded with a roar as did the fifteen skirmishers who joined them. Dircium stepped onto the ramp connecting the wall with the weapons platform and threw down his javelins.

Some things felt better up close and personal. He drew his gladius and stomped across the ramp.

***

Ibis Gustavi, his weight supported on the shoulder of a Legionary, watched as Corporal Sisera followed eight Legionaries out from under the testudo formation. Then, just before they disappeared around the curving ramp, the Tesserarius screamed and jumped in front of the squad's shields.

"You there, gather a squad and help clear the right wall," he ordered grabbing the first Lance Corporal he saw. "Quickly."

Staggering and wincing under the pain from the arrowhead in his shoulder, the Sergeant fought to keep his head clear. Seeing another squad leader, he beckoned him over.

"Take a squad to the left wall and help clear it," he instructed before collapsing.

The Legionary supporting the Optio lowered his weight to the ground.

"What did he want?" inquired the squad leader.

"Pull a contubernium together and help clear the left wall," Private Ottone from 4th Squad told him.

The Velites staged on each side of the gate wall followed the heavy infantry squads up the ramps. Between the skirmishers and the Legionaries, the wall defenders began falling fast. While the militia's commander and General Periander wanted to keep their infantry intact, they couldn't let the city fall around them.

"Companies. We will defend the gates," Periander announced. "Forward to the attack. Remove the Republic forces from the portals."

***

Alerio ducked behind the squad letting them catch the arrows and deflect the spears and pebbles from the slingers. In an orderly fashion, the eight inexperienced Legionaries left the cover of the overhead shields and started up the ramp.

Suddenly, the Corporal screamed before appearing in front of the squad. Without a shield, the Tesserarius ran ahead, charging the defenders on the wall with two gladii. The NCO's action confirmed Lance Corporal Messoris' belief that Corporal Sisera had a death wish.

But it wasn't suicide driving Corporal Sisera.

On the hill beside the entrance to Adrano, Decanus Tescum and his contubernium fought with archers and spearmen. It was a mismatch; the militiamen who launched missiles shouldn't have stood against Legionaries. In fact, they didn't. Most of them died on javelin tips or gladii blades. But, the soldiers on the defensive wall and the oxybeles crew had no targets in the kill zone.

They turned their ranged weapons on the exposed contubernium. And, in a storm of arrows, spears, and bolts, the men of the 10th were plucked off the hilltop. One by one, they fell back and into the embrace of the Goddess Nenia. Only their lifeless bodies made it to the bottom of the hill.

**

Alerio Sisera bent at his waist, dodged a thrown spear, and sprinted forward. A hastily launched arrow bounced off his armored skirt. Another arrow clipped his helmet. The spearman snatched up a second spear. In the face of a charging Legionary, the archers attempted to cock their gastraphetes. Manipulating the belly bows then seating the arrows was drilled into them under controlled conditions. Adding a raging infantryman to the process caused them to fumble a few of the steps. Even so, at the end of arming the crossbow, all they needed to do was release the arrows. The spearman had options, hold and jab, or throw the spear. He must have been the indecisive type because he held the spear but just below his shoulder level.

The gladius blade chopped into the shaft driving the iron head off to the side. Then a hobnailed boot planted flat-footed on the spearman's chest armor. Alerio's weight drove the soldier back on his heels before crashing him onto his back. While stomping the spearman's head with his raised leg, Alerio threw one gladius at an archer and knocked aside the mechanical crossbow with the other blade. As he brought the gladius back, the tip sliced the first archer's neck. A jump landed him in front of the second bowman where Alerio kicked the man's legs out from under him.

Legionaries flowed around the fight and attacked another group of soldiers further along the wall. After Lance Corporal Messoris and his infantrymen passed, a light infantry Veles stopped, reached down, and picked up the gladius.

"That was some fine fighting," he announced while handing Alerio the gladius.

"Do me a favor," Alerio asked as he took the Legion sword. "I need to get to the weapons platform. Kill this cūlus for me."

"It'll be my pleasure, Corporal."

***

Two, ten-man units of militiamen jogged along the wall and stopped near the ramp to the platform with the mounted weapons. They lowered their spears, locked their shields, and settled into a defensive posture.

"Squad halt," Lance Corporal Messoris called, and the eight men and the skirmishers stopped.

"Messoris, what's the holdup?" Alerio demanded while shoving through the ranks.

"As you can see Tesserarius, they've created a hard point at the ramp," the squad leader answered.

"And what are you doing?"

"I am analyzing the situation and weighing the best options, Corporal."

"Did you learn that in Legion training?" Alerio inquired.

"It's important for leaders to preserve their Legionaries," Messoris reported. "A bad decision cost lives."

"I can't argue with the logic," admitted Alerio. "But what did the instructors have to say about standing in a stationary position, down range of a dual bolt ballista?"

"Nothing. No one would do that," the young Lance Corporal offered. "That would be insane."

Alerio raised an arm and indicated the weapons platform with a gladius blade. Two engineers pulled handles on a wheel drawing the thick string back with each spin. Two others shoved the giant crossbow around, so the bolts pointed at a section of the wall. A closer inspection of the oxybele crew revealed they were clearly rotating the weapon around to target the Legionaries.

The realization dawned on the young Lance Corporal. If he meant to, he couldn't have stopped the squad in a better place to have his infantrymen slaughtered.

"Orders, Corporal?" Messoris requested.

"What did your instructors say about the application of force?"

"Direct, violent, and decisive."

"Good," Alerio said. Then, to the squad's puzzlement, the Corporal began to hum. Pausing for a heartbeat, he instructed. "Follow me."

If I today, if I today
See it my Optio's way

Alerio ran straight at the defensive line of shields. His sudden movement left the Legionaries behind for a moment. Then, they charged after the unbalanced NCO.

Stab the javelin and bring on doomsday
Stomp the field where my enemy lay

Three paces from the militia shields, Alerio threw his righthand gladius. It flipped end-over-end towards the face of the soldier on the end of the enemy formation.

If I today

My orders obey

A sidestep, then another, and he came directly at the soldier. Alerio's other gladius rose from an inside guard. The raising blade knocked that soldier's spear up and out of the way. He grabbed the shaft, then hacked the shaft of the militiaman in the second rank moving it out of place. And finally, Alerio's blade struck the adjacent man's spear as the shaft swung over to cover the soldier ducking the thrown gladius.

Barbarians hordes I will slay

Driving with his legs, Alerio shoved the spear shaft into the soldier's face driving him backward. Then the Legionary changed the angle and pushed the soldier off the wall. While the militiaman screamed on the way down, Alerio stabbed the spearman in the second rank.

And they will be damned

For I am a Legion man

The soldiers turned and focused on the single man attacking the end of their lines. He should have already died but that would be remedied shortly. Then, the precise and measured assault by Lance Corporal Messoris' squad reached the soldiers.

The front rank stabbed with their gladii while the second thrust javelins over their shields. On the sides, Velites used their javelins to force the soldiers to remained compacted. It was easier for the heavy infantrymen to kill them in a tight formation.

Yesterday, Tomorrow, and Today

Alerio slipped back between the drop-off of the wall and a Veles. When the clash between the Legion squad and the Adrano unit moved beyond the ramp, he snatched up the other gladius.

"Give me six skirmishers," he said to an NCO.

Armed with the two blades and trailed by six Velites, Corporal Sisera sprinted up the ramp to the weapons platform.

Chapter 32 – Bolts and Home

The four engineers backed away from the oxybele, pulled their swords, and lined up behind four spearmen. Adding to the defenders on the platform, the three engineers from the lithoboloi crossed over to create a third rank.

"Not very formidable," a skirmisher suggested when Alerio and his six men stopped at the edge of the weapons stand.

"I only need one engineer for the oxybele," Alerio informed the Velites. "The rest are a nuisance."

"Launch," the NCO ordered without hesitating. Six javelins on a flat trajectory impelled the four spearmen and two of the lithoboloi engineers in the back rank. "Attack."

***

"Get up," Alerio ordered the surviving engineer.

The Greek's legs folded under him when the Legionary jerked the engineer to his feet. After being shaken until his arms and head wobbled, he managed to lock his knees and plant his feet.

"I don't want to die," the Greek stammered.

"Good. An instinct for self-preservation is a strong motivator," exclaimed Alerio. Directing the man's attention by turning him towards the back of the gate wall, the Corporal inquired. "Can you put bolts into the bowl? I mean without hitting the Legionaries."

"This is a line-of-sight weapon, not an onager. If you can't see what's below the hill, I can't hit it."

"In that case you are no help to me," Corporal Sisera informed the man while drawing back a gladius.

The Greek's eyes got big, he started to shake, then he raised both hands in the air and waved them around.

"Wait, wait," he pleaded. "I can't shoot around corners or down into a bowl. But I can see General Periander."

"And if you can see the target, you can hit it?"

"Yes. And these bolts will cut through his fancy armor like a knife through a well-cooked sea bass," announced the engineer.

"Where are you from?"

"Syracuse, Centurion."

"Not an officer," Alerio corrected. "But I'll promise you this, engineer. If you take the General off his feet with a bolt, you will see Syracuse again."

"And if I miss?" questioned the Syracusan.

"I won't," Alerio informed him. To punctuate the statement, Alerio flipped the gladii into the air where they crossed over his head. He caught both as they spun downwards. "You have one launch. And then, I've got to get back to the shield wall."

Roars and screams reached them from the second weapons platform. Glancing over, all Alerio and the engineer could make out were heavy and light Legion infantrymen hacking on the oxybele and lithoboloi. The engineers and defenders for the mounted weapons were sprawled on the planks.

"There is one possible fate for you," Alerio suggested.

The Syracusan didn't reply. Instead, he put his shoulder against the stock and began rotating the weapon. When the bolts faced towards the back of the entrance bowl, he stepped behind it and sighted down the grooves. Three times he walked to a side and nudged the stock.

"You'll allow me to go to Syracuse?"

"Yes. You'll be free to go home."

"In that case," the engineer said while reaching for a lever.

Yanking the wooden arm disengaged the small hooks holding the sinew and hair string under tension. Released, it snapped up the stock driving the bolts along the grooves so fast it was difficult to follow with the eye. They rose slightly and made a gentle arch. One of the shaped iron projectiles struck an Adrano staff officer in the head. Because of the fountain of splashing red, Alerio missed the impact of the second bolt.

Centuripe General Periander crunched up around his midsection. Arms and shoulders tucked, and his knees were drawn up towards his chest. Resembling a bug laying on its back, he struggled for a few heartbeats.

"Goddess Nenia release his soul and allow him peace," Alerio prayed.

"I thought you would hate General Periander?" the engineer questioned. "Yet you pray for a quick death."

"He was a man and a leader of soldiers," Alerio replied. "That thing, suffering on the road is merely a broken body waiting for death. There is nothing left to hate."

"You are a man who knows death," offered the Syracusan.

"All too well, engineer," Alerio replied. Then, he instructed one of the skirmishers. "Veles. Take this man to the gate and shove him out. After that, the living or dying is his responsibility."

"You do have an interesting relationship with death, Legionary."

But the engineer talked to empty air. Corporal Sisera was already turning off the ramp and sprinting down the wall.

***

The sounds of shields clashing carried from the bowl area at the gates. Alerio reached the down ramp in full stride, slid on the stones to change direction, and bounced off the walls of the curved ramp. He reached the bottom and faced chaos.

Chaos in a Legion attack line was reserved for the shield wall. To have Legionaries standing in the rear with no direction or goal displayed a lack of leadership. Plus, wounded, and exhausted men sat behind those backing up the first two ranks.

"Give me a reserve column here, here, and here," he directed by grabbing Legionaries and shoving them into lines. They would wait there, shuffle forward, and eventually reach the second and finally the front rank. "Find a line and get in it."

Over the shields, Alerio noted the field of soldiers flowing down the street and right up to the Legion shields. An infantryman stumbled back holding a bleeding arm.

"Give me four men to clear the rear and treat the injured," Alerio called out. He didn't wait for volunteers; he corralled the four closest Legionaries. "You are medical. Clear this area and stage the wounded and dead off to the side."

Then he ran to the other side of the thin Legion formation and organized those men.

"Rotate, rotate," Alerio bellowed. His objective was to get fresh men in the front two ranks. But the sloppy exchange of personnel opened gaps that allowed Adrano spears to injure two more men. The entire front stepped back to reset giving ground to the troops of Adrano. Looking around, he shouted. "Lance Corporal Frentani, Lance Corporal Stulte. On me."

The squad leaders came from the sloppy lines of men waiting to move up. Both were sweat soaked and displayed fresh blood spatter.

"Ten more steps and we'll be pushed out of the gates," Alerio informed them.

"We know, Corporal," Frentani replied. "But this is the first maniple. They don't have the experience to hold the line properly."

"Two months ago, they were on their family's farms digging up stumps," Stulte added. "It might be advisable to retreat through the gates instead of defending them."

A vision of the 10th Squad being swept off the hill crossed Alerio's mind, and he ground his teeth.

"We've paid too high a price for this piece of real estate," he explained. "Besides, the second maniple will need access to the city."

"When they get here," Frentani sneered. "If they ever get here."

"You didn't call us together to sacrifice words to the gods, Tesserarius," Stulte suggested. "Is there a plan besides dying gloriously for the Republic?"

"Pull your contuberniums out of the lines," Alerio instructed. "Position each man as a commander of a column. You two pick a side and act like NCOs."

"You expect this herd to perform as a Century?" Frentani questioned.

"We're going to take advantage of their youth," Alerio described. "Quick rotations so the front ranks can do damage, then they can rest. Make sure our line commanders know about the fast exchanges."

"Have you looked at the number of infantrymen the Adrano militia has brought to the party?" inquired Stulte.

"Rapid changes, Lance Corporals. We'll wear them down for the second maniple."

Chapter 33 - The Price of Resistance

"Rotate," Alerio called out.

His order was picked up by the Lance Corporals and passed on to the line commanders. Those experienced Legionaries physically grabbed the men on the shield wall and yanked them back, while pushing the second rank forward. This rude change had happened so often, the men on the front ranks weren't surprised. Only relieved to get off the battle line where they fought with all of their might.

While Corporal Sisera rotated men off the front to keep rested infantrymen defending against the mass of soldiers, he was dealing with a small number of Legionaries. All of them had been to the front and back many times. He wasn't sure if they could survive even a few more rotations.

"Sisera, right?" a voice behind Alerio asked.

"Yes, Senior Centurion," he replied once he turned to see who stood behind him.

"This is going to be difficult, Corporal."

"What's going to be difficult, sir?"

"Extracting your lads and getting the second maniple into the fight," the Senior Centurion answered. He glanced back, eyed the gate wall, looked to the front, and added. "Without losing ground and having to fight to retake the gates."

"Lance Corporal Frentani. Lance Corporal Stulte. Clear the lanes, stand by to disengage," Alerio called out. Along the lines of the first maniple, the Legionaries from the 25th pushed and shoved men causing them to shift and tighten the columns. Spaces opened between the lines for double rows of second maniple infantrymen. Once the formation finished adjusting, Alerio advised. "Standing by, sir."

The Senior Centurion leaned forward as if to check his eyesight. Then he spun on his heels and addressed three waiting Centurions.

"Form staggered columns and get them inserted," Edidi ordered. "I want the first maniple off that shield wall in fifteen, fourteen, thirteen…"

By the count of eleven, NCOs were directing Legionaries forward. At the count of eight, men from the first maniple were elbowed back leaving only the first two ranks fighting the Adrano forces.

"You started this, Corporal Sisera," Edidi suggested. "Finish it."

"Thank you, Senior Centurion," Alerio acknowledged before bellowing. "Frentani. Stulte. We are relieved, pull our ranks."

The line commanders from the 25th Century reached out with both arms, grabbed the infantrymen from the first and second ranks, and snatched them back and away from the enemy spears. As rapidly as they were extracted, the shields of the second maniple snapped forward.

Rather than battling against exhausted, inexperienced infantrymen, the soldiers found themselves face to face with men who understood bloody combat and knew the dangers of losing the fight. And the Legionaries of the second maniple had no intention of failing to win this battle.

"Stand by," a Centurion shouted. His words were picked up by NCOs, squad leaders, and pivot men. "Step back. Advance, advance, advance," he bellowed.

While the shock of the Legion shields and deadly thrusts by gladii devastated the front rank of Adrano soldiers, Alerio collected the survivors of the 25th Century. Leading them, he wove between the fresh Legionaries flowing through the three gates.

"Sir. The 25th Century has been relieved," Alerio informed Centurion Megellus.

"Stand easy, Corporal Sisera," the infantry officer replied. He shifted his position on the hill, gasped from the pain of the arrow shaft in his thigh, and indicated a bare spot. "Have a seat Tesserarius. You and the men have earned a rest."

"Sir. With your permission, I'll go check on our wounded and…," Alerio didn't finish.

Neither man said the other part of the Corporal's request. There would be time later to count, record, bury, and mourn their dead. But Alerio had a relationship with the Goddess of Death and felt it was his responsibility to assure his men passed easily on their journey to the river Styx. The officer didn't know about Alerio's peculiar personal deity, he simply assumed the Tesserarius wanted to get a start on his accounting duties.

"Granted."

***

Elements of the second maniple controlled the hills on both sides while in the center the Legion shields, javelins, and gladii drove the Adrano troops to the base of the slope. Behind the advancing Legionaries, the veterans of the third maniple stepped through the portals, split apart, and marched up the ramps.

While the veteran infantrymen took control of the city's defensive walls, the second forced the soldiers back and towards the commercial district of the city. Having exchanged the Legion shield for a waterskin and a piece of cloth, Corporal Sisera scrambled up the hillside. At the top, he approached the bodies of the 10th Squad.

Arrows pierced Lance Corporal Tescum's legs and arms. But the shaft that took his life bisected his throat and split his windpipe. The sticky red pool around him showed he fell immediately while drowning in his own blood. Beside him, but facing away, was Private Palinurus. Except, the iron bolt from an oxybele must have impacted the Legionary's chest with enough force to carry the big man off the hill. Yet, in his final position, Palinurus appeared to be defending Tescum's right side. It seemed, even in death, the big infantryman kept his word.

Alerio rolled both men onto their backs and began chanting while washing their faces. Although the Goddess Nenia had already visited them, the Corporal wanted to be sure the other Gods recognized the nobility and bravery of his men. Assuring they entered the Elysian Fields was the least he could do for these heroes of Adrano.

**

The leading edge of the 1st Century's cordon collapsed while coming through the main portal. Once on the backside of the gates, they billowed out and reformed. In the center of the Century, 1st Centurion Irrisus stepped beyond the gate wall, ran his eyes expectedly over the wounded, dead, and the backs of the fighting ranks. Seeing it was clear of anyone, not a Legionary, he raised an arm and signaled for the command staff to enter Adrano.

"We're pursuing the Adrano militia and infantry into the center of the city," one of four infantry officers reported. Another asked. "Orders, Senior Centurion."

"There's a good question for you," commented Edidi. Turning to the battle commander, he inquired. "You'll soon have the city, sir. What do you want to do with it?"

Ruscus looked at the dead and wounded Legionaries on the hills. The sight hurt his heart. Then he spied an officer among the infantrymen and walked over.

"You look familiar. What's your name?"

"Centurion Fenoris Megellus, 25th Century of the Crassus Legion North," the officer replied. Then the infantry officer clamped his teeth together against the pain, pushed to his feet, saluted, and announced. "I stand for the lost men of the 25th. Colonel, the 25th Century proudly presents the city of Adrano to you."

Ruscus recognized the Centurion as the one Ambassador Sergius called incompetent, disorganized, and cowardly. His sitting wounded in the midst of the gate defenders disproved all of those descriptions. But there was another term the battle commander would use to replace them, shrewd.

By proclaiming victory of the city and awarding it to the Colonel, Megellus had claimed monetary bonuses from the loot and spoils including the sale of slaves.

"Centurion Megellus. I have two questions for you," Ruscus explained. "What should I do with Adrano?"

"Make an example of the city, sir. We've paid too high a price for this property."

"Very good," Ruscus declared. "Senior Centurion?"

"Sir, Mesalla Legion East is standing by," Edidi replied.

"We will never return and shed Republic blood on these stones again," the Colonel instructed. "Level this hovel."

"Senior Tribune, we've received demolition orders from the battle commander," Edidi informed Istac. "Have reserve units prepare pens to guard the slaves."

While the senior advisors talked, Colonel Ruscus turned back to the infantry officer from the 25th Century.

"The other question," remarked the battle commander. "Who receives the Phalerae?"

Megellus twisted his head around, looked at the top of the hill, and called to a man kneeling beside a body.

"Corporal Sisera. Do you get the Phalerae for breaching the gate first?"

The Legion NCO glanced up from washing the face of a dead Legionary.

"No, sir," Alerio replied. "That medal goes to Lance Corporal Messoris of the first maniple. He was first into the city."

For the remainder of his time in the Legion, Lance Corporal Messoris would have a gold sculpted disk displayed on his breastplate during parades and inspections. It was there so everyone knew of the man's bravery for being the first to breach the city's defenses. Even if he protested every time that a Corporal, he didn't know, pushed him through a hole in the gate.

"1st Centurion Irrisus. Find me Decanus Messoris. And see if you can find him a slot in the second maniple. A man that brave shouldn't be considered inexperienced or unbloodied," Colonel Ruscus ordered as he walked away from Megellus. Then the battle commander stopped and faced back towards the infantry officer. "You will receive the gold crown for taking and holding the gate Centurion. And a second purse to go with the coins from the Ambassador."

"Sir, what coins from the Ambassador."

"Your Century's share of the tribute for saving the diplomatic mission."

"Colonel, we didn't receive anything from Ambassador Sergius," Megellus informed him. "Except abuse."

***

Two days later, the surviving soldiers were naked and in pens. The surviving citizens of Adrano were prodded out of other cages and headed out of the city to be sold. Teams of Legionaries pried apart brick walls while others pushed down granite columns. Once the building materials hit the ground, infantrymen raised dust by hammering them into small pieces.

Wagons had transported the wounded Legionaries to the Legion camp beside the Simeto river. And the 25th Crassus Century, in honor of their performance at the gate, was excused from all duties. But there wasn't joy in the air. A dark feeling hung low to the ground around the Century's area because five of the tents had only one or two Legionaries to represent the contuberniums.

High above the valley and the Legion camp, Colonel Ruscus rode slowly in order to ease the stress on his guard detail.

***

In Centuripe, the 1st Century reached the top road and soon jogged into the main barracks. From the center of the formation, the battle commander dismounted, marched across the courtyard, and entered the building.

"Ambassador Sergius. We will have words. Everyone else, clear the room," Ruscus ordered from the door of the meeting chamber.

He marched into the room pointing at civilians who didn't move fast enough.

"Clear this room. Or I will have you removed," he directed. Staring at the diplomat's staff, he informed them. "I have a punishment post. If you want to visit it, remain in this room."

"Excuse me, Ruscus. But you are interrupting an important meeting," Sergius complained. "I don't see the necessity in…"

"1st Centurion Irrisus. I am going to look into Octavius Sergius' soul," declared the Colonel. "When I look back, if anyone is still in this room, break their legs. They can crawl over the threshold."

"Yes, sir," Irrisus replied while drawing his gladius.

The five Latian staff members escorted the civilians out of the room. Irrisus and the Legionary guards followed, leaving only the two men in the chamber. As the battle commander for a Legion, Ruscus didn't bother looking back. He knew his orders were obeyed.

"Now that you've ruined my morning, Ruscus," Ambassador Sergius said as a reprimand. "What can I do for you?"

"It's Colonel Ruscus of Mesalla Legion East. It would behoove you to remember that," Ruscus warned. "You will use my title, and follow my instructions, or I will set my Legionaries loose and they will turn the hills of Centuripe into a mountain of rubble."

"Surely, you wouldn't," Sergius ceased talking. He grew nervous under the gaze of the Colonel's unblinking eyes. They seemed to be looking deep into his. Changing tone and tactics, the Ambassador inquired. "What do you want me to do?"

"You owe the 25th Century Crassus a monetary bonus," the battle commander explained.

"There will be no tribute payments to the Republic. Their Corporal destroyed thousands of Kentoripa vases," replied the Ambassador. "You see Colonel Ruscus, there are no tribute coins to spread around as bonuses."

"That's not my problem. That's your issue as is finding coins for the 25th," Ruscus advised. "If you don't have the ready cash, a note drawn on a temple in the

Capital will suffice. And make it a primary God's temple. Their patron is Senator Spurius Maximus and you do not want the old General to travel to a lesser temple to cash in the chit."

***

A week later, Adrano and its defensive walls were reduced to a collection of broken stones and uninhabited dirt streets. At the Legion camp, sacrificial meat rotated on spits and the aroma teased the men standing in formation with their Centuries.

"Legion, stand by," called out Senior Tribune Istac.

Trumpets blared to accent his voice. His words were picked up by Tribunes and infantry officers. Without the distraction of combat, the infantrymen, weapons engineers, cavalrymen, supply men, and animal handlers heard the calls and stopped talking and shuffling around.

A rousing cheer greeted Colonel Ruscus when he rode from the command tents. Approaching a wooden platform built for the occasion, the battle commander brought his horse to the rear of the structure. Dismounting, he climbed the stairs and stood looking sternly at the Legion. Finally, the cheering died down.

"Mesalla Legion East. Are your Century funds full?" he boomed.

A roar of approval for the coins he distributed from the sale of Adrano goods rose from the Legion. It crashed over the battle commander in waves. He waited for the adoration to settle.

"Our victory was complete but came with a terrible loss of life and horrible injuries to your fellow Legionaries," he called out. "Of all the Centuries who suffered, one took the brunt and will have to hold the majority of remembrances. Centurion Fenoris Megellus and the 25th Century Crassus lead the charge, opened the gate, and held it. Along with squads from our first maniple, they upheld the highest traditions of the Legion. For his leadership abilities, I am awarding the gold crown to Centurion Megellus."

Adding to the praise of the infantry officer, all the Centuries of infantrymen called out his name.

"Congratulations, sir," Optio Gustavi offered. "You might not want to keep the Colonel waiting."

Fenoris Megellus remained unmoving in front of the 25th along with the Optio and the Tesserarius.

"That is your clue to approach the reviewing platform, sir," Alerio coached. "Is it your leg? We can get you a horse."

At the mention of the arrow wound, Megellus reached down, felt the indention, and the rough scab over the stitches. The memory of pain, fever, and immobility broke his hesitation. He marched to the platform with a slight limp.

Senior Centurion Edidi met him and escorted the infantry officer up the steps.

"Centurion. For breaching the gates and holding the ground until relieved, I present you with the gold crown," Ruscus announced loudly. He placed a band of braided gold on the officer's head. While the Legionaries screamed their approval, the battle commander leaned in and handed Megellus a pouch and a piece of parchment. "A bonus from me for your Century. And a letter of credit from Ambassador Sergius drawn on the Temple of Mercury."

"I don't understand, sir. From the Ambassador?"

"It's his way of making amends," explained Colonel Ruscus.

Centurion Megellus saluted and marched back to the 25th. The Colonel gave a short speech and ended it by calling for Lance Corporal Messoris to come forward and receive his gold Phalerae. As expected, the first maniple exploded in shouting with the prospect of one of their own being honored.

While waiting for the young Decanus to arrive at the platform, Colonel Ruscus had a few moments to reflect. The chit for the 25th was a way for the Ambassador to atone for his mistreatment of the Century and their Centurion. And the extra coins from the Colonel served the same purpose.

**

"Tesserarius. Take the coins and this parchment. It's a draft for funds from the Ambassador," Megellus explained. "It should be more than enough to cover the funeral costs for the priests and the ceremonies."

"This will be more than enough, sir," Alerio replied. "With thirty-five remembrances, our share of Adrano has been seriously depleted. This will refill our fund's chest and leave us extra. The bonuses are a fitting reward."

"I understand but we didn't come to Centuripe to get rich," the infantry officer said. "We came for a mission and now we're reaping the rewards."

"You're correct, sir. It's just…"

"Just what Corporal?"

"It's sad, sir, that the debt of appreciation is being repaid to so few of us."

Act 8

Chapter 34 – Wayward Hero

"Enna is a toothache. Shaped like a massive molar. The city has cliffs all around as slick as a tooth's side," the Optio for the 24th Century described. "They sent us there to take the city and keep the Qart Hadasht mercenaries from coming around it."

"That's why you weren't at Centuripe when we took the barracks?" guessed Optio Gustavi.

"We landed at Catania and the Senior Tribunes were afraid Qart Hadasht mercenaries would cut across Sicilia and attack the Legions," the NCO informed Gustavi. "We were the first to land, so we drew the Enna assignment. They sent Mesalla Legion East after you when they landed. We chopped wood and did nature patrols where we frightened forest creatures. At least you saw action and earned bonuses."

Gustavi peered over his shoulder at the forty-five Legionaries of the 25th Century. Some of them were still favoring wounds. They were the lucky ones. Thirty-five of those who marched out to save the Ambassador were in Hades celebrating in the Fields of Elysium. If a person was a believer. Non-believers would say the thirty-five were buried in graves above the Simeto River.

"I'd trade back the bonuses for my Legionaries," Gustavi mentioned.

The other Sergeant glanced back at the almost half sized Century. He swallowed a lump of embarrassment.

"I didn't think," he apologized.

"Neither did the Colonel of Mesalla Legion East."

***

The Crassus Legion North continued its marched south towards Syracuse. NCOs and a few Legionaries left their Centuries and went to visit with friends in other units. The shuffling was ignored as long as an Optio or Tesserarius remained with the Century as well as most of the Legionaries.

If was different for the Centurions. They were expected to go and consult with the Senior Centurion during the march. All the infantry officers made the daily trek to the front of the column during the trek.

"Centurion Megellus. I haven't seen you for two days," remarked Publius from the back of his horse. "Don't you like me anymore?"

"I like you just fine, Senior Centurion," Fenoris Megellus responded.

"Then why haven't you come to see me?"

"You are up there at the head of the column," Megellus replied. "I'm back here with a half Century and a sore leg. And as you and Senior Tribune Nictavi pointed out, a half Century of misfits lead by an incompetent isn't good for anything except guarding the wagons."

"You know he said that before seeing the gold crown warrant," Publius explained. "Or reading the revised reports from Colonel Ruscus."

***

Rather than wear the actual gold braided crown, the gold crown award was displayed as a medal on the Centurion's chest armor during parades and inspections. On the morning the 25th caught up with the Legion, Megellus had pushed himself until he suffered cramps in his thigh and staggered from another bout of fever.

Reluctantly, he allowed his NCOs to convince him to ride in one of the wagons. Further reducing his appearance as a top line Legion officer, an early morning rain created muddy conditions and he was covered in splatters of drying dirt.

Adding to the infantry officer's misfortune, the Century's caravan converged with the head of the Legion's main column. Not only was the Centurion dirty and recovering in a wagon, but the reports of the successful missions were in sealed parchments and the award for holding the gate resided in Megellus' personal belongings.

A cavalry patrol spotted the caravan and alerted the staff officers riding near the front of the Legion.

"I'm bored," Nictavi announced. "Come on Senior Centurion, let's go see for ourselves."

Three Greek wagons coming from a river valley certainly deserved to be investigated. Publius kneed his horse and the Legion's two senior advisers followed the mounted Legionaries.

"Isn't that your Centurion Megellus wobbling around in the wagon?" Nictavi observed. "He appears to be drunk."

"He is," Publius admitted. "And there seems to be only about half the correct number of Legionaries for a Century."

They trotted between the mounts of the cavalry and reined in beside the first wagon.

"Centurion Megellus. What is the meaning of this?" demanded Publius.

"Senior Centurion, 25th Century Crassus reporting in," Megellus stated. Then he remembered the reports and bent to untie a waterproof pouch. Suddenly his head throbbed, his vision blurred, and he fell onto the packs stored in the bed of the wagon.

"He's drunk, disheveled, and sleeping during a march," Senior Tribune Nictavi said. "If you want my advice, I'd say the only place for a half Century of misfits under the command of an incompetent officer is in the back, way in the back."

"An excellent idea," Publius declared. "Fall in behind the pack animals as the Legion's rear guard. Relieve the current Century and have your officer join me when he sobers up."

"Sir, Centurion Megellus isn't..."

"Optio. Do not pour scented water over a pile of merda and tell me it's a flower," the Senior Centurion scolded. "You have your orders, follow them. If you are able."

Gustavi's face flushed red, and he stammered. The delay in speaking saved his career and probably his life. Senior Centurions controlled the punishment post and the wood used for crosses.

***

The column continued to march southward with Publius restraining his horse to keep the animal walking beside the 25th Century. The Senior Centurion fixed the infantry officer with a steady gaze and Centurion Megellus clinched his teeth and set his jaw. Moments of silence followed the 'I like you fine' exchange. Finally, Fenoris Megellus spoke up.

"I am medically unfit to march to the head of the column. As are half my Century due to injuries suffered in saving the ungrateful Ambassador," Megellus announced. "And in capturing the city of Adrano."

Senior Centurion Publius had a problem. Due to his and Senior Tribune Nictavi's hasty judgment of an ill Centurion and the conclusion that an incompetent officer had allowed another Legion to appropriate his men, they had insulted Megellus.

Not just insulted but, had ordered the wounded and grieving Century to guard the wagons and animals. For two days, before Corporal Sisera delivered the messages, the men of the 25th had marched through the leavings of horses, ponies, mules, sheep, and goats.

When Coronel Bacaris saw the letters from his old friend Colonel Ruscus, the Legion's battle commander exploded in delight. Then when he read about one of his Centuries completing two major operations and their infantry officer earning a gold crown, he demanded to meet the Centurion.

"Nictavi. We've been sitting on our backsides the entire time we've been in Sicilia," Bacaris explained while waving the parchment around. "Our infantrymen have had no chance for glory. Now an opportunity has fallen into my lap. I have a real hero to show off to the Legion."

"Who would that be, Coronel?" the Senior Tribune inquired.

"Let me see," Bacaris said as he read the missive again. "A Centurion by the name of Fenoris Megellus. It mentions he and half his Century were wounded or killed. I imagine Publius has our hero and his men riding in the medical wagons."

"I imagine so," Nictavi stuttered. "Orders, sir."

"Bring Centurion Megellus up here so I can meet him," the battle commander instructed. "Or, if his wounds are too severe, I'll ride back to medical."

"I'm sure he's able to ride, Coronel," Nictavi lied. He had no idea of the extent of the Centurion's injuries. "I'll go find him and have him present himself to you, Colonel."

The Senior Tribune nudged his mount into motion and the animal trotted down the column. Once out of the battle commander's sight, he kicked the horse into a gallop. He needed to speak with the Senior Centurion as soon as possible.

"Publius. Where is Centurion Megellus and the 25th?" Nictavi asked as he reined up hard beside the senior infantry officer.

"Pulling drag and doing the merda two-step," he answered. "Just where we ordered them to go two days ago."

"Do not ask questions right now," pleaded the Senior Tribune. "Get back there. Clean Megellus up and dressed in presentable attire. I'll bring a horse for him."

"Hold on Nictavi. What are you going on about?"

"Our Colonel wants to meet the hero of Adrano."

"Who?"

"Centurion Fenoris Megellus, of the 25th Century, Crassus Legion North," the Senior Tribune blurted out. "and his battle commander, one Colonel Bacaris, wants to meet the hero, now. Is that clear enough?"

"Oh, great Coalemus," Publius declared upon realizing his mistake.

"You are not alone," Nictavi assured the Senior Centurion. "It seems we have both been worshiping at the altar of the God of Stupid."

***

"It's a pleasure to meet you, Centurion," Colonel Bacaris said in greeting.

"Sir, I can truthfully say the same," Megellus replied.

His horse, being part of the Tribune's stock and accustomed to being near its herd mates, stopped beside the battle commanders. The infantry officer and the Colonel's knees were almost touching. Nictavi would have preferred more space so he could hear their conversation better and maybe intercede if Megellus started to tell the Colonel the truth.

"I didn't know what to make of Ambassadors Sergius' earlier letters."

"Sir, not to be indelicate, but the Ambassador is not a fan of the Legion," Megellus commented.

"I realized that after receiving Colonel Ruscus' reports," Bacaris explained. "How is medical treating you and your infantrymen?"

It was subtle but both Nictavi and Publius sucked in air and held their breaths.

"Truthfully, sir, the doctors have been helpful," Megellus lied. "But we need to reach the marching camp so my men can properly heal."

Nictavi and Publius exhaled softly, and the tension faded from their necks.

"I know it's hard to convalesce on the march," commented the battle commander. "Once we're in camp, I want to hold an officer's feast and have you talk about your experiences at Centuripe and Adrano. In the meanwhile, let me know if you need anything."

"I will, Colonel, and thank you."

On the way back to the 25th, Megellus turned his eyes towards the Senior Centurion.

"I assume now I can move my Century to their rightful place in the march," he growled. "And have my men seen by a doctor and not a field medic?"

"Yes, of course," Publius assured him.

***

The Senior Centurion walked his horse beside the marching column and tried to forget the last few days. Again, he attempted to understand the Centurion.

"I would appreciate it if the hero of Adrano rode up and talked to me every day," Publius explained. "You once were a scheming foul up. Now I'm not sure what you are."

"Senior Centurion, I am an officer who watched almost half my men die in combat," Megellus stated. "When you bury that many fine Legionaries, you realize that eating merda from staff officers isn't worth it for yourself."

"What are you saying?"

"If you want me to attend officer's meetings and smile at the staff officers, I need extra rations for my Century," Fenoris Megellus replied.

"The Colonel has been up my cūlus about not seeing you," confessed Publius. "And all this time all you wanted was additional food?"

"My lads are healing and need the extra rations," the infantry officer informed the Senior Centurion. "It was a nightmare on the slopes of Adrano. And worse once we

306

breached the gates. Food is the least I owe my Legionaries."

"You will have the additional rations."

"And you will have the hero of Adrano."

Chapter 35 – Seize Siege

There were ten squad tents, an NCOs' tent, and an officer's tent. From the streets bordering the Century's area, it appeared to be a normal encampment. Not until the messenger walked down the center, did the reality come to him. Half the tents were empty or were occupied by a couple of men. Mostly, the knowledge came from the lack of noise. In other camps, eighty infantrymen made a lot of noise. In the area of the 25th Century, muted would best describe the mode.

"Centurion Megellus. Consul/General Otacilius Crassus requests your attendance for a conference in Syracuse," the young Tribune announced.

He spoke to the backs of three men who were bent over a drawing. When three heads looked around and three pairs of hard eyes locked on him, the young nobleman felt a chill flash through his body.

"I'm Centurion Megellus. When?"

"You are further directed to bring an aide. The orders specify, an infantryman of your choosing."

"When?" Fenoris demanded.

"Sunrise, at the number three gate," the young staff officer answered. "Do you require directions, Centurion?"

One of the men extended a finger and placed it on the drawing.

"No, Tribune. I will be there at dawn," Megellus assured him. Then he returned to the map of Syracuse's defensive wall and studied it. "Corporal Sisera. You will attend me at the meeting. Afterward, I want a complete accounting of their defensives on the other side of the wall."

"Yes, sir," Alerio acknowledged.

"It could be a trap, sir," Optio Gustavi suggested.

"Another reason to take Sisera," advised the officer. "Tesserarius. Before the Syracusans capture the General and his staff, search for an escape route."

"Yes, sir. I can do that," Alerio responded. "There's a swamp on the northwest side of the city. If we can make that, we can hide until dark."

"Corporal Sisera, I was joking," the Centurion offered.

"I wasn't, sir."

The messenger backed away while the intense officer and his serious NCOs went back to analyzing the city's defensive wall.

***

In the distance, four men stood around a campfire. While the firelight didn't travel far, it did illuminate the pebbled surface of a road. Once the eyes picked the road out of the darkness, they readily followed the surface to where it vanished under the planks of a gate.

"We're not the first to arrive," Alerio pointed out.

"I can see that," Megellus replied. "Are aides supposed to offer opinions?"

"This one does, sir."

"That's fine when we're alone. But follow the lead of the others when we're with the General."

Before they reached the campfire, the crunch of hobnailed boots on pebbles alerted the four men. The two aids separated and took up defensive positions on either side of the fire.

"Senior Tribune, good morning, sir," Megellus greeted the only face he could make out in the flickering light.

"Centurion Fenoris Megellus, may I introduce Consul/General Otacilius Crassus," Nictavi said with a salute to the man beside him.

"Good day, General," Megellus offered. "If I may ask, why am I here, sir?"

"After reading the reports from Adrano and speaking to Colonel Bacaris, I decided I wanted your opinion of the Syracusan defenses," Otacilius Crassus replied.

Megellus laughed then attempted to cover his mouth to stifle the chuckles.

"Is something funny, Centurion?" questioned Nictavi.

"I apologize to you General and to you Senior Tribune. It's just that I brought Corporal Sisera along to study the defenses," Fenoris informed them. "I've been teaching him map drawing. He's coming along nicely with his scale, perception, and shading."

"Are you an artist then?" inquired General Crassus.

Megellus drew back his shoulders and puffed out his chest.

"I sir, am a Legion officer. The proud Centurion of 25th Century," Fenoris answered. "Nothing more and nothing less, General."

"Good. I look forward to seeing your Corporal's drawing," Crassus commented.

A board banged on the far side of the gate before it swung open. Torches lined the road from inside the gate to a large tent. A uniformed man marched between the lights and stopped at the portal.

"I am Captain Lith, commander of the King's guard," the man standing in the shadows stated. "Representatives of the Republic, follow me."

He performed a crisp turnabout and marched away.

"Into the hands of Adiona," offered a familiar voice.

"And so, we send our prayers to the Goddess of Safe Returns," Megellus added. "Good morning, 1st Centurion."

"For now, I am simply the aide for General Crassus," Lichenis advised. "You might remember Centurion Quadantenus from the 8th Century. He is the acting aide for the Senior Tribune."

"I recall hearing from my Century about an unpleasant evening with Centurion Quadantenus' men."

"I hope you'll let bygones be bygones," the infantry officer from the 8th Century recommended.

"Gentlemen, let's not keep the King waiting," Crassus suggested as he began strolling towards the gate.

The Senior Tribune fell in beside the General, Lichenis and Quadantenus moved up close to them leaving Centurion Megellus and Alerio bringing up the rear. Once the delegation cleared the gateway, the door slammed shut and the locking braces dropped into place.

"Your thoughts, Corporal," Fenoris inquired in a low voice.

"This can only go one of two ways, sir," Alerio whispered. "There are too many soldiers staged in the dark for other choices."

"What ways?"

"Talk or die," Alerio offered.

***

Captain Lith waited in front of the tent flaps for a large cloth structure. When General Crassus reached the entrance, the flaps were thrown back to reveal a banquet on a long table.

Alerio peered between the senior men's shoulders.

"Eat. I hadn't thought of food before dying," he mumbled. "At least we won't go hungry."

"Corporal Sisera, shut up," Fenoris hissed.

"Centurion Megellus. If you can't control your aide, maybe it's best if he waits outside," Nictavi instructed. "These are serious negotiations. I will not have them thrown off course by a mere Corporal."

"That's fine with me sirs," Alerio offered. "I don't care much for fancy talk. But do you think I can have a taste of lamb before I'm ousted?"

"Keep your mouth closed, Tesserarius," pleaded his officer.

"Can I have just a few pieces of meat before I'm exiled?" Alerio asked.

"That does it," growled the Senior Tribune. "Corporal Sisera, you will remain outside, and no food will be sent to you. Move aside."

"I apologize for my aide's behavior, sir," offered Megellus.

Alerio stepped to the side while the delegation continued into the tent. Delicious aromas drifted out before the tent flaps closed.

"Captain Lith. Would your soldiers have any camp stew available?" inquired Alerio. "I seem to have missed breakfast."

"You are an undisciplined oaf with the manners of a goat," the Syracusan Captain stated. "Your officers want you hungry. Then so shall it be."

Alerio leaned against the fabric of the tent and grinned.

"Do you want me to just stand here?"

The Captain of the King's guard bristled, reached out, grabbed the Legionary's shoulder, and shoved him towards a campfire, about twenty paces from the tent.

"You act like a pack animal then you should be with the animal handlers," Lith directed. "Go sit with your betters."

Alerio allowed the toes of his boots to drag as if he was too lazy to pick up his feet. And he kept his head and his eyes down to show he was uninterested in his surroundings. The officer and the handpicked soldiers of the guard watched the insolent man walk away.

"If that's the best they can do," suggested one of Lith's soldiers. "Then Syracuse has nothing to worry about from the Republic."

"It's actually a little disappointing," the Captain replied. "Be sure none of the Legion officers leave the tent and begin analyzing our defenses. I'm going around front to meet the King."

"Yes, sir," the soldier replied

***

Alerio arrived at the campfire and was ignored by three disinterested handlers. Animal wranglers and wagon drivers didn't have much power or authority in the city's military. As such, the opportunity to abuse a Legionary came as a pleasant distraction.

"Sit downwind of me, dog," one said. He added a bark then clarified. "I don't want to smell you."

Alerio lifted an arm and extended a finger. He spun it in the air as if testing for wind.

"Got it," he announced. The Legion NCO shuffled around until he was downwind of a gentle morning breeze. As he moved, Alerio reached into a pouch and pulled out a small wineskin. "I stole this from a nobleman's tent and can't decide if it's good vino or not."

"Pass it over," a wrangler offered. "I'll let you know if it's a good wine."

Alerio took a short stream and passed the skin to the man. With a smirk on his face, the animal handler lifted the wineskin and allowed a few drops to drip into his mouth. He swished it around his cheeks, swallowed, then he squeezed the wineskin hard.

"Hold on there," demanded another handler. "Let me try the wine before you drink it all."

He took the wineskin, did the drip test before taking a mouthful that overflowed and drizzled down his beard.

"That is good wine," the wrangler announced. He shook the empty wineskin. "It's a shame you don't have more."

The third handler's shoulders drooped in disappointment, and he focused on stirring the food cooking in an iron pot.

"Oh, that's not a problem," Alerio stated. He reached into the pouch and lifted out two more of the small wineskins. "I took three. The rich man won't miss them. I hope."

The three wranglers laughed at the idea of stealing from the wealthy. And the possibility of the thief getting caught and punished only added to their pleasure. When you spend your days getting mistreated by soldiers and working with stubborn animals, any diversion was welcome.

"Bring those wineskins over here and have some stew," the third animal handler offered. "We have plenty."

***

The sun rose over Syracuse and details of the city's defenses became apparent. But over the shrubs and bushes around the animal handler's camp, only a small section of the wall, the archers' walkway, and a gate, were visible.

"My mother pointed out the bird she wanted butchered for dinner. He was old, useless, and ate the other bird's grain. Three times I chased that dumb bird around the bird pens," Alerio related a story to the handlers. "On the fourth trip, the stupid bird appeared. He came from the other direction running directly at me. He must have gotten turned around. With one chop of the ax, I killed the old bird. As proud as any hunter, I held the carcass up for my mother to see. With an odd look on her face, she pointed to the top of the pens. Sitting up there was the ancient bird. I had killed one of the young ones."

"Old and clever," a handler agreed. "We see it all the time. The ones we think are dumb and won't work, are just sly and sneaky."

"I know Legionaries like that," Alerio offered. "I might be one of them."

The handlers chuckled and one declared, "You're too young to be old and devious."

"Speaking of devious, my officer has a horse that seems to go limp occasionally at the walk," Alerio said. "She trots fine or when turned out to pasture. Otherwise, the animal seems okay. We can't figure out if she's faking the injury or has a problem."

"That's easy enough to check," a wrangler explained. "You'll want to grab the long neck muscles in the front. Rub them up and down. One will likely cause the horse to flinch."

"And that's the problem?" questioned Alerio.

"No. that will tell you which side has the problem," another of the handlers chimed in. "With that knowledge, you'll know which side of the sternum muscle to knead and massage to give the animal relief."

"And help it heal," another offered.

"Back up a couple of steps," begged the Legionary. "There is a sternum muscle? I thought that was a bone."

"In humans, yes. But on a horse, the pectoral muscles are closer together and wrap the sternum."

Alerio poked himself if the center of his chest. Tapping with his fingers, he started at his neck and worked his fingers down to his stomach.

"I don't understand," he pleaded. "All I feel is bone."

"Come with me. Our draft horses are just around these bushes," a handler informed him. "I'll show you."

"Thank you," Alerio expressed his gratitude with a bow. "That will be very helpful."

***

Four horses were hobbled. And not too far away, two empty wagons sat in the grass just off a road.

"We unloaded the tent, table, and dining equipment then moved the transports over here," the handler explained. At one of the horses, he wrapped his fingers around the long front neck muscle. "You can see the horse makes no sudden move away from any pain or discomfort. That's because the horse is healthy."

While the wrangler manipulated the muscle, Alerio leaned over being sure his shoulder touched the man's back.

"I see what you're doing," the Legion Corporal uttered. "How much of the muscle are you feeling?"

The handler, recognizing a willing student, began a long explanation while working his hands up and down the muscle. But, Alerio was a farm lad and grew up around horses and other animals. From a young age, he assisted his father in treating a variety of animal injuries.

While the animal handler talked, Alerio raised his head and studied the Syracusan defenses. From the vantage point in the open field, he perused a long section of the wall and the location and number of ramps leading up to the archery walkway. Then, he scanned the weapons' platforms with the oxybeles and lithobolois and mentally positioned them in relationship with the gates. Finally, he identified the positioning of the onagers and counted tents in the camp of the soldiers assigned to defend this area of the wall.

"I see," Alerio commented. He reached around and clumsily squeezed the horse's sternum muscle. "Oh, I feel the muscle. Are you sure it's a sternum?"

"Didn't you hear what I said?" questioned the wrangler. "Come on, we better get you back to our camp."

The two men leaned away from the horse's chest. As they began walking back to the handler's camp, the top of the King's tent was visible over the bushes.

"You there," a voice challenged.

Slowly, Alerio turned towards the speaker and bowed.

Standing not far away was the oxybele engineer Alerio had captured in Adreno, use to kill General Periander, and then had a Veles escort out of the besieged city. The man wore the rank of an officer in the Syracusan army.

"Lieutenant of Artillery, good day, sir," Alerio greeted him. "Any chance of you returning the favor?"

Chapter 36 – Expulsion & Absolution

"Consul Crassus. Surely, you realize that you cannot do a total siege of Syracuse," Hiero II stated. He raised a ceramic mug and took a sip of wine. "The southern portion of my city is shoreline and docks. Resupplying my people is not a problem. Also, I have sent a message to the Qart Hadasht Capital asking for their terms to help me."

Consul/General Otacilius Crassus sat across a small table from King Hiero. Senior Tribune Nictavi occupied a chair slightly behind the General and off to the side. Mirroring his position, an advisor to the King sat within an arms distance of his ruler.

1st Centurion Lichenis, Centurions Megellus, and Quadantenus were on one side of the tent and Captain Lith and four guards occupied the other.

"We will not lay siege to Syracuse expecting to starve you out. Or, to pressure you to surrender," Crassus informed the King. "Long before the concept of attrition comes into play, my Legionaries will come through your walls. Once in, we will defeat your military, take what we want, and sell your people into slavery."

"That's bold talk from a man whose army is outside my walls," observed the King.

"It's not bravado. The Legions have done it before," Crassus replied. "And King Hiero, we have the will to do it again."

Something in the General's tone irritated Hiero. He turned and consulted with his advisor. While the Syracusans talked, the swoosh of a tent flap being opened cause Captain Lith to march to the entrance. After a conference with a Lieutenant, he left the tent.

"Your Legions laid siege to Centuripe and Adrano," Hiero remarked after the consultation. "Yet, each situation ended differently. Why?"

"Centuripe has high walls and a large army," replied General Crassus. "As you know, they have clashed with your forces many times over the years. However, it wasn't the strength of their army that brought about the result. Their council showed wisdom and decided the best approach was a treaty with the Republic."

"And what tribute did they pay for the pleasure of living under the Republic's boot?"

The General leaned over and consulted with the Senior Tribune. Moments later, he smiled and held out both arms as if pouring something out onto the tabletop.

"None, King Hiero. There was no demand for Centuripe to pay a tribute to the Republic," Crassus informed him. "Good business and common sense prevailed over becoming a spoil of war."

"And that brings us to Adrano," Hiero remarked. "The city sits..."

His advisor tapped Hiero on the arm and the King stopped talking and listened for several heartbeats.

"I am corrected. The city of Adrano sat at the top of a high slope," Hiero described. "A high wall protected them as did a well-trained militia. Additionally, they employed professionally manned oxybeles, lithobolois, and onagers."

"And, my Legion walked through their bolts, arrows, and stones. We entered the main gate and defeated the militia," Crassus bragged. "Then, after selling the population for a mighty profit, we dismantled the city because we could. Yet across the Symaethus Valley, Centuripe thrives."

"An interesting tale of opposing cities," Hiero observed. "Do you really believe Syracuse will fall as rapidly? My military as easily defeated and the profits as high?"

Before the Legion General answered, both flaps on the tent were thrown back. Captain Lith and a Lieutenant marched to the center of the tent. Following the two officers, two large soldiers dragged a man in and stood him upright. Bruises and cuts marred his face, and he seemed to have a gash on his forehead, based on the bloody rag he held there. The prisoner sagged and if not for the soldiers, he would have toppled over.

"What is the meaning of this?" demanded Hiero II when he saw the uniform of a Legionary.

"Sir, this man was spying," Captain Lith answered.

***

"Is this how you treat members of a delegation?" General Crassus challenged. He jumped to his feet and stepped away from the discussion table.

Momentarily, the confidence left Centurion Megellus and he sagged against the wall of the tent. He recovered his composure and straightened up. Then he stepped away from the edge and began asking questions.

"Does my Corporal have a tablet or parchment where he marked down the sights he saw? Did he speak to anyone about the defensive procedures?" Megellus asked. "Did he attack anyone, insult an officer, act suspiciously? Tell me, Captain Lith, how was he spying? And how did he get the marks on his face?"

A silence fell over the tent. Taking advantage of the stillness, the Senior Tribune inserted his opinion.

"Corporal Sisera. What mischief have you gotten into?" demanded Nictavi. "I told you this was an important meeting. Now, look at what you've done."

Alerio didn't reply. He grimaced as he smiled at the Senior Tribune through cut lips.

"Captain Lith. I as well would like an answer," King Hiero commented. "How was the Legionary spying?"

"Sir. I will let Lieutenant Papyrus of the Syracuse Artillery explain."

The artillery officer stepped forward, saluted his King, and indicated Alerio with a jerk of his thumb.

"Corporal Sisera is a breaching specialist for the Legion," Papyrus informed the room. "I first saw him in the flat before the gates of Adrano as we started the defensive launchings."

"You were in charge of the oxybeles and lithobolois at Adrano?" Fenoris Megellus shouted while starting to leap at the Syracusan officer.

In anticipation of violence, the King's guards lowered their spears. Before the infantry officer leaped, an arm wrapped around Megellus' waist holding him in place.

"Stand down, Centurion," 1st Centurion Lichenis advised. "Let this play out. No good can come of throwing your life away."

"We stand for the lost men of the 25th, sir," Alerio offered. He braced, even though the pain of standing rigidly erect showed on his face.

Megellus stood upright, shook off the 1st Centurion's arm and repeated, "We stand for the lost men of the 25th."

Silence settled on the interior of the tent until the King spoke.

"Please continue Lieutenant Papyrus."

"Thank you, sir. I watched Corporal Sisera strolling through our rain of iron and rocks as if it was a spring shower," the artillery officer related. He indicated Megellus. "That officer ran to his side and fell with an arrow in his leg. Sisera picked him up and walked him to the blind spot in front of the main city gate. There I lost sight of the Legionary."

"When did you see him again?" coached Lith.

"Shortly after the Legion breached the gate," the Lieutenant described. "We were resetting to repel the next wave when Sisera came along the wall. Brandishing two swords, he leaped on a line of spearmen. He was in the process of killing them when a squad of Legionaries arrived."

"Hold on Lieutenant," Hiero interrupted. "You're saying this Legion Corporal attacked a line of spearmen, single-handedly?"

"Yes, sir. As I said, he is a breaching specialist," Papyrus insisted. "Surely, his skin has been forged by Hephaestus. When I saw him within our walls, I knew why he was here. Preparing a plan to breach the walls of Syracuse."

"General Crassus. Do you truly command men with weaponized skin?"

"King Hiero," Crassus responded. "It has been rumored that some Legionaries have been blessed by the God who forges weapons for the Gods of Olympus."

"I have much to consider," Hiero stated while standing. Before leaving the tent, he added. "There is no doubt, the Republic is formidable. But so is the Qart Hadasht Empire. Can either defeat the other without destroying themselves?"

Once King Hiero II and his advisor left, Captain Lith indicated the opposite exit. Following General Crassus, the Legion delegation walked out and took the road to the gate.

***

"Corporal Sisera. You have to hold still so I can finish," the medic complained.

He waved the thin silver needle and waxed sheep intestines thread in front of the NCO's face.

"I have to get this drawn while it's still fresh in my mind," Alerio replied. "Sew somewhere else, if you must."

"Only the cut on your forehead requires sutures," the medic informed him.

"Put a compress on it for now," Alerio ordered.

Drops of blood dripped onto his cheek, rolled off, and fell onto the sheepskin parchment under his hands.

Across the commander's tent, General Crassus and Colonel Bacaris studied Centurion Megellus. Behind them, Senior Tribune Nictavi glared at the infantry officer.

"I propose charges be brought against Fenoris Megellus," Nictavi suggested. "His scheme put you at a disadvantage during the negotiations, General."

Crassus thought for a heartbeat then called across the tent.

"Corporal Sisera. We are waiting for proof that your Centurion isn't a complete fool," Crassus warned. "If you want to save his career, I suggest you show us the value of his imagination."

Alerio drew a final line, marked a distance on it, and leaned back.

"Sir. We now have the defensive positions for that part of the Syracusan wall," he announced.

"Bring it here and explain what you've drawn," instructed the Senior Tribune. "We don't have time to decipher scribbling. But I'm sure you can describe what's on the parchment."

Alerio used two hands on the skin to prevent it from folding and smearing the fresh ink. He crossed the room in step with the medic who held a cloth over the gash. After placing the map on the Colonel's camp table, he took control of the compress and backed away.

"What do you think Bacaris?" Crassus asked the battle commander.

Bacaris touched a few places on the map, allowed his finger to trace ink from a gate to the weapons' platforms, then to an onager position.

"With this map, I can plan a breach and plot safe lanes of attack for our infantry," the Colonel stated. "It's excellent intelligence, General."

"Centurion Megellus. You and Corporal Sisera are excused," Crassus said releasing the two.

"Thank you, sir," Fenoris replied while taking Alerio's arm and guiding him towards the exit.

They were two steps from the opening when the Senior Centurion burst into the tent.

"King Hiero has sent a representative to the Legion staff area," Publius reported. "He wants to talk."

"More negotiations?" suggested Nictavi.

"According to guards accompanying the King's advisor, Hiero said the Qart Hadasht Empire doesn't have breaching specialists with weaponized skin," Publius replied. "I don't know any army that does. But it sounds like Syracuse wants to make peace with the Republic."

"Will you go to the treaty talks, General?" Colonel Bacaris inquired.

"No. I have duties to attend to in the Capital," Crassus answered. "For political reasons, it's best if General Mesalla handles the details."

***

Fenoris Megellus tightened his grip on Alerio's arm and pulled him out of the tent.

"It seems the Sicilia campaign is all but over for this year, sir," Alerio commented as they walked towards the 25th Century's area.

"That may be true for the marching Legions," the infantry officer observed. "But sixty towns and cities signed treaties with the Republic, and they need to be enforced."

"It sounds as if you aren't leaving the island, sir."

"I'm not. The Senate will authorize garrisons and I'm going to request one," Megellus informed the Corporal. "It'll make it easier to select the position I want for the next campaign."

"As a Construction Officer, sir?" asked Alerio.

"Before the Legion breaks up, distribute the funeral funds and extra coins to the men. Then I'm detaching you to the Capital for a couple of things before you're released from the Legion."

"What things, Centurion?"

"Open an account for me at the Temple of Mercury," Megellus instructed. "Then see Senator Maximus and deliver a chit and a letter."

"I can do that," Alerio informed him. "But you never answered my question. What duty will you request, sir?"

"Infantry officer for a Century of heavy infantrymen," Fenoris Megellus stated.

"I'd be proud to serve with you again, sir."

"And I'd be proud to have an NCO of your abilities, Corporal Sisera," Megellus replied. "Now get over to medical and get that gash stitched. As it is, it'll probably leave a scar."

Chapter 37 – Rare Coins of War

When Alerio reached the Capital, he rented a coach. Not because he didn't enjoy walking around the city. He did. But it was dangerous to stroll around with sacks of gold coins. He stopped at a temple and deposited the Centurion's money before taking the carriage to Villa Maximus.

"I didn't expect this," Senator Spurius Maximus stated while waving two chits around.

"But you said the Legion provides an opportunity for glory and bonuses," Alerio remarked. "If I remember correctly, sir. You said, if you do a heroic deed, you'll receive two things; a bonus and the chance to do another difficult mission. We did a near-impossible mission, then another, and were awarded bonuses. What's not to expect, sir?"

They were seated across from one another in the Senator's office. The chits in question had been issued by the Temple of Mercury. One was for the Senator from Ambassador Octavius Sergius via Centurion Fenoris Megellus. The second draft was to be forwarded to the father of Fenoris Megellus. Both showed large sums on deposit with the Temple's head priest.

"The truth, Corporal Sisera, is few Legionaries are ever in a position to reap glory and coins from their deeds," Maximus explained. "Those that do are usually put in the lead of the next assault so they may die gloriously. And while they do set an excellent example for the rest of the Legion, no bonuses are paid to the dead."

"I apologize, Senator. I was under the impression that bonuses were common," Alerio ventured. "After all, you fronted the coins for the Century. I thought that you planned to turn a profit on the investment."

"And I will earn one. But from the trade with towns in Sicilia not from bonuses," Maximus proclaimed while waving the chits in the air. "The Legion's Senior Centurion and Tribune, the battle commander, and the General have shares of the spoils from conquests. And a smaller portion goes to a few Legionaries or Centuries that lead assaults or perform exceptionally well."

"The 25th did that, sir," Alerio bragged. "because you invested in the Century."

"I can see the results," Maximus admitted. He gazed at the vouchers and then across the desk at the Corporal. "And yet, I am surprised. For you see Alerio Sisera, it's rare for the men doing the fighting to earn coins directly from war."

The End

Infinite Courage

Author Note

Infinite Courage is book #8 in this series. In each of the books, I include historical events, ancient technology, lifestyle items, Legion details from the mid Republic era, and ancient Gods, all thoroughly researched. I love history and want my readers to as well.

One reader wrote to me, "First books based on Roman History that I have really enjoyed." A big thank you to that reader, and to you, for making Clay Warrior Stories a success.

Infinite Courage takes place in 263 BC. After the intense fighting between Carthage and Rome at the start of the First Punic War, it's surprising that the Carthage Empire disengaged in the second year. This allowed Rome to consolidate its hold on the eastern half of Sicily.

I am currently researching for book #9 set in 262 B.C. when the Carthage Empire reengaged.

There was no Ambassador Sergius or General Periander. But, the tale of Centuripe and Adrano presents a puzzle. Why did a wealthy city like Centuripe, with a powerful army, sign a treaty after a brief siege by the Legion? Contrast that with a poorer city like Adrano that during a siege, angered the Legion enough to be attacked and depopulated. For those who follow Alerio's routes, I use the current names of the cities so readers can map the topography, settings, and locations used in the stories.

Writing adventure and staying close to history is sometimes frustrating. I really wanted to write a major battle at the walls of Syracuse. But King Hiero II signed a treaty with Rome in 263 B.C. before the battle started. A good move for Syracuse, and a letdown for this writer.

If you have comments or want to contact me, please e-mail me.

E-mail: GalacticCouncilRealm@gmail.com

To sign up for my newsletter, and for blogs on ancient Rome, go to my website.

www.JCliftonSlater.com

Thank you for reading the historical adventures of the mid-Republic. Until we meet again in book #9 Deceptive Valor, Alerio and I wish you good health and vigor.

Sincerely,

J. Clifton Slater

I write military adventure both future and ancient.

Books by J. Clifton Slater

Historical Adventure – *Clay Warrior Stories series*

#1 Clay Legionary   #2 Spilled Blood

#3 Bloody Water   #4 Reluctant Siege

#5 Brutal Diplomacy   #6 Fortune Reigns

#7 Fatal Obligation   #8 Infinite Courage

#9 Deceptive Valor   #10 Neptune's Fury

#11 Unjust Sacrifice   #12 Muted Implications

#13 Death Caller   #14 Rome's Tribune

#15 Deranged Sovereignty

#16 Uncertain Honor   #17 Tribune's Oath

#18 Savage Birthright   #19 Abject Authority

Novels of the 2nd Punic War – *A Legion Archer series*

#1 Journey from Exile   #2 Pity the Rebellious

#3 Heritage of Threat   #4 A Legion Legacy

Military Science Fiction – *Call Sign Warlock series*

#1 Op File Revenge   #2 Op File Treason

#3 Op File Sanction

Military Science Fiction – *Galactic Council Realm series*

#1 On Station   #2 On Duty

#3 On Guard   #4 On Point

Printed in Great Britain
by Amazon